She was the one...

As soon as his flesh touched hers, Bren felt as if an electric current had been set loose within him.

No wonder he had been so strongly called to her. No wonder the very sight of her damn near made him crazy.

Miranda Lynch was the only woman in this world he could bond with, the only woman in existence who could save him from being the last of his kind. He'd thought this special woman his mother had always told him would come one day was a myth, and yet here she was, standing before him with her hand in his.

There was no place in this world for the Korbinians, not anymore. Their time had passed. Logically he could dismiss Miranda Lynch; rationally he knew what she promised would never work. But a primitive instinct he could not deny now accepted this woman as his, and he wanted her so sharply that he could think of nothing else.

Books by Linda Winstead Jones

LINDA WINSTEAD JONES

is a *New York Times* bestselling author of more than fifty romance books in several subgenres—historical, fairy tale, paranormal and, of course, romantic suspense. She's won a Colorado Romance Writers Award of Excellence twice. She is also a three-time RITA® Award finalist and (writing as Linda Fallon) winner of the 2004 RITA® Award for paranormal romance.

Linda lives in north Alabama with her husband of thirty-four years. She can be reached via www.eHarlequin.com or her own Web site, www.lindawinsteadjones.com.

LAST OF THE
Ravens
LINDA WINSTEAD JONES

Silhouette Books

nocturne™

SILHOUETTE BOOKS

ISBN-13: 978-0-373-61826-2

Recycling programs
for this product may
not exist in your area.

LAST OF THE RAVENS

www.silhouettenocturne.com

Printed in U.S.A.

Dear Reader,

Every year, my writers' group descends upon a bed-and-breakfast in Tennessee for laughing, eating and drinking, karaoke, lots of talk, massages—and plotting. At one of these retreats a couple of years back, we were in the middle of an afternoon plotting session when somehow, for some reason, the subject turned to birds.

For years I've had a vague idea knocking around in my brain—a shifter in the Tennessee mountains and a woman who's the target of a would-be killer. It never went very far. It was just one of those misty, unformed ideas that seem to kick up in the middle of the night. And then, during this plotting session, someone mentioned ravens and it all came together. The hero I'd been thinking of wasn't a werewolf, but a man who turns into a flock of ravens.

From there, the idea started to gel. Miranda Lynch sees and hears ghosts; she helps them find justice. Bren Korbinian is convinced he's the last of his kind…until he touches Miranda and realizes what might lie before them if he's brave enough to take what she can give him—and if they can escape from those who will do anything to keep them apart.

My heartfelt thanks to all the members of Heart of Dixie who guided the plotting conversation to birds that weekend. It just goes to show…you never know where the next idea might come from.

I hope you enjoy!

Linda

With thanks to all my Heart of Dixie friends for the laughter, the support and the camaraderie.

My life would not be the same without plotluck, retreats and squeees.

Prologue

"Don't you trust me?" Jessica asked.

"Behind the wheel of a car? Never."

Miranda gripped the padded handle of the passenger door and held her breath as the car took a sharp curve too fast. The rolling north Georgia mountains were brilliant green with the coming of summer, and the rock formation just beyond the passenger window sped by much too close for safety or comfort. Miranda didn't say anything about Jessica's driving—she'd given up that futile task years ago—and still her older sister laughed at her reaction.

The setting sun dipped lower on the horizon, coloring the sky pink and yellow and orange on this beautiful April evening. Flowering plants on either side of the

road screamed of life that fought to survive in an unfriendly environment, while hearty evergreens on the
hills above seemed ancient and indestructible. Soon it
would be dark, but this fleeting moment was breathtak-
ingly beautiful.

Miranda's design degree had been newly awarded.
She and Jessica—her only family—had plans for a new
and exciting interior design business in Atlanta, and
even if they did have terrible luck with men—the Lynch
love curse, Jessica called it—Miranda knew she should
be happy. She should be content. This was a good time
in her life.

But an inexplicable discontent gnawed at her, the
way it sometimes did. For the past few days she'd occasionally caught herself holding her breath for no
reason at all, and now and then she got the oddest feeling
that someone was watching her. She'd even turned
around a couple of times, thinking she'd catch someone
spying on her. Not that anyone had reason to spy on an
ordinary girl like her!

Miranda had had good instincts since she'd been a little
girl, and she'd learned to trust her first impressions when
it came to the people she met. Her initial reaction to a
person was usually strong and unmistakable; at first sight,
she liked or disliked those she met. On the few occasions
she'd ignored those instincts she'd later regretted it.

There was something beyond ordinary instincts
within her, something she tried very hard to dismiss.
Jessica knew about her little sister's uncanny intuition,
but not even she knew about the other little oddity.

On rare occasions Miranda got butterflies and

chills and knots, as well as a peculiar feeling that all was not well when outwardly it appeared that everything was fine. It had been years since she'd suffered a deep sensation of unidentifiable discontent like the one she was experiencing now; a week after that last troubling incident, her seemingly perfectly healthy mother had passed away suddenly, her kind heart failing without warning.

This time it was just nerves making her feel odd, Miranda told herself. Graduation. A new business. Life! Her future was bright, and nothing would get in the way of her plans.

Jessica took a corner too fast and again Miranda instinctively tightened her grip on the armrest. The bright lights of the truck that had crept into the wrong lane blinded her, much as the sun had not so long ago. The sisters barely had time to scream.

Bren awoke with a start. Something was wrong. Not just a little wrong, but very wrong. Disastrously wrong. In spite of the intense sensation of doom, the fire crackled in the fireplace, and the television played on at a low volume. All was as he'd left it in this half-finished mountaintop house he called home.

It had been a tiring day, as usual, and he'd fallen asleep on the couch shortly after grabbing a bite to eat. He was like the cobbler who had no shoes; he spent all day building vacation and retirement houses for other people, and he never had time to finish his own place. His mountainside house, which was finished and impressive on the outside, was habitable within, but still needed trim, paint, interior doors and a hundred finishing touches that would one day make this a home.

Unable to shake the feeling that something was wrong, he jumped off the couch and walked out onto the deck, running his fingers through black hair that was long past due for a trim. A burst of late-evening spring air woke him fully, filled his lungs, made him hungry for something he couldn't name. Still, he couldn't shake the feeling that the world had shifted.

The life Bren had made for himself was simple, and to be honest there was little that could happen to shake it. His parents were gone, and he had no one else of importance in his life. No brothers. No cousins. Certainly no wife or children. Brennus Korbinian loved his life, made the best of every day, but he knew full well that he was the last of a dying breed. The time for his kind had passed, long ago. He accepted that fact, had accepted it years ago. What choice did he have but to accept?

In the shadows he stripped off his shirt and glanced beyond the deck, down the steep curve of the mountain. There was nothing to see but the tops of trees—and one structure with an annoying red rooftop. He scowled at the cabin that was situated farther down the mountain, a little ways down the winding road that led to the highway below. Bren had offered the owner twice as much as the place was worth, but the stubborn man refused to sell. Thank goodness the cabin was rarely used. Bren needed privacy; it was all he required of life.

All was dark at the intrusive cabin tonight. No lights shone from the windows, and Bren hadn't seen a car in the drive as he'd made his way home hours earlier. Even if someone was there, they'd have to have binoculars or a telescope to see anything they shouldn't.

And still, he wanted that cabin. Once he had it, this entire mountain would be his. Like his father before him, he'd spent years snatching up pieces of property in order to make it so. When he had that plot of land down the hill, the privacy he required would be his, finally and completely.

Bren stripped to his skin, then easily stepped up onto the railing that surrounded the large, deep deck. He glanced down into the vast space beneath, felt the sweep of evening air against his skin, held his breath as deep inside he acknowledged the certainty that yes, something in the world had shifted. He also accepted that he did not know what that something was—and did not need to know. His world was small. Everything he needed was right here.

He dropped, catching air against his bare skin for a moment and then erupting into freedom. If anyone had been watching, they would've seen a man one moment and a flock of black birds the next. They would watch as those birds swept down the mountainside, moving in concert, flying as one, until they convinced themselves that they could not have possibly seen what they thought they'd seen.

The last of the ravens flew into the darkness, and in this form, which was as natural to him as human flesh and bone, Bren knew that somewhere in the world all was not as it should be.

But that did not concern him. Not at all. He caught

a fierce wind and a cacophony of caws echoed down the mountain he called his own.

Miranda awoke slowly, wondering where she was and how she'd gotten here. What day was it? Where the hell was she? It didn't take her long to realize that she was in a hospital. The shocking memory of the accident came back to her in a flash. She didn't remember the collision itself, but she recalled vividly the headlights on the semi that had crossed into the wrong lane, and she remembered screaming.

Jessica!

"You're awake."

Miranda's head snapped to the side. Not a good move. Her head was wrapped in a thick bandage and she had a headache that made her skull pound furiously. Still, she was relieved to see Jessica standing there, untouched, wearing the same pink sweater and jeans she'd been wearing when she'd picked up Miranda.

The bright sunlight shining through the window behind Jessica made her look less than substantial. It had been just after sunset, last Miranda remembered, so the light meant she'd been unconscious all night....

"I love you," Jessica said, not coming any closer.

She must feel horribly guilty to get so emotional. Jessica didn't do emotion, not so blatantly. The love was there but it remained unspoken, except in the worst of times. "I love you, too," Miranda said, and she lifted a hand, motioning with her fingers for her sister to come closer. Jessica didn't budge; she stayed in the bright sunlight.

Miranda's arm was bandaged, as well as her aching head, and she couldn't help but wonder why she'd been hurt so badly while Jessica didn't have a scratch on her. The light shifted and Miranda found herself blinking hard to clear her unsteady vision. The sounds of hospital activity continued in the hallway. Footsteps passed by quickly, as did squeaking carts and whispering voices. It all sounded so far away, so unimportant.

"Jessica?"

"You're awake!"

Miranda moved her head more slowly this time, as she looked toward the door and the excited voice. Her friend and roommate, Autumn, rushed in, tears in her eyes... "Thank goodness. I was so worried!"

Miranda attempted a smile, which didn't seem to work very well. "I'm fine, really. Just a bump on the head, I think." She lifted the hand that didn't have an IV connected to it and patted the thick bandage. "What are you doing here? Did Jessica call you?"

Autumn paled, and she bit her bottom lip. Tears ran down her cheeks. "Oh, honey."

"What?" Miranda looked toward Jessica to ask what was going on, but there was no one standing in front of the sunny window. Miranda blinked hard, then craned her neck to see where Jessica might've gone.

"I didn't want to be the one to tell you." Autumn hiccupped and sniffled.

"Tell me what?" Miranda asked. There was a knot in her stomach. "Where's Jessica?"

Autumn shook her head and wiped away a tear. "It was a truck...head-on, the state trooper said." She took a deep breath and finally whispered, "Honey, I'm so sorry. Jessica didn't make it. She died instantly, so there was no pain. She probably never even knew…" Autumn's breath caught in her throat. She couldn't go on.

Miranda tried to sit up but couldn't. Every bone and muscle in her body ached. "What do you mean she didn't make it? Jessica was just here. She was standing right over there!" She pointed at the window on the empty side of the stark hospital room. Autumn shook her head and more silent tears slipped from her eyes as a voice whispered in Miranda's ear. *I love you.*

Chapter 1

Four years later

There were those who could not be allowed to mingle with the innocent. Monsters, some would call them. Evil, the leaders of the Order of Cahir proclaimed. Or so she'd heard in her time in this dark, dank place.

Roxanna sat on a narrow cot, her knees drawn up, her chin down in an instinctively protective manner. She was hungry. The old man fed her now and then, biscuits and cookies and fried chicken, but she wasn't hungry for food. In the past year she'd seduced a dozen men and taken their souls, strengthening herself, building an unimaginable power. But now she was hungry again. She was weaker than she'd been when they brought her here, which was likely just as they had planned. Even if she hadn't been chained to the cot, she wouldn't have been able to make it very far if she tried to run.

She'd be easier to kill now.

Roxanna lifted her head and looked at the redheaded one. At the moment they were alone, just one weakened sorceress and one guard. Even though he had taken part in her torture as they tried to discover if she was working alone or with a coven, there was a part of him that desired her. Another part was afraid of her and what she could do. If she could call him to her, if she could take his soul, she'd be strong enough to escape. This time she wouldn't be so easily found.

"I could use some water," she whispered.

"Later…" the redhead began.

"Please."

He hesitated, scowled, then poured water from a jug into a paper cup and carried it to her. If their hands touched, if she could use all she had learned on him…

Their hands did touch; he did react, with a gasp and a widening of his eyes. She stared into those eyes and stroked with one finger. A moment more and he'd be hers.

"Kill her," the old man said. She hadn't heard him come down the stairs but he was there, behind the redhead. "She's weakened enough now that it won't be difficult." The man before Roxanna didn't immediately do as he was told; he was close to being hers. "Kill her now, or I kill you."

At those words, the redhead reacted quickly. Water splashed over Roxanna's dress, the same stained dress she'd been wearing for almost a month. He drew a knife from a leather sheath at his waist, and without hesitation he drove the blade into her chest. Once, and again, and then again.

Roxanna fell back on the cot, her chains rattling. She'd known she'd die a violent death, had dreamed of it, tried to heed the warnings. And yet now she was dead. With her last ragged breath, she decided that no matter what she'd done, no matter what they said, she was not a monster.

"I don't need a vacation," Miranda insisted stubbornly.

"You do," three voices responded in concert.

She pursed her lips, but arguing with this bunch was a waste of time. Autumn and her husband of two years, Jared Sidwell, stood side by side and glared at her over sweet iced tea. Cheryl Talbot smiled and nodded.

FBI Agent Roger Talbot flipped a burger on the grill and belatedly he agreed with the other three. "This last job was a doozy. It drained me, and I didn't have to do what you do. You're pale and you've lost weight and there are dark circles under your eyes. Let's be honest here. You look like crap."

"Roger!" Cheryl chastised. "There's no need to be so...so..."

"Honest?" he said, lifting his head to look at his wife with undeniable love.

Miranda had met Roger Talbot three years ago in the line of work she'd taken up a year after the accident that had killed her sister and in return given her what some called a "gift." Some gift. No one wanted an interior decorator who saw ghosts in the rooms they wished to adorn. No one wanted to walk into a room and find the woman they had hired to bring together paintings and curtains and upholstery fabrics talking to Grandma— who'd been dead seven years. Miranda knew that to be true. She'd been there. She'd tried so hard to live a normal life—but the spirits she'd begun to see after the accident continued to haunt her. The only way she could find any peace was to help them.

When she'd first heard from a murder victim, she'd tried to ignore the bothersome specter. The man—the ghost of a man—had been annoyingly persistent and would not leave Miranda alone. After a few days she'd given up and gone to the police. Naturally they'd dismissed her as a nut and sent her on her way, but the ghost did not take the hint and get lost. Instead, the spirit of the murder victim had stuck to her like glue, an unrelenting stalker no one could see, a dead man insisting on a justice only Miranda could deliver.

The only way she could get rid of him was to hand him off to someone else. The man wanted his murderer caught and punished—naturally. It had taken a while, but eventually Miranda had found someone who would listen to her. That someone had been FBI Agent Roger Talbot. They'd been working together—more or less under the table, when it came to official business—for years. For the first couple of years she'd been able to keep her ability secret, but eventually word had gotten out. There were plenty of people who thought she was a nut, or worse, a con artist, but there were also more than enough people out there who wanted her services.

Jessica had been right. Less than five years after that

fateful night Miranda had clients lined up out the door. She was very much in demand. In some circles she might even be called famous. Miranda Lynch, who'd discovered an uncanny ability to talk to ghosts after the horrific car accident that had taken the life of her sister, was a hot commodity.

These days when she felt like someone was watching her, she was probably right.

Roger and Cheryl were several years older than Miranda, but they had become like family to her. Roger was a big brother, protective and sometimes teasing, and Cheryl had become almost a surrogate mother, even though she was only ten years older than Miranda. Cheryl cooked healthy meals; she introduced her young friend to shoes that were comfortable *and* cute, insisting both qualities were essential; she made sure Miranda went to the doctor when she was sick. Their three kids felt like family, as well, especially fifteen-year-old Jackson, who looked so much like Roger he might as well be a younger, thinner clone. They were the center of Miranda's personal life, pretty much the only personal life she had. The Lynch love curse seemed to be fully in effect, since every unattached man Miranda met was either repulsed by her ability or else wanted to make a profit from it.

Autumn and Jared had met the Talbots through Miranda, and in the past year or so there had been occasional cookouts and birthday parties like this one. Jared and Roger weren't exactly close friends—they didn't have much in common, since Roger was in law enforcement and Jared was in computers, and Roger liked to hunt and fish and Jared's idea of fun involved computer games or paint-ball fights—but Autumn adored Cheryl as much as Miranda did. These four people had become the only family Miranda had left and at this rate they were the only family she would ever have. The last attempt at having a significant other in her life had ended so badly she'd sworn off men. She was twenty-six years old and a determined old maid who devoted more of her life to the dead than she did to the living.

Not exactly the life she'd planned for herself.

She really should listen to these people when they told her she needed time off, but she had clients waiting, meetings to make and obligations to fill. Sure, beyond law-enforcement consultations most of her clients just wanted to know that their loved ones still lived on, somehow and somewhere, or else they wanted to know where the will or the family jewelry had been hidden.

"I have a cabin in Tennessee," Roger said.

"I know." He'd been trying to get her to take advantage of the place for the past two years, but she was usually too busy to take an entire weekend off, much less go on a real vacation. There was always so much to do! People died every day. Most of them traveled directly to their place in the afterlife, but some of them reached out for her after they should've passed on.

"I don't get to use it nearly often enough," he continued, studying the burgers, instead of her. "Cheryl doesn't like the cabin much."

"I like the outlet malls, which are only forty-five

minutes or so away," Cheryl responded with a wide smile. "I don't like the single bathroom that's the size of the hall closet, and I hate that my cell phone doesn't get a signal there. It's medieval to be so out of touch. It doesn't help that the man who owns the only other house on the mountain glares daggers at us every time we cross paths. I swear that psycho wants the damn mountain all to himself. I don't know what he's doing up there that he can't stand the idea of neighbors, but there must be some kind of nefarious dealings going on. The man has to be hiding something."

Miranda looked at Cheryl, hoping for support from that quarter. "There's a psycho on the mountain and your husband wants to send me there for a vacation?"

"A psycho and outlet malls," Cheryl said with a wide grin. "Sounds like a fair enough deal to me."

"*You* don't like it," Miranda argued.

Cheryl shrugged. "Not all that much, but it is nice and quiet there, and Roger's right. You look like you could use a little nice and quiet. A couple of weeks—"

"A couple of weeks?" Miranda interrupted shrilly. "I was thinking of maybe a long weekend."

"So you *were* thinking of taking a few days off?" Autumn asked, a hint of hope in her gentle voice.

"I said *maybe*." Did she look that bad? Could everyone around her see that the work of talking to ghosts was draining her, robbing her of sleep, making her feel much too old for her twenty-six years?

That was certainly possible. It was as though she didn't only understand the emotions of the spirits she talked to, she experienced them. She didn't only hear and see how they died, she felt their pain. She was tired all the time, and lately if she got four hours of sleep it was a good night. It wasn't all that unusual that those closest to her might see the effects of the strain.

"*Maybe* is a start," Roger said. He took the burgers off the grill and put them on a platter. "We should've done steaks," he said beneath his breath.

Thank goodness, a change of topic. "It's my birthday and I wanted your burgers," Miranda said.

"And chocolate cake!" Jackson called, walking out of the kitchen door and into the backyard bearing a huge birthday cake complete with fudge icing and decorative yellow roses.

"What more could a girl ask for?" Miranda said, her eyes flitting from Autumn and Jared to Roger and Cheryl. Two couples, each so different, each so close— each a part of something intimate and special that Miranda had given up on ever knowing. She finally pinned her eyes on Roger and sighed. "Fine. A long weekend will be enough, though."

"Two weeks would be better," he countered. "Fresh air, complete quiet, outlet malls…"

"A psycho," Miranda added.

"Korbinian's not a psycho," Roger argued with a sharp and slightly censuring glance to his wife. "He's just odd as hell, and he's pissed because I won't sell him the cabin. You leave him alone, and he won't bother you. I'll run you up on Saturday."

"Can I go?" Jackson asked, his voice bright and his eyes lighting on Miranda briefly. Fifteen-year-olds were not particularly good at hiding their emotions, especially where women were concerned. Roger's son had had a crush on Miranda for the past several months.

A living being liked her for herself, and he was really cute. Too bad he was a starry-eyed kid.

"We're not going to stay long," Roger warned his eldest son.

"That's okay," Jackson responded.

Roger nodded. "Sure, you can ride with us."

"What about you, Cheryl?" Miranda asked.

"No thanks," she answered quickly. "I'll leave it to the Talbot men to see you there. The girls have dance class on Saturday, and besides, I suspect we won't be in Tennessee long enough to make a visit to Pigeon Forge and the outlet malls." She sighed in feigned distress. "Another time. Now, let's eat!"

With the window to his four-wheel drive truck rolled down to let in the cool mountain air, Bren heard the chatter of change on his mountain. Birds flew; critters scrambled. Either some tourist had taken a wrong turn and was horribly lost, or Talbot was at his cabin. Damned, stubborn man. Sure enough, there was a familiar car parked in the drive of the small, red-roofed cabin that marred the side of Bren's mountain. He drove by slowly, and as he did the front door opened to frame the big man who owned the place—and refused to sell. Bren's last offer had been ridiculously high, and still Talbot had turned him down without even taking time to consider selling.

Bren braked a bit when he caught sight of a smallish woman standing behind Talbot. That was not Mrs.

Talbot, who was a tall, thin brunette. This woman was a short, shapely blonde. Was she a mistress? A new wife? Hell, a cabin this isolated would be the perfect place to carry on an affair. No wonder Talbot wouldn't sell!

Spotting the truck, Talbot stepped onto the porch and waved, almost as if he wanted Bren to stop. Bren kept his eyes on the curving road ahead as he drove up the mountain road. No way would Talbot be able to drive all the way to the house at the top of the mountain, not without four-wheel drive—not that he'd ever been all that social.

It was no mistake that getting to the Korbinian house was such an effort. Bren didn't want visitors; he didn't like surprises.

He glanced in the rearview mirror just in time to see the blonde woman step onto the porch. She had long, straight hair that was as pale as Bren's was dark, and she was smallish without being frail-looking. She had a womanly shape he could appreciate even from this distance. Nice. He couldn't see her face well, and still he felt something unexpected. A pulling, almost. A draw that made him consider turning around and driving back down the hill just to see her better. He fought the urge and kept going, slowly.

Behind her was a teenager Bren recognized as having been here before. If Talbot had brought his son along, the blonde wasn't a girlfriend. For some reason that hit him with a rush of relief. Maybe she was entirely unattached. Maybe she was free. He shook off the thought. When the sight of a passably pretty stranger made his thoughts wander this way, it was time to get laid.

With that realization, his thoughts returned to the woman down the hill. If the pretty blonde wasn't with Talbot, then why was she here? Not that he cared.

Unless Talbot planned to sell the cabin to her, in spite of his refusals of Bren's generous offers. These days many people made permanent homes in the mountains, rather than just vacation homes they visited a few times a year. What if the woman planned to stay? Attractive and shapely or not, that would be a disaster.

Miranda settled in after Roger and Jackson left. There was more than enough food for the week in the cupboard and the fridge, and while she didn't have a vehicle of her own—she didn't care much for driving since the accident, especially on winding mountain roads— Roger had made arrangements with Duncan Archard, who owned the gas station at the foot of the mountain.

The cabin was small, and it was furnished with a collection of mismatched pieces that had been discarded from the Talbot household over the years—and perhaps, she suspected, picked up off the side of the road. Many of the pieces were in rough shape, though they were still usable. There was no style to speak of, and Miranda's design sensibilities itched. She couldn't help but look at the small rooms with an eye to possibilities. There were four rooms and one horrendously small bath. The two bedrooms were utilitarian at best. The main room was comfortable but sparsely decorated. A bookcase stuffed with old books had a figurine of a black bear sitting atop it, and there was a chipped bowl sitting in the center of the coffee table. The kitchen was small and was stocked with the barest of necessities, as well as the groceries she had bought on the way into town. The curtains in the kitchen window were made of a fabric that sported a repeated image of ducks. Shudder.

Perhaps the cabin was too small to ever be grand and impressive, but with a little imagination and some work it could be attractive and cozy, an adorable cottage in the Tennessee woods.

But bad taste aside, the place was completely quiet. The bed and the couch were both quite comfortable. As Cheryl had warned, there was no cell signal here. With more than a touch of relief, Miranda turned off her cell and stored it in a bedroom drawer. She hadn't realized how much she'd needed to get away until she'd walked into the isolated cabin and felt a rush of something like peace. Her friends had recognized her need for rest before she had, but she could no longer deny it. She probably wouldn't need to call on a driver at all this week. She was going to sleep late and nap and read and go to bed early. There was no television, so she wouldn't be inundated with the bad news of the world. No politics, no disasters, no sad stories—as long as she could ignore the bits of news that would be sure to pop up when she checked her e-mail on the laptop. For one week, everything beyond this mountain could wait.

She wasn't even worried about the psycho up the road. Roger had explained that Brennus Korbinian owned a real estate brokerage and his own construction company. Her brief glimpse of him as he'd driven by in his expensive truck had soothed her somewhat. Korbinian was younger than she'd expected a crotchety loner to be, and though she had not gotten a really good look at his face she'd seen longish black hair and one sharply defined jaw. He was just a rich guy with a weird name who was annoyed that he couldn't own this entire mountain. He wasn't a psycho, though he was a spoiled brat, and he wouldn't ruin her week of rest. She probably wouldn't see him again, unless she happened to be sitting on the small front porch as he drove by. As there was absolutely no reason for her to sit on the tiny front porch when out back there was a large deck with a fabulous view, she was quite sure she'd had her first and last glimpse of him.

Since ghosts usually remained near the site where they'd died, perhaps she'd even have a quiet week where her ability was concerned. This place was isolated, not all that easy to get to and sparsely inhabited. She needed a rest from the ghosts she spoke to much more than she needed a rest from people. The spirits she spoke to had no sense of time and were likely to pop in at any time, usually at two or three in the morning while she was trying to sleep, if she happened to be within a few miles of the site of their deaths. Their emotions and demands drained her. Maybe here, so far from any highly populated area—

"I thought you would never get here!"

Miranda spun around and found an older woman sitting in the rocking chair near the cold fireplace. Ghosts were not usually so substantial that they looked real; not since Jessica's appearance after death had Miranda seen a spirit so solid. "Who are you?" Best to find out what the ghost wanted and send her on her way. Otherwise, the plan for a week of rest had just gone out the window. Miranda waited to be assaulted with anger or sadness or confusion, which was normal in these instances. The ghosts who came to her always wanted something from her.

Instead, she was surprised to feel awash in love and peace, in spite of the harsh words. The dark-haired woman sitting in the rocking chair smiled. "He has been waiting for you. He just doesn't realize it."

"Who…?" Miranda began, but before she could continue the ghost disappeared. The sensations of love and peace were gone in an instant, just as the ghost was gone.

Miranda swore under her breath. So much for her week of rest! "You'd better let me sleep tonight," she mumbled, staring at the empty chair.

It was well after dark when Bren climbed onto the deck railing, naked and curious and a little annoyed. Behind him the house was unlit. No lamps shone to illuminate and reveal his secret to any who might be watching. There was only the moon above, and its light was not enough to fight against the complete and deep darkness of his mountain.

Down the hill bright lights burned in the cabin that was a blight on his life. Who was the woman? Why was she here? Was she there alone or had Talbot and his son remained, too? Bren found that even now, hours after he had glimpsed her, he wanted a thorough look at her face. More than that, he'd been thinking of her and wondering why she was here since he'd walked into the house, annoyed after seeing Talbot at the cabin.

Perhaps he would see and know more with the senses of the raven than he did as a man. In the form he hid from the world he would fly around the cabin, peer through the windows with 154 eyes, and maybe he would finally understand why he had not been able to get the blonde out of his mind.

Maybe he'd get a close look at her and realize she was not so pretty and tempting, after all.

Bren dropped from the railing and burst, and as a flock of ravens he swooped toward the cabin. He caught the wind with his wings, he became a part of the night air and he flew. There was no other freedom like this one, no feeling to compare to gliding through the sky.

The lights of the cabin appeared to be brighter than they had through human eyes, and he felt the woman's presence more strongly than before. Even in this form, he was pulled toward her as if by a powerful magnet. She was alone in the cabin; he knew it long before he swooped down and saw that Talbot's car was gone from the driveway. He felt the presence of the woman in a way he had never felt another; her heartbeat was in tune with his. He could feel and hear her breath even from here, and if he could he would gladly fly through her window and encompass her, caressing her with the tips of silky black wings and studying her face with many eyes.

The flock swooped down and circled the cabin, and Bren glimpsed the interior through the cabin windows. Some of the curtains were closed, but the large sliding glass door that looked over the mountain was uncovered, for who could possibly see into the cabin from that vantage point?

The blonde sat on the couch with a book in her hand, legs drawn up beneath her, hair falling over half her face, a crocheted afghan across her lap. As he watched she lifted her head, alerted by the sound of wings that caught the air, or else by the same instinct that called him here. She looked into the night, into him, and Bren felt as if he'd been pierced by blue eyes.

The woman dropped her book to the couch and stood, and wrapping the afghan around her shoulders, she walked to the sliding glass door. Bren did not make a hasty escape but remained where he was, circling the cabin, watching her through ravens' eyes, unable to tear himself away. What was it about her that called to him so strongly? It was more than her beauty, more than his curiosity, more than the fact that he'd been too long without a woman in his bed.

She was curious, too. Hearing him but surely unable to see much in the dark of night, she opened the sliding glass door and stepped outside. The deck was accessible only from the house so she felt safe enough, he imagined. She'd heard something, perhaps *felt* something, and had come outside to explore.

She stepped to the railing and looked into the night sky, catching sight of the assemblage of birds, which moved in unison, which moved as one. Instead of being alarmed by their number and their closeness, she smiled.

Miranda watched the big black birds fly before the brilliant orb that was the moon. The mountains, the moon, the birds. Before her was a heart-stopping picture unlike any she had ever seen before, beautiful and unexpected. She was a city girl, and sights like this one were unknown to her.

She had no pets at home, and if she ever did decide to get one, she wouldn't choose anything as exotic as a bird. But she did have a soft spot for ravens, always had. Maybe a story or poem she'd read long ago had stuck with her, maybe some past image had been planted in her brain, because she couldn't resist the rare knickknack or book where ravens were concerned. Over the years her collection had grown. It was no wonder she was fascinated with the birds. They were dangerous and elegant, impressive and puzzling, intelligent and savage. And beautiful.

Soon she'd make her way to bed, but for now she found herself enjoying the night air and the ravens, the peace and quiet and the absence of ghosts—the one who had appeared so briefly earlier in the evening had not shown herself again. She leaned casually against the deck railing. Why didn't Roger and Cheryl come here more often? There was something special about these mountains. They touched her soul in a way she could not explain, and though she was not ready to admit it aloud, she was deeply grateful to her friends for all but forcing her to come here.

The birds she'd been watching changed direction and swooped away from her, disappearing into the wooded land just beside and beneath the cabin, this sturdy structure that looked to be perilously built onto the side of the mountain but felt solid enough. Miranda walked to the side of the deck and looked down, but it was too dark to see much of anything below. She did hear the rustle of wings and the crackling movement of birds in the underbrush for a moment, and then all went still. She strained, listening closely, but the birds were completely silent.

And then she heard another sound, one that was not at all birdlike. It might've been the movements of a large animal. Or a man. "Who's there?" she called sharply, almost hoping to be answered by a growl or a bark. All went silent but she knew something, or someone, was down there. "I'm going to ask you one more time," she said sharply, "and then I'm going to get my gun." She did wish she'd thought to ask Roger for a pistol or a rifle! Not that she knew how to use a firearm. "Who's there?"

After a short pause and another rustle of underbrush, a voice answered. "I'm your neighbor from up the hill."

Korbinian, the psycho real estate agent. "What the hell are you doing here?"

"It's my mountain," he said, just a little bit testily.

"Not all of it," she responded, shaking a finger at the darkness. "Wait right there."

Miranda ran into the house, dropped her afghan and grabbed the flashlight that was sitting on the coffee table close at hand. Power outages must be common here, because the cabin was lousy with flashlights and candles. She could only imagine how complete the darkness would be here where no city light could reach.

She ran onto the deck and turned on the powerful flashlight, shining it down to the place where she'd heard movement and that voice. At first she saw nothing, and then her light found him.

Korbinian stood far below, partially sheltered by the thick growth on the slope that cut down the side of the mountain. What she could see was that longish, straight black hair, the solemn face and a bare chest. It wasn't cold, but it was certainly much too cool for anyone to be out bare-chested—even if that chest was as nicely muscled as his was. The exposed arms were not too shabby, either.

A barely dressed stranger who had no business being here was talking to her, and she was taking the time to admire his muscles? She'd lost what was left of her mind.

"Come closer," she commanded harshly, using the light to gesture into a clearing below her and just a few feet from where Korbinian stood.

"I'd rather not," he responded.

"Why not?" She shone the light on his face and he shaded his eyes with one lifted hand.

"I'm naked."

Miranda did not have an immediate vocal response for that, though her heart skipped a beat and her temperature rose slightly. Eventually she asked, "Why?"

"I'm a naturalist," he said.

"A what?"

"A nudist," he clarified. "I like to hike naked."

Miranda studied the brambles below and wondered why on earth anyone would tramp through the brush bare-assed, without the protection of clothing. The night was chilly and she thought about making a joke about naked men, cold weather and shrinkage, but she didn't know Korbinian nearly well enough to do so. Still, the thought crossed her mind.

"What are you doing here?" Korbinian asked.

She kept the light trained on his face as she leaned into the deck railing. Maybe he was naked, but he was far below and thought she had a gun. "I'm a friend of the Talbots. They offered me the use of their cabin and I took them up on it."

"You're on vacation," he said.

"Yes."

"For the weekend?"

"For the week," she said. It really hadn't taken much effort for her friends to convince her that a long weekend wasn't long enough. His jaw hardened in obvious displeasure, so she added, "Maybe two. It's so peaceful here I might call Roger and tell him I'm going to stay a while longer."

"You'll get bored," Korbinian argued.

She should be annoyed with him, or frightened, or at the very least concerned. But she wasn't. "I don't think so. I understand there are kicking outlet malls not too far away."

"I didn't see a car."

Why was Korbinian arguing with her? Why didn't he just slink back into the woods, embarrassed at getting caught out and about without a stitch of clothing? She should be the one to end this strange conversation. All she had to do was turn off the flashlight and go inside, making sure all the doors and windows were locked.

But she didn't. "Roger gave me the name and number of a man who will drive me wherever I want to go."

"I'll drive you," he said quickly, almost as if he

wanted to get the words out of his mouth before he changed his mind.

This was just too odd. Miranda very briefly shone the light onto the man's chest and shoulders and nice arms. Once again she noted that he had a fine physique, and she imagined he spent more time building houses than selling them. With a body like that, no wonder he wasn't embarrassed!

"No, thanks," she said cautiously. "I'll probably stay right here, after all." Sleeping, reading, doing nothing at all.

"Do you have a name?" he asked brusquely.

"Doesn't everyone?"

"You don't have to tell me if you don't want to," he said. "It would just be nice to be able to call you something besides the blonde."

"Why are you calling me anything at all?"

"You're on my mountain."

"Our mountain," she countered. "For this week, at least." She leaned over the deck railing a little, secretly wishing for a better look. It wasn't like her to be so bold and so curious, but there was something about Korbinian that appealed to her. Her instincts had been sharpened since the accident, and at this moment she was quite certain that there was no reason to be afraid of Brennus Korbinian. "My name's Miranda. Miranda Lynch."

"Call me if you change your mind about that ride, Miranda Lynch. The name's Korbinian. I'm in the book." Korbinian stepped back into the darkness of the forest, moving into the shadows and away from the beam of her flashlight. Too bad. He must've startled the birds because suddenly she heard them again. They rustled and cawed, and soon burst from the trees and took flight.

Miranda moved her flashlight slowly back and forth, the light cutting through trees and brush but only to a certain point before darkness took over. Unable to see any sign of Korbinian, she said in a soft voice, "You scared the birds."

Alone in the darkness, Miranda's stomach clenched and flipped. She grasped the deck railing and took a deep, calming breath. Before her conversation with Korbinian she'd been perfectly content, but suddenly she was keenly aware of her solitude.

Chapter 2

It was Sunday and he didn't have to be anywhere early, but years of habit had Bren up at dawn. While it was still early he headed down the mountain, driving slowly even though he knew the road. His eyes strayed toward the Talbot cabin as he approached, and he wondered what on earth had possessed him when he'd told Miranda Lynch to call him if she needed a ride. His days were more than full, and he wasn't running a taxi service for the woman who'd intruded on his mountain.

Still, he slowed as he passed the cabin, and when he caught sight of her on the deck, sitting there admiring the view with a cup cradled in her hands and a blanket across her lap, he stopped. He sat there for a moment, then he cursed and backed up so he could pull into the driveway. He turned off the engine and pushed open the door, angry with himself for stopping but unable to stifle the urge to get a good up-close look at the woman who had all but lured him to this cabin last night.

He couldn't get onto the deck from here, not without a few acrobatic tricks, so he stopped near the spot in the very small excuse for a front yard where the ground sloped sharply. The deck was solidly built onto pillars that were buried deep into the side of the mountain. He could transform and be on that deck in a matter of seconds, but since he'd spent a lifetime hiding what he could do that wouldn't be a smart move, tempted though he was. So he called the woman's name, perhaps a bit more sharply than was necessary.

Miranda Lynch walked to the railing, much as she had last night. This time she had that afghan around her shoulders and she continued to hug the cup against a morning chill. Her fair hair was slightly mussed; she hadn't bothered to comb it yet, he imagined. There was an interesting flush to her cheeks, one caused by the crisp morning air. He couldn't discern her shape beneath that blanket, but he had seen it well enough last night. She was petite and finely formed. Her heart-shaped face was framed by a mop of pale hair, and her blue eyes were almost too large for her face. Standing so close, he could tell that there was a light sprinkling of freckles across her pert nose. Miranda Lynch had a girl-next-door look. She was cute, not gorgeous, and still he felt an incredible draw to her that was anything but natural.

"Mr. Korbinian," she said, smiling gently and then taking a sip from the blue mug. "This is a surprise."

"I'm going to the grocery store, and since you don't

have a car I thought I'd see if you needed anything." His offer was voiced more sharply and abruptly than was necessary, he supposed, but since he wasn't exactly sure why he was making it at all he didn't feel guilty.

Her eyebrows shot up in surprise. "I didn't have you pegged as the neighborly type."

"You don't know me, so why am I 'pegged' at all?" He could only imagine what Talbot had told her about him. They hadn't exactly been on the best of terms in the past few years.

She didn't have an answer for that, so she took another sip, a slow one this time as if she was savoring the warmth and the taste rather than trying to come up with a response. He imagined the liquid—tea? coffee?—on her tongue, the way she would taste it, savor it, swallow it. A woman drinking coffee should not make him hard!

"I don't need a thing," Miranda said, "but thanks for asking. It was very sweet of you, Mr. Korbinian."

He couldn't remember the last time anyone had called him sweet. Maybe never. "Call me Bren."

Miranda's head snapped away from him and to the side, as if she'd been alarmed by a loud noise to her right. His hearing was quite good, and he hadn't heard a sound. She whispered low, mouthing something he couldn't hear, then a moment later she said in a slightly louder voice, "I will not!" Then she looked at him, and her eyes were bigger than before, her face paler. "It really was nice of you to stop by but I have everything I need and I've come here for peace and quiet so…"

"So thanks but no thanks and get lost," Bren said, taking a step back.

"I don't mean to be rude, but yeah," she said, and then again her head snapped around and she whispered so low that a man with ordinary senses would not have been able to hear, "Go away!"

Bren got into his truck, happy to make his escape. Miranda Lynch was pretty and he was most definitely drawn to her in a way he could not explain, but she was also a nut who talked to herself. It had been a while since he'd been seriously involved with any woman. His perplexing attraction to the stranger proved that he was in bad need of female companionship, but the last thing he needed in his life was a blonde with a screw loose.

"You've scared him away!" the ghost said. "Call him back, it's not too late!" The ghost waved a slender hand as if Miranda should jump off the deck and chase Korbinian down the mountain.

Miranda waited until she heard the truck moving away from the cabin before she turned to the spirit. She'd seen a lot in the past four years. Murder victims. Distraught mothers who'd left their living children too soon. Ghosts who didn't realize they were dead. Those who came back one last time to tell a loved one goodbye. This was her first actual matchmaking ghost.

"I'm on vacation," Miranda said calmly. "Come back next week and we'll talk."

"Not next week," the woman said. "Good heavens, I've waited for you all this time and now you want me to wait another week?" She put hands on slender hips and struck a defiant and elegant pose. "You have to get close enough to touch Bren. Once you touch him he'll know that you're the one. Once you touch him…"

"I have no intention of ever touching Brennus Korbinian," Miranda said as she turned away from the ghost and headed back to her chair. The view from the deck was breathtaking, but it was difficult to enjoy with a ghost at her elbow. Still, she tried. She ignored the woman who chattered away, but she could not help but hear.

"He's really not so gruff once you get to know him. He is quite handsome, don't you think?"

Of course he was, but while Miranda couldn't lie to the ghost she wasn't about to agree aloud. She certainly didn't want to encourage the specter in her blatant matchmaking attempt.

"I do wish he would shave more often and get an occasional haircut," the woman said, perching on the deck railing as if she needed the support, when in fact she could just as easily have hovered on air. "But all in all he's quite a catch." She ticked off Korbinian's selling points. "He's rich, he's handsome and he's very attentive and kind once you get to know him."

Miranda shooed the woman away with one hand, encouraging her to move out of the way. Her too-solid ghostly image was blocking the view.

"He's lonely, you know, that's why he's occasionally gruff."

"Move," Miranda said simply.

The ghost smiled at her, as real and solid as any living person could be. "Tell me that you think Bren is handsome and I'll depart to let you enjoy the scenery for a while."

"That's blackmail."

"And it must be the truth," the ghost added. "I will know if you're trying to pacify me."

"If I tell you with honesty that I find Brennus Korbinian handsome you'll leave me alone?"

"For a while."

Miranda pursed her lips. She really should not allow herself to be blackmailed by a ghost; it set a bad precedent. Still, she wanted her peace and quiet. She wanted an unobstructed view of the distant and magnificent mountains. "Fine. He's attractive."

"*Very* attractive."

Miranda hesitated only a moment before responding. "Yes, he's very attractive."

"What do you find most appealing?"

"Go!" Miranda said, and at last, the ghost obeyed, leaving Miranda with an unobstructed view of a vast green paradise and a niggling sensation in her gut that robbed her of the peace that view should afford.

Since he obviously needed to get laid, as his reaction Miranda Lynch proved, Bren pondered the possibilities as he walked through the familiar grocery store aisles, mindlessly tossing staples into his cart. He hadn't exactly been a monk, but he'd always avoided keeping a woman too long or promising more than he could give. The downside to being the last Korbinian was accepting that he would never find the one woman he could bond with, the one who could give him children and share his life. She did not exist.

He could marry, he supposed, but there would be no children, and he had never before met a woman he felt he could share his secret with. His body, yes; his secrets, never.

In order to keep his life as he wanted it—solitary— he had to keep his intimate relationships shallow and short-lived. He didn't want any woman in his house; he didn't want any woman thinking he could offer more than a night or two. In the past he'd had a couple of relationships that had lasted a few months, but a few months had always turned out to be too long.

Bren had almost finished checking out when he realized that the cashier was flirting with him. She smiled, she commented on each of his purchases, she leaned forward, breasts shown to their best advantage. He hadn't seen her here before. She had the face and body a man would remember, and thick, long dark hair that had been pulled back into a massive ponytail. Tammy, according to her name tag, was the perfect solution to his current dilemma. He needed a woman who wouldn't drive him to distraction. One he could have a little fun with and then walk away from without guilt or second thoughts. One who didn't talk to herself and get under his skin and vacation at the cabin that was a blight on his mountain.

The problem was, this beautiful woman who was flirting outrageously did nothing for him. Nothing at all. Miranda Lynch takes a sip of coffee and he gets hard. Tammy thrusts her boobs in his direction and slowly licks her lips and looks him in the eye with an unmistakable come-hither expression—and nothing. *Nada.* Shit.

It was a long hike down the winding road to the gas station and convenience store at the foot of the mountain, but it was a pretty, mild spring day, and after just a few hours in the cabin Miranda found she was tired of sitting. She could only take so much vacation, apparently. Her restlessness had nothing to do with Korbinian's morning visit, she told herself. Nothing at all.

As she walked carefully along the side of the road, Miranda admitted to herself that her friends had been right when they'd insisted that she needed some time off. She constantly pushed herself hard, feeling that with every murderer she helped to catch she was honoring Jessica's memory. With every burden of grief she eased, she felt as if a bit of her own grief was released. The death of a beloved sister was not in vain. if Miranda put the abilities that had been awakened in that accident to good use.

That didn't mean she enjoyed reliving violent deaths and soothing the tears of those left behind. It was simply what she had to do to honor Jessica's memory. This was not the life she had planned, but in the end it was the life she'd made. What choice did she have?

Suddenly Miranda realized she was not alone on the winding tree-lined road.

"You're sad," the ghost said as she kept pace with Miranda's easy, cautious stride.

"I thought you were going away," Miranda said without so much as altering her step. "In fact, you promised that you would."

"Your sadness called me back," the woman said. "We don't have to talk about Bren if that makes you feel any better."

Miranda sighed. "It does, actually." She glanced at

the amazingly solid-looking specter at her side. The woman appeared to be maybe fifty or so, and her dark hair had a few strands of silver-gray shot through it. She was pretty; perhaps had once been a great beauty. Unlike Miranda she was tall; she was elegant and commanding in a way a woman of five-two could never manage. "Do you have a name?"

"Of course," the ghost answered simply. "Doesn't everyone?" It was the same flippant answer Miranda had given Korbinian last night. Had this meddling ghost been listening in? Probably.

"What should I call you?" Miranda persisted. If the woman was going to insist on hanging around, she should call her something.

"My friends call me Dee." The ghost looked pointedly at Miranda, her eyes amazingly alive and bright. "I believe I can call you a friend, and I promise you that you can call me the same."

"You're haunting me," Miranda argued, though she had to admit that Dee had been less than tormenting. Maybe she'd been a matchmaker in life and had carried that proclivity into the afterlife. Most spirits remained earthbound for more pressing reasons, but anything was possible, she supposed. "Friends don't haunt friends."

"I'm only haunting you a little," Dee said, and then she laughed lightly. "I would not feel pressed for time if you had not been so late!"

"How could I be *late?*" Miranda asked.

"Two years I've been waiting. Two years!" She didn't sound angry, just frustrated. Dee took a deep breath. Odd, since ghosts really didn't have to breathe. "But we're not going to talk about that now. We're going to talk about why you're so sad."

There was no use in arguing the point. "I miss my sister."

"That's only natural," Dee said with sympathy.

Miranda didn't allow herself to share her feelings openly, not anymore, but since no one else could see or hear Dee, what difference did it make? Ghosts frequently spilled their guts to her. Perhaps there was nothing wrong with her doing the same. "Jessica was my only family, and her death was sudden and unnecessary and..." Miranda fought back tears. "I miss her," she said again. "Even years later some days I feel so alone. I have some wonderful friends, but still, I feel like I'm isolated from everyone, like I'm separate. Does that make sense?"

"You will have another family one day," Dee said. "You won't always be alone."

Miranda shook her head. Her abilities were a complication, she had found, and romantic relationships didn't work. The Lynch love curse remained in effect.

"You *will*," the ghost insisted in response to the silent reaction.

They continued to walk, both of them silent. Miranda's steps were short ones to accommodate the steepness of the hill, and Dee simply kept stride, always directly beside. When they hit a stretch of road that was not so steep their speed increased, then as it dipped down they slowed again. Miranda found she was oddly glad of the company, even if her only friend in Tennessee was an interfering ghost who thought the local grump was the catch of the decade. Maybe Korbinian wasn't a psycho, but he wasn't exactly dream date material, either. Who was these days?

The road that led to the cabin and then farther up the mountain to Korbinian's place was narrow. She couldn't imagine two cars of a normal size passing without tires leaving the road and easing onto the perilously crumbling shoulder. The narrow strip of dirt along the sides of the road was uneven and narrow, and beyond the edge was a slope that varied in height from a few feet to a frightening vast drop. Miranda found it best to stay on the pavement. It wasn't as if there was any traffic along the road to deal with.

At least, not much traffic. When she heard the approaching vehicle she knew it had to be Korbinian. He'd been gone for hours, so he must've done more than grocery shopping while he was out. Not that she cared where he had gone or what he had done. Miranda moved to the shoulder as far as was safe, glancing down to the tangled green and brown growth on the slope below. She took small, cautious steps, waiting for the vehicle to come around the corner and pass. If she was lucky her neighbor wouldn't feel he had to stop and offer her a ride.

She caught sight of the front of Korbinian's massive black truck. As soon as he rounded the corner he'd see her and move to the other side of the road, and even if he didn't, as long as he kept his tires on the pavement she'd be fine. Too close for comfort maybe, but safe enough. The driver came into her line of vision, and she caught sight of his shaggy dark head and stern face. A cell phone was pressed to his ear and he was talking with animation and passion to whomever was on the other end of the line. Passion for work, she imagined, unless that was a girlfriend and they were arguing. It was definitely not a *happy* conversation.

How come he got a cell signal and she didn't? Talk about unfair. That was Miranda's last thought before Dee shouted, "Look out!" and pushed. A ghost should not be able to gather the strength to physically disrupt the living, but this one did. Miranda felt the force against her shoulder as she lost her balance and scrambled wildly to regain her footing. Korbinian's head snapped up and he spotted her, and he quickly swerved his vehicle to the side. But it was too late. Miranda tumbled off the side of the road.

Bren ended the call without warning, put the truck into Park and set the brake, then threw the door open and jumped out, running to the side of the road and leaving his truck crossways in the narrow roadway with the door standing open. He'd been trying to finish up his business call before he hit the next curve, where cell service ended, and he hadn't been paying attention, here where he never saw another car much less a pedestrian.

He looked over the precipice where Miranda Lynch had stumbled and disappeared, and breathed a sigh of relief when he saw her sprawled on the ground just a couple of feet below. She'd been winded and there were leaves and twigs caught in her long hair and on her pale pink sweater, but other than that she appeared to be unhurt.

"What the hell were you doing walking on this road?" he snapped.

Blue eyes looked up at him. He had never known that

eyes could actually shoot daggers, but hers did. "I'm fine, thank you," she said coldly, still not moving.

Properly chastised, he took a couple of steps down the steep slope so he could help her. Loose dirt and fallen leaves made his footing uncertain, so each step was cautious. "Are you hurt?" he asked.

"Thank you for your concern, but it comes too late," she said, struggling to sit up. The ground here was not too steep, so she should have been able to manage on her own in spite of the loose dirt and leaves. Still, he offered a hand. A hand she ignored as she struggled to stand without assistance. As she had this morning, her head snapped to the side and she whispered, as if there was someone there, "I will *not* take his hand! The idiot ran me off the road!"

Obviously she'd scrambled her brains, though he wasn't sure that had happened when she'd fallen. They'd been pretty much scrambled when he'd met her. And still, his body responded to the very sight of her.

She worked her way to her feet without assistance, even though righting herself on the uneven ground would've been much easier with a hand to hold on to. So, she was stubborn, as well as scrambled. After a moment Bren found himself working to restrain a smile. The woman would go to any lengths to avoid touching him, apparently. A twig with a few leaves attached had wound itself snugly in a tangled length of blonde hair. One lucky leaf had landed on a tempting swell of pink sweater. He remained steady, hand offered, in case she changed her mind about accepting help, but she was determined to make it on her own.

When she had regained her footing, she shooed him out of the way so she could climb back up to the road. He obliged, taking two long strides up the slope to the shoulder of the road, then turning to watch her try to do the same on her short legs. After taking a couple of steps only to stumble back down the hill a bit, then failing in her attempt once more, she looked up at him— ah, there were those daggers again—and shot out her hand in a silent and decidedly surly request for help. Bren reached out and clasped her hand, taking it firmly in his own.

As soon as his flesh touched hers, Bren felt as if an electrical current had been set loose within him. Before he had the chance to explain away the phenomenon, again the unexpected happened. Clear as day, Bren saw his ancestors, the Korbinians who'd lived thousands of years ago, breaking from human form to a flock of birds so massive they blocked out the sun. As if he were there, he saw a time when his kind was prevalent and united and powerful, when they ruled the skies and the night.

Then he felt and saw this woman beneath him, a part of him as she was meant to be, as she had been born to be. She smiled, a lover's smile. Her body took him in, and together they found pleasure like none other he had ever known.

He saw himself on the deck of the house where he now lived alone, but in the very real vision he stood there with his sons who, like him, were human and yet more than human. They all transformed to take to the skies together, blocking out the moon as they took flight across this mountain they called home.

She was the one. She was Kademair. No wonder he had been so strongly called to her. No wonder the very sight of her damn near made him crazy. Miranda Lynch was the only woman in this world he could bond with; the only woman who could save him from being the last of his kind as he had always accepted he would be. He'd thought this special woman, who his mother had always told him would come one day, to be a myth, and yet here she was, standing before him with her hand in his.

"A little help?" she said in frustration, and only then did Bren realize he'd been standing there holding on to her for a too-long moment.

He gave Miranda's hand a tug, pulling her gently up the hill until she was once again standing on the narrow shoulder of the road. She released his hand as soon as she was able, shaking her head mightily, a move that dislodged a few leaves but did little to right the effects of the fall. Bren reached out and gently pulled the largest twig from her hair. She found the move too personal, too intimate, and slapped his hand away.

"You should watch where you're going," she said sharply.

His voice was much calmer as he responded, "You shouldn't be walking on this road. It's too dangerous."

"Dangerous? How about talking on the cell phone while driving a monster truck up a narrow winding road? *That's* dangerous. What carrier do you have?" she asked, picking that lucky leaf from the swell of her breast. "I can't get a signal at all."

"There's nothing past the next curve," he said, trying

not to see this woman in an all new light, trying to forget the mental image of her beneath him. The vision had been so real he could still feel her; he could smell her; he knew how her flesh felt against his, how her body gave and took. Forgetting was impossible, even though he wasn't sure he wanted what she could offer.

There was no place in this world for the Korbinians, not anymore. Their time had passed. Logically he could dismiss Miranda Lynch; rationally he knew what she promised would never work. But a primitive instinct he could not deny now accepted this woman as being his, and he wanted her so sharply that he could think of nothing else.

Chapter 3

Bren insisted on driving her back to the cabin, and Miranda only protested once, quite mildly. She no longer felt like walking to the store and then making her way back up this mountain road. The fall hadn't been dramatic by any means, but it had shaken her, just as standing there with Bren's hand clutching hers, his dark brown eyes boring into her as if he saw something new and striking on her face, had shaken her.

At least Dee was gone. The meddling ghost had better not show her face again, after pushing Miranda off the road. Miranda squirmed in the passenger seat of Bren's truck, disturbed on many levels. Dee must be quite powerful to be able to move earthly objects. It wasn't easy for a spirit to physically affect anything at all, much less generate a push vigorous enough to move a living being. If Dee decided to stick around, there was likely nothing Miranda could do to stop her. What if Dee was actually strong enough to tag along back to Atlanta and even to jobs across the country? What if she could never get rid of the matchmaker? Scary thought.

Bren pulled sharply into the short driveway in front of the Talbot cabin, and then he turned to Miranda with accusing eyes and a firmly set mouth. She couldn't help but notice—again—that grumpy or not, he was very good-looking. Good-looking but not pretty. There was nothing soft about the man, not in his facial expression or the cut of his jaw or the fire in his eyes—eyes that were the color of dark chocolate, she noted as she stared into them for a moment. What she could see—and *had* seen—of his body was definitely not at all soft. He had a workingman's body, sculpted and impressive and hard. If she'd met him years ago, before her life had changed so dramatically, maybe she'd be attracted to him. Maybe.

Who was she kidding? If noticing the precise color of his eyes and admiring his body wasn't attraction, what was?

"Why were you walking down the road?" he asked sharply.

"Exercise," she said. "And I thought I'd pick up a couple of cans of soda at the gas station."

His expression was accusing, as sharp and hard as everything else about him. "I offered to buy you anything you needed while I was out."

She glanced at the collection of grocery bags in the backseat. They'd been jostled when he'd stopped so suddenly, and his purchases were now in a state of disarray. A few cans had escaped the plastic bags, and a box of cereal had turned upside down onto the floorboard. Oh, my. The tough guy ate Froot Loops. "I'm perfectly capable of—"

"Obviously you're not," he interrupted harshly. "I'll be back in an hour to drive you to the store."

"I really don't need—"

Again he interrupted her. "I'll be back in an hour. I can either take you shopping or I can sit in the driveway and wait right here in case you change your mind and decide to take off on foot again."

"You wouldn't!"

"Try me."

Miranda sighed as she opened the passenger door and took the long step down to the driveway. She was still a bit shaky, but when she looked back into the truck and once again Bren's powerful eyes caught hers, she allowed herself to listen to the instincts that had so seldom disappointed her. Brennus Korbinian was a grumpy, annoying, nudist in a place where to be in a state of undress was not at all wise. He didn't watch where he was going when he drove. He was definitely bossy.

But deep down he was a good person, and yes, whether she wanted to admit it or not, he was attractive, as Dee insisted he was. It had been a long time since Miranda had allowed a man to take her anywhere on anything that might resemble a date, and like it or not, she thought that he considered his offer to run her to the grocery store a date of sorts.

She'd only be here a few more days, so maybe it

wouldn't hurt to let a good-looking man take her to the grocery store. It wasn't as if a week was time enough for what might be a casual interaction to turn into anything more serious. "Fine," she said. "One hour." And then she slammed the passenger door and walked toward the front porch, digging the keys to the cabin out of her jeans pocket.

Korbinian stayed in the driveway until she had the door closed behind her. She didn't look out the front window, tempted as she was to do so, but she did listen as he drove away. Miranda glanced around the main room of the cabin as she brushed a spot of dirt from her jeans. "Dee, show yourself." The specter had some explaining to do.

In spite of Miranda's command, the main room remained quiet and ghost-free. As she headed for the bathroom to make repairs to her appearance, she decided if getting pushed off the side of a mountain was the price for peace and quiet, she'd take it.

Fifty-eight minutes after he'd dropped Miranda at the Talbot cabin, Bren was back in her driveway. At home he'd called the plumber who'd been cut off when Bren had tossed his cell aside, put away his groceries and unsuccessfully tried to wipe away or even explain away the visions that had come to his mind so strongly when he'd taken Miranda's hand.

He sat in the driveway and waited, wondering if he should go to the door and ring the bell like a proper gentleman caller. Was Miranda sitting in the cabin waiting for him to collect her? Would she expect him to open the passenger door for her and carry her grocery bags and make nice? His fingers tapped nervously against the steering wheel; his eyes remained fixed on the front door. He wasn't known for making nice. Being a loner had its costs, and a lack of social skills was one of them.

Surprised as he was, the woman's appearance should not be entirely unexpected. Bren's father had long considered himself the last of the Korbinians, but he'd been wrong. The old man had been nearly sixty when he'd met Denise Brown, a childless divorced woman more than twenty years his junior. They'd married three weeks after meeting, and Bren had been born less than two years later. Maybe if they'd met earlier Bren would've had brothers, but they hadn't, and he'd been an only child, just as his father had been.

According to Joseph Korbinian, as the population of their kind diminished, so did that of the women they were meant to be mated to. In ancient times when the Korbinians had flourished, so had the Kademair, those women with whom they could bond and mate, those women who had the genetic ability to nurture and give birth to Korbinian children. The decline was simply nature, Joseph had explained to his only son. There was no longer a place in the world for those who could walk as men and also take flight, no place for a rare species that had once served as revered messengers and warriors. In ancient times the Korbinians had been honored, but a thousand years or so ago those they served had turned against them in jealousy and mistrust. After a bloody war the species that walked as man and flew as ravens had lost, and those who'd survived had gone into hiding.

And now all that was left of what had once been a fine and special race was one man. Bren was the end of it, unless he followed his instincts and took Miranda as his mate; unless he made this woman the mother of his children—the mother of the Korbinians. The savior of an entire race. But if there was no longer a place for them in the modern world, should the race be saved? Or should it be allowed to die, as nature so obviously intended?

He couldn't deny the doubts that warred with these new thoughts. Maybe Miranda wasn't Kademair, after all. Maybe his father had been right. Bren wondered if he craved what he could not have so much that he'd created this scenario with a convenient and attractive woman.

She didn't make him wait long. Miranda stepped onto the front porch, displaying no sign of her earlier accident or of annoyance that he had remained in the truck, instead of going to her door. She'd changed clothes and now wore black jeans, short black boots, a deep-teal sweater and a simple but strange little black hat that was slightly quirky and somehow suited her. The narrow brim framed her face, along with that blonde hair, which he now knew was not one shade but a hundred or so, golden and ash and pale brown all woven together. A red purse on a long chain dangled from one shoulder. She'd put on makeup, he noted as she walked toward the truck. Not a lot, but her lips were soft and pale pink, and her eyelashes were darker than they'd been an hour ago. There were no longer any leaves or twigs in her long hair, which had been brushed into a golden sheen.

Bren leaned across and opened the door for her from the inside, and she stepped onto the running board and then climbed in, hair swinging, pink lips seductive, jeans hugging her legs and fine ass just so. The way he felt right now, she could've come out in baggy flannel and he'd be turned on.

No, what he was experiencing went well beyond *turned on.* He'd never felt an attraction like this one— and he still didn't know if it was a pull he'd follow. Destiny or not, he would not be led by biology or mythology or whatever the hell this was. His life—and hers—was in his hands, and the decisions to be made could not be made lightly.

"Do you need anything besides groceries?" he asked as Miranda closed the passenger door and he backed onto the road.

She sighed. It was a very nice sigh, indeed. "Is there a decent antique or furniture store nearby?"

"There are a couple of them along the highway."

"I'd like to thank the Talbots for letting me stay here by buying them something for the cabin."

"Like what?" he asked.

"Maybe a couple of lamps," she responded. "Something decorative, or maybe a small end table. The cabin is very nice, but it's pretty, uh, sparsely furnished."

She almost choked on the words *sparsely furnished,* which gave him an idea of what she was up against. Bren smiled. "Are there ducks and bears?"

Her head snapped around. "Yes! How did you know?"

"The cute-animal theme is a common decorating mistake in these parts."

She relaxed. He could feel, as well as see, her response. "You sound as if you don't approve. What, you don't have dancing black bears and cavorting ducks at your place?"

"No," he answered decisively. "There are also no deer heads or stuffed bass, no geese in frilly white hats and, while we're on the subject, no wax fruit in the kitchen."

"You must have had an enlightened decorator," she teased.

"No decorator. I did it all myself."

She studied him critically; he could feel her gaze on him. "Most men are very utilitarian when it comes to decorating."

Bren shrugged. "You'll have to see my house and judge for yourself, I guess."

She clammed up, perhaps no more comfortable with the idea of visiting his home than he was at the idea of inviting her there.

They hadn't been gone more than fifteen minutes before Miranda knew agreeing to let Brennus Korbinian take her anywhere was a huge mistake. Their simple trip felt too much like a date, even though the antique store he took her to was definitely not a normal stop on any courtship route. The long warehouse was dusty and overstuffed, filled to the brim with a mixture of new and old pieces, some of them treasures, most of them junk.

She loved the crowded, dusty store, and strangely enough Bren seemed comfortable there. He knew the woman who owned and ran the place, an older lady he called Mabel, and the greetings they'd exchanged had been simple and cordial. With the owner of the antique store he was anything but grumpy, though he wasn't exuberant in his interactions, either. Mabel was helping another couple look for something specific, leaving Miranda and Bren to wander through the lovely mess alone.

They hadn't been browsing long when Bren asked almost casually, "So, how do you know Roger Talbot?"

It was an innocent enough question, she supposed. In the Atlanta area Miranda had gotten a lot of press, some of it praising, more of it denigrating, the occasional bit meant to be amusing, she supposed. Even though her work often took her out of state, away from home Roger always managed to keep her involvement under wraps. He had not been so lucky at home base. Locally, word of her talents had been out for a while now.

Obviously no one around here would be reading the Atlanta papers, so she was tempted to make up a believable story for Bren, something that had nothing to do with seeing ghosts or solving crimes. He would probably believe whatever she told him, unless he happened to do a Google search on her. Some days she hated the Internet! Nothing was secret anymore. Nothing was private.

Besides, she'd been here before, she'd played that game. She meets a man. She likes him and he likes her. Why spoil it right off the bat with the truth? All goes well and then he finds out what she can do and it all goes to hell.

Miranda picked up a small glass bowl and studied it carefully, afraid to look directly at Bren. She tried to convince herself that she didn't like him all that much, anyway. If she scared him off here and now, what had she lost? Nothing. "I talk to the ghosts of murder victims at crime scenes and pass the information on to Roger, who uses what I find out from the departed to collect the evidence he needs to arrest and convict the guilty."

All was silent. Miranda listened intently to the horrendously loud ticking of a nearby ancient clock as she studied the light from the front window breaking through the glass bowl in her hand. Bren didn't laugh, he didn't gasp, and unless he moved soundlessly he hadn't stepped away from her in horror, either.

"Sounds like tough work," he finally said in a lowered voice. "No wonder you needed a vacation."

Miranda twisted her head slightly and looked into Bren's face. No, he wasn't kidding her. He wasn't scared or repulsed, either. There was a touch of sympathy in his eyes, but not so much that she thought he felt sorry for her. She hated pity as much as she did disbelief. Maybe more.

He shook a finger at her, and she noted that he had a workingman's hands, long-fingered and callused and rough and beautiful. "You weren't talking to yourself this morning or after you fell off the road. You were talking to a ghost."

"I was. You don't seem at all surprised," she observed.

"It takes a lot to surprise me." He smiled. For a man who didn't smile often, he did so very nicely. "To be honest, I'm relieved. For a while there I thought you might be a little bit off your rocker, talking to yourself and all."

"I do sometimes talk to myself," she said, experiencing the strongest rush of ease she'd felt in a long time.

"Yes, but you probably don't tell yourself to go away."

She drew back a little. "You heard that?" This morning

when she'd tried to order Dee to go she'd whispered so softly and Bren had been standing so far away…

"Yeah." He motioned to one ear with one of those long, fine fingers. "I have the Korbinian hearing. You can't pull anything over on me."

Heaven above, she liked him. Cheryl's psycho, Roger's irate neighbor who was determined to own the entire mountain, a man who'd literally run her off the road and then chastised her for being there. She liked him much more than she should. He was alternately funny and pensive, grumpy and hospitable, and he did look fine in those worn jeans. And then an alarming thought occurred to her, a thought that wiped away all her ease.

"You're being nice to me so I'll convince Roger to sell you the cabin!" She put the glass bowl down too hard. "I should've known," she muttered to herself.

"I am not," he said without anger.

"You *are*. That's why you offered to give me a ride, that's why you stopped and helped me after you ran me off the road." She threw her hands up in the air. "If you didn't want me to help you get the cabin, you probably would've left me there to fend for myself. You probably would've gotten a good laugh and just kept on driving."

Finely shaped eyebrows arched. "You don't think much of me, do you?" he asked, calm as could be.

"No, I don't." Miranda defensively crossed her arms and took a pose that clearly said *Keep away*. Clear as it should've been, Bren wasn't listening.

"Do you want to know why I offered you a ride?" He took a step closer and she backed away. "Do you really want to know why I found myself outside the cabin on your first night on the mountain?"

Naked, as she recalled.

Again he moved forward and she moved back, until she found herself trapped in a kind of hole fashioned from an antique wardrobe and a noisy clock. *Tick tock, tick tock.* "Do you really want to know why I didn't run from you when you made it very clear that was what you wanted?"

"Yes," she whispered.

He leaned in, cupped her chin and lifted her face, and then he placed his mouth over hers. She was so surprised by the move that for a moment she didn't react. She simply stood there and accepted; she experienced; she felt. Yes, it had been a long time since she'd been properly kissed, and this simple touch of mouth to mouth was more than proper. It was extraordinary. The kiss rocked her to her toes, it paralyzed her, it shook her to the center of her being and fired up a wave of desire that was strong and primitive and totally unexpected. She heard the ticking of the big clock and the beat of her own heart, she felt Bren's lips and the wobbling of her knees and a tingle that shook her and took her to a place she had not been in a very long time.

Desire. She couldn't say the sensation was entirely unknown to her, but it was something she'd denied herself for years, and she had never experienced it so fully, so deeply or so quickly. Bren's lips moved gently and she shuddered. Her lips parted and so did his, and for a moment she was frozen, unable to breathe, unable to describe the connection and pleasure she experienced. When he removed his mouth from hers it took all the will she had not to grab the front of his shirt and pull him back.

"That's why," he said, and then he turned away and left her standing there, shaken and confused and very tempted to chase after him.

Bren helped Miranda carry her purchases into the cabin he had so long coveted. If he had his way he'd buy the place and raze it to the ground. A good look at the interior did nothing to change his mind about those plans.

A couple of decent lamps and a decorative bowl were hardly going to help matters. What the cabin that marred his mountain really needed was a good fire.

"Cozy," he said beneath his breath as he surveyed the orange sofa and matching overstuffed chair. "Ugly as sin, but cozy."

Miranda laughed. "Tell me what you really think, why don't you?"

They had managed to ignore the kiss, at least openly. He couldn't forget it and he knew she hadn't forgotten, either. He could almost swear there was an electric current running between them, a current that repelled and attracted at the same time, a current that changed the smell and the feel of the air he breathed.

Bren had known at first touch that she was the one for him. Sexually, reproductively, to the soul and to the bone, Miranda was for him. From that moment he'd felt as if he was being led—hell, *dragged*—into a life that was predestined and he had no choice in the matter. But just because she was here and they had some kind of ancient connection didn't mean they had to act on it. Her presence and his knowledge of the possibilities didn't mean he had to follow his impulses. For a moment the kiss had chased his doubts away and he'd been ready to dive in, body and soul, but the doubts were back. He would not be led, not in a matter as important as this.

He wondered if Miranda felt anything out of the ordinary. She was Kademair, but that didn't necessarily mean she knew, as he did. That didn't mean she looked at him and realized he was meant, biologically at least, to be the father of her children. Did she struggle with the possibilities, as he did? Maybe she was blithely and wonderfully ignorant of how momentous their meeting was.

The father of the rebirth of a species or a childless bachelor and the last of his breed—that was his choice. It was not a choice to be made in an instant, no matter how natural one path seemed to him at this moment. The natural path would take him directly to Miranda Lynch's bed, into her body. With everything he was, he wanted to peel those black jeans away from her skin, taste her, arouse her, claim her in a way he had never thought to claim any woman.

If he were an animal there would be no choice to be made. But he was not an animal, he was a man. Difficult as it was, he would attempt to think rationally. He would try to push back his natural attraction until he was sure of what he wanted.

His well-ordered life could change in an instant. Did he want the dramatic change this woman's appearance offered?

Miranda showed him where to place the lamps, while

she put her sodas and skim milk in the refrigerator, commenting on how rude the cashier at the grocery store had been. It was true. Tammy had not been happy to see Bren return with another woman. Bren had barely spared a glance for the cashier, unnaturally taken as he was with Miranda, but he'd noticed.

"So," Miranda said while her head was in the refrigerator and she didn't have to look him in the eye, "why do you want this place so badly, anyway?"

"It's an eyesore."

"This cabin might not be up to your standards, but it's hardly an eyesore," she said, closing the refrigerator and turning to face him. "Are you really such a loner that you want to have this entire mountain to yourself?"

He didn't want to answer that question, not yet. Was he still a loner? "Why is your friend Talbot so determined to hang on to it? I've offered him more than enough to buy a better place elsewhere."

"I suppose it has sentimental value," she said as she left the galley kitchen. "It belonged to his father. Back in those days the cabin at the top of the mountain wasn't much bigger than this one, he said."

"No, it wasn't," Bren admitted, remembering his father's cabin, the place where he'd spent most of his childhood. His mother had demanded more, for herself and for her son, and for many years they'd moved between a proper house in Townsend and the cabin on the mountain. The house in Townsend, nice as it had been, had never felt like home.

The conversation about this mountain and the cabin was small talk, but in the air something momentous lingered. A kiss and the electric energy in the air danced between them. Everything had changed, could change, and surely Miranda felt that on some level. Bren wasn't good at romance; he didn't know how to woo or chase or smoothly seduce, and he still wasn't sure what he was going to do about this woman who had worked her way beneath his skin. The possibilities remained endless.

He was straightforward in everything he did, including sex, so he asked, "Do you have a boyfriend at home?"

"No," she answered quickly.

She didn't wear a ring, but that was less than conclusive. "A husband or fiancé?"

"No." She didn't ask him why he wanted to know. After the kiss she shouldn't need to ask. "What about you? Is there a girlfriend out there wondering where you are on a beautiful Sunday afternoon?"

"No," he responded as simply as she had.

"A Mrs. Korbinian?"

"Not yet," he said, looking her squarely in the eye.

For some reason that answer brought a hint of color to Miranda's cheeks. She tried to ease the tension in the room with a laugh that sounded all wrong, as she removed her hat and tossed it onto the couch as if it were a Frisbee. "What's wrong with us? The ghost thing scares a lot of men away, but you…what's your excuse, Korbinian? Why are you still single?"

"Maybe one day I'll tell you." If he stayed here much longer he wouldn't be able to leave. He had the best of intentions, but if he stayed in Miranda's company he'd soon be physically incapable of walking away, and the decision he wrestled with would be made. Bren headed for the door, but he did turn to look back at Miranda. She was a hard woman to leave. "Dinner tomorrow, my place, I'll pick you up at six."

He didn't give her a chance to refuse his offer, but left quickly—while he still could.

Chapter 4

Miranda showered and put on her pajamas early in the evening, determined to get the rest that had brought her to the mountains. She would relax if it killed her! She made soup for supper—chicken noodle soup right out of the can, since real cooking wasn't what she'd call restful. To be honest she wasn't all that hungry, but she made herself eat a few spoonfuls.

After soup she sat on the deck for a while, enjoying the spectacle of near and distant vistas, but her eyes were drawn too often to the house at the top of the mountain. Korbinian's house—in no way could it be called a cabin—had been built with an eye to fitting into the environment, so it didn't exactly pop out. The roof was a dull, dark green; the deck, which ran the length of the house, seemed almost a part of the wooded landscape.

If not for the little bit of light shining through large windows, which surely afforded Bren a stellar view, she could almost think his house was a part of the mountain he wanted to claim entirely as his own.

She couldn't get a good handle on Brennus Korbinian. Yes, he looked at her like he wanted to eat her up, and they were both unattached and healthy in a world where in so many cases that was good enough for everyone involved. Miranda had never understood the appeal in a one-night-stand, but plenty of women—and men—her age did. If she was ever going to consider a casual sexual relationship, Bren would be perfect.

She understood her attraction to him, but why was he paying her so much attention? Korbinian was successful and good-looking, so he shouldn't be exactly desperate for female companionship. Lack of social skills aside, he should have women lined up at his door, if that was what he wanted. He didn't strike her as one of those men who had to conquer every woman they met, as if sex was a game and they thought themselves master players. She'd met guys like that, men who moved in too quickly, got too close, smiled too widely and too intimately. Bren wasn't like that, not at all. In the beginning he had been anything but friendly, and he was very low on the smarmy meter—even though he had hiked to the cabin naked, which she surely would've taken as a warning sign if she didn't instinctively like him at least a little bit.

Over time his attitude had changed, subtly but significantly, to one of cautious friendliness. That was hardly the way of a snake.

Over time. Ha! She'd known him one day, if you

could call carrying on a conversation with a distant naked man knowing him.

Her instincts where people were concerned were better than normal, yet they were far from flawless. Could she trust those instincts where Bren was concerned? Had her hormones overridden those instincts…as well as her common sense?

Much too early in the evening, the lights from those windows at the top of the mountain went out, and she could no longer see the lines of the Korbinian house. The mountain was black, ominous and filled with secrets. Did Bren retire so early? Likely so. He was in construction, after all, and probably would get an early start in the morning.

Not her. She was going to sleep until noon! She was going to lie in the bed and do nothing. It had been a long time since she'd treated herself to a real rest.

The same flock of birds she'd seen last night appeared once again, swooping toward the cabin and then taking a sudden upturn as they approached the deck. Miranda knew a couple of women who were afraid of birds, but she'd always been fascinated with them. They could fly; she flew only in her dreams. They were entirely free; she was mired in responsibility and an abnormal ability she did not want.

Ravens in particular appealed to her, always had, and she wasn't sure why. They were sleek and beautiful and smart. Something about them must be special, given all the poems and legends in which they played an important role. Maybe she was drawn to them because they were forever tainted by a mythical relationship with death, and death was a very real part of her new life. Her fascination with the blackbirds had only grown stronger after the accident, so maybe that was the explanation. Long before she'd been pulled into the world of the dead, maybe something inside her had known it was coming…

The flock of birds swooped down and lit in a nearby dead tree, where their shapes were made clear thanks to the moon behind them. Some sat still, others hung from dead branches by their large claws. They played; they watched her; they fluttered black wings and cawed to her as if attempting to carry on a conversation. Miranda found herself smiling as she watched them frolic, as if they had come here for the specific purpose of entertaining her.

Were ravens night birds? She didn't think so, but twice now she'd seen these birds take over the night sky. They came to her by night. What an odd thought, to believe that these wild creatures were hers in any way.

A sharp, crowlike scream split the night, and then the ravens burst from the tree as one, leaving the perch as suddenly as they had landed, all of them taking flight at once as if on some silent command she couldn't hear with her inadequate human ears. She thought the birds would soon be gone, leaving her alone once more, but apparently that was not their intent. For a few moments the ravens flew before her, their motions graceful and in symmetry. They became a part of the night, swooping and twirling as if their every move had been choreographed. Miranda grasped the deck railing and leaned forward, almost sensing that she was somehow a part of their display. Her heart pounded hard and she could not wipe the wide smile from her face.

She reached out a hand, which they ignored; she laughed for no reason.

Too soon the ravens rose and disappeared into the darkness, circling the cabin high above where she could no longer see them. As quickly as they had come to her, they were gone. Miranda's wide smile faded as she hugged herself against the chill of the night. She stepped inside.

How was it possible to mourn the loss of a flock of wild birds?

Miranda had promised Roger that she wouldn't work at all while she was here, but that didn't mean she couldn't check her e-mail. She'd put off the chore until now, since like cell service, there was no high-speed connection in this isolated place. She'd have to do with dial-up. Barbaric!

Getting her laptop connected did turn out to be a test of her patience, but she managed. Her e-mail downloaded with agonizing slowness. Most of the messages were from potential clients or old clients who had new questions and wanted to meet again. After scanning a couple of the work-related messages, she moved on, leaving the remainder unread. This was, after all, vacation. They could wait.

There was one long and disturbing message from Autumn. In the upscale suburban neighborhood where Autumn and Jared had a very nice home, a young mother who lived on the next street over had been murdered on Friday night. At first the police thought she'd surprised a burglar, but now they were talking to the husband. Even though it looked like yet another sad domestic-abuse case, Autumn didn't much like being left at home alone while Jared traveled on business. She'd been hearing strange sounds at night and was having trouble sleeping, and until she knew with certainty what had happened to the poor woman, she would not rest easy. She didn't ask, but Miranda expected her friend would like her to try to talk to the ghost of the murdered woman when her vacation was over and she got back to work.

There was also a message from Roger in which he chastised Miranda for reading her e-mail, as if he'd known she couldn't go more than a couple of days without checking in. She answered Autumn briefly but ignored Roger for now. Let him think she was doing as he commanded.

She couldn't help but wonder what he and Cheryl would think of her odd relationship with Bren. Was it a relationship? Not really. She'd met him. He'd almost run her over with his truck. He'd given her a ride and kissed her once, in public. That didn't exactly constitute a relationship.

The birds had moved on, and Miranda found herself lost in a stark and unusual and oddly unwelcome silence. No city sounds, no television, no wings flapping or birds cawing. Such silence was downright unnatural! She thought about putting a CD in the portable player Roger had sitting against one wall of the main room or plugging in her MP3 player, just for the noise, but she didn't do either of those things. She decided to embrace the silence, which was so much a part of this mountain.

She often felt alone, as she had told Dee earlier in the day, but she'd never before felt so isolated. It was the

view of mountains that appeared so untouched and un-
inhabited, she imagined, the fact that but for one man
on the top of the mountain, she was physically, as well
as emotionally, separate. She wondered if this was how
people who'd lived long ago, when the world had not
been so populated, might've felt. Isolated. Vulnerable.

Miranda started to turn off the laptop, then hesitated.
She wasn't quite ready to disconnect from the rest of the
world, and when she turned off the computer, that's what
she would be. Completely disconnected. Instead of
signing off, she went to a search engine and typed in
Brennus Korbinian. So she was a potential stalker. She
hated the fact that anyone could type in her name and in
minutes read all about her life, and here she was snooping
into Korbinian's past. Her curiosity was justified, she
reasoned. There was something decidedly unusual about
the man, and if she was going to have dinner with him
tomorrow night she needed to know more.

What if he kissed her again? What if he wanted much
more than a kiss next time?

Again, waiting for results was agonizingly slow. It
took minutes rather than seconds for the information to
come up on her screen. There were articles about Bren's
involvement in the community, which surprised her. He
didn't just want this mountain all to himself, he fought
against overdevelopment, even though he made his
living building and selling homes. Very nice, expensive
homes, judging from what she saw on the Web site for
his real estate company. There were a number of Realtors
listed, but he was not among them. The company was
his, but apparently he spent his time building homes, not

selling them. Miranda smiled. No, Bren would not make a great salesman. She could just see him, brusque and without any finesse at all, telling potential buyers to make up their damned minds or quit wasting his time.

She scrolled down the page of results until she came to an obituary for Bren's mother, Denise Korbinian, who'd passed away a little more than two years ago. Feeling more stalker-ish than ever, Miranda clicked on the link to read the entire story, which came complete with a photo.

"Dee!" she said aloud, and then she glanced around the room to see if calling the ghost's name had conjured her up. Apparently not. Dee, Bren's *mother,* perhaps still felt guilty about her little stunt on the road. As well she should.

Below that link on the main search page were quite a few articles and sites in foreign languages. She also found Bren's father's obituary. Joseph Korbinian had preceded his wife in death by six years, almost to the day. Curious, and anxious to wipe away the new knowledge that her current haunt was Bren's mother, Miranda continued her search.

Moving on to name meanings, she discovered that both Brennus and Korbinian meant Raven. Miranda got a strange chill down her spine as she looked at the words on the computer screen. Her own name meant "admirable." Boring. Raven was much cooler—and odd, considering her collection at home and the birds who had visited her here.

Odd, but not exactly freakish. It was just a name! With that thought she turned off the laptop, taking a moment to glance at the clock in the bottom right-hand corner before the screen went black. She'd spent far too long browsing the Internet for info about the man who was going to feed her tomorrow night. The fact that she'd had to deal with dial-up service hadn't helped matters at all.

She stored the computer beneath the desk and walked through the cabin, turning off lights as she went. Once she thought she saw Dee out of the corner of her eye, but when she turned the specter was gone. "Coward," Miranda muttered.

Even though her mind was spinning, Miranda quickly fell into a deep sleep. She dreamed of black birds and silky soft wings that brushed her flesh with a touch as gentle as that of a lover.

It was a dream and more than a dream, an acknowledgment of the bond between them and a powerful fantasy, rolled into one.

Bren stood on the railing that surrounded his deck, as he so often did, and transformed in an instant into a flock of ravens that flew without a single doubt or reservation to the cabin below. Miranda's bedroom window was open, as he had known it would be, and he burst into the room. She was not surprised to see him as a flock of blackbirds that flew in unison, that saw and thought and moved as one. She was waiting for him on her bed, naked and smiling and gesturing with a crooked finger for him to come closer.

As if he needed any invitation. He hovered over her, his wings brushing against her body, black feathers stark against pale, delicate flesh. He was seventy-seven ravens that moved over and against her in a wave, caressing her body with wingtips she welcomed. She smiled and accepted him for who and what he was, opening her arms wide so that his wings feathered against them from shoulder to wrist. She did not flinch, not even when his wings came near her face. She knew he would not hurt her; she knew he was hers to command in all ways.

Her gentle smile told him she liked what she felt. Her welcome told him that she knew who and what he was, and there was no fear within her. Not of him.

"My Kademair," he said, his mind speaking to hers in a voice only she could hear.

"My raven," she responded aloud.

He brushed the tips of a dozen wings along the soft exposed flesh of her flat belly and higher, across the swell of her breasts. A wing brushed across a taut pink nipple, once and then again. Miranda closed her eyes and threw her head back, exposing a slender throat he caressed with the wings that had carried him through the night air to her. He heard her heartbeat, sensed the warmth rolling off her body.

"My Bren," she said, reaching for him.

And in the blink of an eye he was there, a man to her woman, flesh to her flesh. Lips and hands replaced feathered wings. The press of his body along hers was unlike anything he had ever experienced, but then, she was his Kademair, and they shared a connection that was unknown and even unimaginable to mere men.

Her hands rested lightly on his hips while he kissed her throat with leisure, replacing the caress of feathers with the brush of his lips and the tip of his tongue. He drank in her warmth, fought to refrain from filling her too quickly when there was so much pleasure to be had in simply touching her. Her soft breasts pressed against his hard chest, and her sigh was more arousing than any sound he had ever heard. He was close to being inside her, but it was too soon. She was ready for him physically, he was certainly ready for her…but she did not know all. She did not yet understand how momentous their coming together was.

She wrapped her legs around his hips, shifted her body until Bren was closer and harder than before. He hurt with wanting her; he needed her like he needed air in his lungs and a night sky to fly across. He was being pulled to her and into her by a force beyond his control, as if who they were, who they were meant to be, dragged them to a place where their will no longer mattered. Had it ever? Did he really have a choice?

"Do you know?" he whispered in her ear.

"All I know is that I want you," she responded. She scooted her hips down, bringing herself closer to their joining. "I want you in a way I have never before wanted anything. There is no room in me for anything beyond that need, not when it's so great." Her flesh was warm silk against his own, and he drank in the warmth with her body pressed to his. Where had she been before this? Why had she hidden from him? Her beauty was remarkable, her need for him an aphrodisiac that drove all thoughts but having her from his mind.

The tip of his penis touched her silky wetness, almost entered her body, and she moaned in satisfaction and need. Eyes closed, body open and inviting, lips parted, heart pounding...she was his. Bren no longer cared about anything but the end to this. She was his; he was hers. The heat they created was undeniable, and he had been a fool to think either of them had a decision to make. This was meant to be. He pushed into her body and she accepted him with a moan and a gasp. Her hips lifted, her legs caught him tightly and pulled him deeper.

An urgent tapping against the bedroom window made Bren's head snap around. The warm and willing woman beneath him vanished, leaving him alone and cold as a soft voice spoke within his mind.

Save me.

Miranda awoke in a sweat, dragged awake from the most startling and unexpectedly delicious dream by what sounded like a pecking against the window. A bird's insistent beak, pebbles being thrown against the glass, fingernails...

The noise came again and she sat up slowly, running her fingers through her hair and grasping for reality. For a moment she thought a dream had awakened her, a bad dream brought about by Autumn's disturbing e-mail about a murderous burglar. And then she heard it again. That sound wasn't a part of any dream; someone was out there. No one was tapping against her window trying to get her attention—someone was trying to break into the cabin. Miranda glanced at the clock on the bedside table and found it dark. The power was out. She reached for the phone on the nightstand and lifted the receiver to discover that it, too, was dead.

This was no bad dream, though she fervently wished

that it was. She had no cell service, and there was no one within miles but the man she'd been dreaming about. No way could she scream loudly enough for him or anyone else to hear. Like it or not, she was on her own, and as isolated as she had felt earlier. She was alone.

Heart hammering, Miranda slipped from the bed into inky darkness. She knew where the intruder was by the sound of him trying to work his way past the lock on the front bedroom window, which faced the narrow road and the empty driveway. She'd like to think that the intruder thought he was breaking into an empty cabin, but since he'd cut the phone lines and the power, she couldn't be sure that was the case. If he realized she was here, then he knew she was helpless, so to cry out and confront him with threats at this point would be useless. Best to make a quick, quiet escape. But how?

Miranda left the bedroom, moving through the completely dark space with only memory, the feel of the floor against her bare feet, and searching hands in the air before her as her guide. There were flashlights in just about every drawer in the cabin, but to switch one on would warn the intruder that she was awake, and then he'd stop being cautious and quiet and force his way in. His caution bought her a little time.

In the main room a touch of moonlight through the sliding glass door kept her from complete darkness. She snagged a flashlight from the desk drawer closest to that door and then she eased the door open and stepped onto the deck to look out over a vast and deserted moonlit landscape. In the moonlight the green trees looked black and forbidding. The dead tree where earlier the ravens had stopped and spoken to her was stark and cold. She glanced up the mountain to where Bren's house was located. Without a single light on, she could only place it by memory.

"You could get your ass down here and save me," she whispered in frustration as she tiptoed to the railing and looked over. What good was a studly and interested neighbor if he couldn't be summoned when she needed him? Her stomach flipped over as she looked to the ground below. It was a long way down, but what choice did she have? From inside she heard the tinkle of breaking glass; her intruder had gotten impatient or brave or clumsy and was no longer taking care to be quiet. There was no time to lose.

Miranda made her way to the far side of the deck, where the drop was slightly less overwhelming than elsewhere. From here she'd gazed down upon a naked Korbinian—had it been just last night?—and had felt herself perfectly safe, since she was so far off the ground and he was so far below. Now she was going to have to try to make her way down, preferably without breaking her neck or any other vital body part.

No longer listening for sounds from inside the cabin but concentrating entirely on escape, she stuck the flashlight into the elastic waistband of her pajamas and sat on the wooden railing. The night air was colder than she'd expected on her bare arms, chasing away the warmth of her erotic dream and making her wish she'd grabbed a robe or a sweater on her way out of the bedroom. Shoes would have been nice, but she was not going back into the cabin, not even for appropriate footwear.

She'd lived alone for years, and in all that time she'd never worried excessively about the dangers. Oh, she locked her doors and windows and she took all the normal precautions, but never had she expected anything like this. Why here and now, when there was nowhere to run to for help?

Miranda said a short prayer as she swung off the deck and grabbed the support post that held the deck up off the rocky, unfriendly, much-too-distant ground below. She hung on, and as she did she heard footsteps from inside the cabin. Those footsteps made her heart climb into her throat, and she clung to the post with all her might, knowing if she made a sound he'd know exactly where she was. Did the intruder have a weapon? Of course he did. A gun, most likely. Maybe a wicked and sharp knife. If he saw her here, if he leaned over the railing with a weapon in his hand, she'd be a sitting duck.

Miranda tried to ease her way down, slowly and cautiously. Splinters stung her bare arms, arms that strained to keep hold. She scraped her bare feet and ankles against the rough wood. A fall from this height would kill or cripple her, but now that she was here, she wasn't sure she could make it all the way down. She held on with her legs, which were wrapped around the rough wooden post as they had been wrapped around Bren in her dream, thankful that her pajama bottoms were more substantial than the little shortie top, which was comfortable but offered little protection in this situation.

She had a horrible thought that made her forget the

pain in her arms and her legs. Was that Bren in the cabin? Was he truly the psycho Cheryl had said he was? Were his lack of social skills and grumpy nature signs of some psychotic disorder? Her taste in men had reached a new low, if that was the case. For the first time in years she'd attracted a man, and the next thing she knew he was breaking in with foul intent. She was so good with the dead and absolutely dismal with the living! Her hormones were definitely interfering with her instincts, if she was so off base about Bren.

The footsteps she'd heard in the cabin moved onto the deck, and Miranda went very still. Instinctively she held her breath. Through the slats above her head she saw the shape of a man. His steps were slow and his boot heels thudded ominously on the wooden deck. She didn't dare breathe as he walked to the railing that looked out over the valley, whispering darkly, "Where are you, Miranda Lynch?"

She couldn't see his face, not through the narrow gaps in the deck floor, and the voice she heard was not familiar to her, though it was such a low and angry whisper she wasn't sure identification was possible. But he'd said her name. He knew her; he had come here for her.

Breathing became essential, but she did so as shallowly and quietly as possible. Her arms ached, but she didn't dare move. The man above might hear her. She clung to the post with all her might, hanging on for dear life—literally. Her arms were growing weak; they trembled. How long could she hold on? The man above finally turned away from the railing, and between the boards above, illuminated by moonlight, she saw in his hand what she had feared he might have. A gun.

In her line of work she'd talked to quite a few ghosts who'd been killed with such weapons. No violent death was pleasant, but she'd had the sensation of hot metal entering the body, destroying the bone and flesh in its path, described by the victims too often not to fear it. The intruder didn't go inside, but stopped there on the deck, standing still as if listening very hard. Listening for her, she imagined.

She couldn't last much longer and she didn't dare move. Her arms continued to tremble; her stronger legs kept her from falling to the ground, thank goodness, but she didn't have much hope that they'd hold out much longer. Her entire body shook so fiercely she was afraid the man above would hear the rattle of her bones.

Suddenly she was no longer alone. Strong arms were wrapped around her, supporting and comforting. Those strangely substantial arms kept her steady. "Hang on," Dee said, her ghostly voice for Miranda alone. "He's coming…he's coming."

Miranda shifted her body slightly and when she did, the flashlight she'd stuffed in her waistband fell free. She squeezed her eyes tightly closed in horror as the flashlight crashed to the ground below, landing loudly and then rolling away. The man on the deck took a step toward her; he breathed loudly in what seemed to her to be satisfaction and perhaps excitement. A gunshot from above or a fall to the ground below? Which would be the better way to go?

She heard the birds before she saw them. Their caws

broke the night, and for some. reason she couldn't explain she felt a rush of relief as they neared. The way their wings disturbed the air spoke to her; they had been called here by her distress.

The flock of large birds swooped under the deck overhang and swarmed the intruder long before he could reach the railing directly above Miranda. Their shrieks of outrage and the surprised cries of the man they attacked with beaks and claws covered the sounds of Miranda's quick descent down the post. She might not have made it without Dee's assistance, and even though Miranda had been surprised by the ghost's display of unusual strength just that afternoon, she was now very glad of it. She was vaguely aware that above her the intruder ran into the house and slammed the sliding glass door shut behind him. He ran noisily through the cabin and exited boldly through the front door. Soon a car engine revved, and the birds that circled above the house screamed a protest.

She could swear they shouted her name, each syllable a shriek called by a different raven. *Mir-an-da. Mir-an-da.*

Miranda had almost made it to the ground when her arms gave out and Dee's support was no longer enough to keep her aloft. She fell with a short and automatic scream, as the car that had been parked out front raced down the hill, the noise of its engine obscenely loud in the otherwise silent night.

She landed hard on her left leg and tumbled down the steep hill, but was able to find purchase on the uneven ground and right herself. The sound of the intruder's car faded and died away, the swish of birds' wings increased in volume and pace and then stilled completely. Miranda took a deep breath and strained to hear, since she could see nothing from this vantage point. Was she right in thinking the car was going down the hill? Was it possible it was headed up, instead?

His voice came out of nowhere. "Are you hurt?"

Miranda scrambled to her knees. Caught in a combination of shadow and moonlight, Bren stood, naked as he had been last night, as he had been in her dream. Her first reaction was one of relief. He hadn't been in the car that had made its escape; he wasn't wearing the boots that had clomped through the cabin in search of her.

Her second reaction was definitely mixed. Bren was naked and fine and tempting, leanly muscled and entirely male. Since she'd just been dreaming about him in such a state, her body reacted as any woman's might, even given the dire circumstances. Something low inside her clenched and trembled, and she could almost feel him entering her, slow and thick and inevitable. Suddenly she was not cold at all. In fact, she grew quite warm. Her heart still beat too hard, she was scared, she was going to be bruised and sore tomorrow…but she was safe, at the moment. She was safe thanks to a flock of birds that shouldn't have been in flight at this hour and a man who liked to tramp around the mountain naked in the middle of the night. A man she was drawn to much too strongly.

"Are you hurt?" he asked again, more intensely this time as he took a step closer to her.

"I think I'm fine." She held out a hand, palm forward,

to command that he stay where he was, and he obeyed. The inky shadows that fell across his body were interestingly placed, and she wasn't sure she wanted to see more of Bren. Not at the moment, anyway. She could see just enough to know that cold or not, shrinkage was *not* a problem. She wasn't sure she could take any more than that. "A man broke into the cabin," she said. "Did you see him?"

Bren shook his head. "Not well. It's dark, and he had something over his face. He's gone now," he added in a soothing voice.

"Why are you here?" she asked, still not rising to her feet.

"Couldn't sleep," he said. "Thought I'd take a walk to clear my head."

"I told you he'd be here," Dee whispered, popping back in for a moment. And then the ghost was gone, and Miranda was once again alone with Bren.

Chapter 5

North Carolina, near the town of Silvera

Duncan Archard presented his report solemnly, trying to hide the excitement that had been building inside him for hours. He'd spent fifteen of his thirty-six years studying and shadowing the last Korbinian, collecting a scattered history of the species, watching from afar as the last of an unnatural breed lived out his life. At the first sign of misuse of power, Brennus Korbinian was to be eliminated.

This was much worse than an abuse of power, in Duncan's opinion.

Ward Quinn, long-time leader of the Fifth Division of the Order of Cahir, studied the written report carefully, his gray head bent, his weathered hands gripping the paper too tightly. When he was done he read the report again, his eyes snapping up to the top of the page. The second time he read more slowly. Duncan waited for the questions that were sure to come.

"Are you sure?" Quinn asked in a low, commanding voice. They were alone in a farmhouse kitchen. Mrs. Quinn slept in the bedroom upstairs, after all this time still oblivious to her husband's true purpose. Other warriors of the Order, dedicated men like Duncan, had been stationed all over the world, their assignments much like his. Watch. Report. Keep peace at any cost.

There were other stations like this one situated here and there, other leaders like Ward Quinn who had spent a lifetime fighting monsters of one sort or another. Last Duncan had heard there were sixteen active divisions around the world; he was too low on the totem pole to know everything, so by now there could very well be more.

"I'm sure."

"Korbinian has been interested in women before." Quinn slapped the report down on a weathered oak table. "He's even had a few relationships, as is to be expected with a man of his age. What makes you so certain this one is Kademair?" He had no qualms about taking out unnatural beings that posed danger to others, had in fact done so many times—personally—but as long as the subjects lived peaceably among the natural world, he was content to allow them to live.

"She arrived on Saturday," Duncan said. "By Sunday afternoon they were grocery shopping together. For a man who keeps to himself most of the time, this is not normal behavior."

"That's hardly proof."

Duncan pulled a photo from his jacket pocket. "This is the woman in question. Recognize her?"

Quinn glanced down at the photo on the table, his expression grim. "Of course."

"There's no proof that Kademair are always gifted in one way or another, but it is alluded to in several of the ancient texts…"

"And talking to the dead is most definitely a gift," Quinn said. "Not one I'd choose for myself, but still… I'm afraid this does change things."

Duncan felt what could only be called a rush of excitement. He'd joined the Order to kill monsters, not to observe them until he was as old as the man before him. "Yes, it does," he said, his voice calm even though he was anything but.

Quinn glared across the table, his pale eyes sharp and surprisingly clear for a man of his years. "Still, it is not our way to eliminate beings as a precautionary measure."

Duncan shook his head. He wasn't as judicious as his boss and mentor. He could've made this report by phone or e-mail, but the farmhouse was just a few hours drive from his home base, and he wanted to look the old man in the eye as he made his argument. "As it stands, Brennus Korbinian is the last of his kind. He's not a sixty-year-old man like his father was when he found his Kademair—he's barely thirty years old. If he joins forces with Miranda Lynch, they might have a dozen children. We can't be at all sure that they would be as circumspect and law-abiding as their father. Could we even watch them all when they grew to manhood? Could we ever be sure that one of them wouldn't use his powers for something less than noble or, heaven forbid, go public? One is all it would take, you know that, Ward." He didn't have to argue that when those Korbinians had sons of their own, the Order would need to start a serious recruitment program to be able to watch them all, and it wasn't as if they could advertise in the newspaper. Instead of the end of his kind, Brennus Korbinian would be the father of a new wave. "Best to stop it now."

Quinn's eyes met Duncan's. Outwardly Ward Quinn was shabbily dressed and rumpled, the sweet, slightly absentminded grandfatherly type. But his eyes were sharp and even hard. He was not a man to be taken lightly. "I cannot speak for everyone around the world, but this division of the Order has never committed murder in the name of convenience. You're suggesting that we act as a prophylactic to keep Korbinian from reproducing."

Duncan didn't bother to argue that point. "With good reason."

Quinn rapped the table with his bent, wrinkled fingers. This was an odd conversation to have in the warm, traditional kitchen where Mrs. Quinn had prepared many a fine meal for her husband and his associates, but it was not the oddest Duncan had ever participated in, in this very room. "When we first studied Ms. Lynch's case, you didn't suggest that we eliminate her," Quinn said in an accusing voice. "Even when her abilities became public knowledge, you did not support such a drastic measure."

Frustrated, Duncan said, "She can't prove she talks to ghosts. There are too many alternative explanations, and people don't always believe what they can't see. But a man breaking apart into a flock of blackbirds in front of a television camera would be tough to dispute. The situations are not the same," he said tersely. "It's not necessary that we eliminate them both," he said, trying to sound sensible. "One can do little harm without the other." Korbinian had been quiet for years. Would having his Kademair taken away spur him to action? Duncan would reveal no preference to Ward, but in truth he'd much rather see Korbinian eliminated than the woman.

Even before he spoke, it was clear Quinn was not convinced. His eyes narrowed. A wrinkle in his brow deepened. "I need more than a trip to the grocery store to convince me that Lynch is Korbinian's Kademair. Go back to the mountains and watch them. If she is who you think she is, things will progress rather rapidly."

"And then?"

Quinn's jaw clenched. "Then we will talk again." He pushed away from the table and his expression changed. He gave Duncan a grandfatherly smile that raised goose bumps. "Tea?"

He didn't dare move any closer. Miranda was frightened, he was naked, and Kademair or not, they barely knew one another. She had no idea the power of the attraction that pulled them toward one another. If only he could learn to carry a change of clothes with him as he flew…

"We'll call the sheriff," he said sensibly.

"The man…he must've cut the phone lines," Miranda

said, tilting her head to look up the hill to him. "I couldn't get a dial tone." She was scared. She was shaken. It made Bren furious to know that someone had done this to her. Her world should not be shaken this way; it wasn't right. He wanted to surround her in any way he could and protect her from any who would harm or even frighten her.

"We'll go to my house and call." He kept his voice even, revealing nothing of the anger inside him. It wasn't time.

Miranda turned and glanced toward his home, possibly imagining the long and difficult walk they had ahead of them. She was currently in no shape to walk far, and the steep road ahead was tough even on a good day.

"If you don't mind that I leave you alone for a few minutes, I parked my car a short distance up the road."

She looked at him suspiciously. "You did?"

"The hills on this part of the mountain are less steep than those near my place. Makes for a more pleasant stroll."

She nodded gently, obviously relieved. "Do you by chance have clothes in the truck?"

"I do." Bren had heard the intruder's vehicle make its way down the hill to the highway. At this moment there was no one on this mountain but Miranda and him—his senses affirmed that fact. Miranda would be safe here for the brief time it would take for him to fly home, pull on a pair of jeans and drive back down.

She fluttered her fingers in an agitated dismissal. "Then go, but please—" she drew her arms in and hugged herself against the cold of the night "—don't be too long."

Bren turned and walked back to the road, well aware of Miranda's eyes on his bare ass. Good thing he'd never been shy.

When he was certain he was out of her sight, he burst into his raven form and flew home. He swooped across treetops and shot directly to the deck of his isolated house, where he took human form once more and rushed inside to pull on a pair of jeans. He was out the front door in less than a minute, barefoot and shirtless but no longer naked. He drove almost madly down the hill, taking the darkened downward curves much too fast for anyone who didn't know them by heart. In moments he was in Miranda's driveway. She'd made her way up the hill at the side of the cabin to the road and was waiting for him in the driveway, arms folded against the night's chill.

She glanced at her broken bedroom window as he stepped out of the truck, then at the door the intruder had left standing open when he'd made his escape. "I should grab a couple of things, I suppose. My purse. My laptop." She shivered. "Some clothes."

Bren took her arm and led her toward the front door, noting with anger that she limped just a little, favoring her left leg. "Try not to touch anything. We'll get your purse and a coat and we'll lock the door as we leave. Everything else can wait until the sheriff has had a chance to look around."

Miranda nodded, numb with shock and fear. Bren almost wished he'd followed the bastard down the mountain, but he couldn't bring himself to leave Miranda alone—not then and not now. Whether or not she was his Kademair, he couldn't abandon her when she was shaken like this.

Whether or not. Ha. After the dream he'd had there should be no doubt about who and what she was. It was no mistake that she was here on this mountain, no co-incidence. She was here for him; she just didn't know it yet. After they collected her purse, the keys to the cabin and a thick sweater he helped her put on over her pajamas, he guided her outside and opened the passenger door to his truck, assisting her as she stepped up. She was shaking still, might shake all night after the fright she'd had.

Now was likely not the time to tell her that she was destined to be the mother of his extraordinary children.

Bren's house was more impressive up close than it was from a distance, and that was saying something. She couldn't see much of the exterior, as it was the middle of the night and there were only two low-wattage outdoor lights burning near the driveway, but the interior took her breath away.

The great room he led her into was massive and furnished with expensive, warm, comfortable pieces that looked as if they'd been assembled with a decorator's eye and a fondness for comfort. The colors—primarily burnt orange, dark brown and a touch of gold—were warm and homey. A fireplace dominated one stone wall, and the remnants of a fire built earlier in the evening smoldered there, giving off some heat. Before Bren called the sheriff he put Miranda in an overstuffed chair near the hearth. She was glad of the heat that rolled off the smoldering logs, gladder still when he returned and added a log to the fire, stoking it to life, creating more heat. Firelight danced over Bren's bare arms and chest. At least he was wearing pants, so she was not completely distracted by thoughts she shouldn't be having about a man she'd just met.

It wasn't like her to be so easily sidetracked. She'd always been cautious where romance was concerned, and had been more so than usual in the past couple of years. She didn't ogle men; she didn't have fantasies and dreams about men who were all but strangers to her.

When the fire was going well, Bren turned and sat on the floor before it. He looked up at her. "The sheriff will be here in the morning."

"In the morning?" Her heart climbed into her throat.

"He said since no one was hurt, he'd go back to sleep and come out to look at the cabin by the light of day."

Not hurt. Ha! She'd scraped her arms climbing down that wooden post, her left leg hurt, and she was going to be bruised all over tomorrow, she was sure of it. But there wasn't anything to be done, she supposed. She was alive and relatively unharmed, and the intruder was gone.

Bren attempted a smile that was too tight. She'd seen, briefly, a real smile from him, and this was not it. He was trying to comfort her, she imagined, trying to make everything seem right with that smile. "It was probably someone who got lost or who thought the cabin was deserted, as it usually is."

Miranda shook her head. "No, that man was looking for me specifically." She shuddered. "I heard him say my name."

"What?" Bren shot to his feet, no longer attempting to make light of her scare. "Are you sure?"

"Of course I'm sure," she responded. "He had a gun, too. He *wasn't* lost and he *knew* damn well that cabin wasn't deserted."

"I'm calling the sheriff again."

As Bren passed by her chair, Miranda reached out and snagged his wrist. She barely knew him, and yet there was comfort in the simple touch. She needed no one; she relied on no one. And yet she was soothed by the feel of her fingers on his wrist. Heaven above, she needed this. "No. The sheriff is right. There's nothing to be done tonight. There are too many places the man might've gone, too many turns he might've made, and I can't describe him or his car."

"It was a dark, two-door sedan, a Toyota," Bren said.

Miranda didn't release her hold on his wrist. She liked the feeling of warmth and connection too much; she needed it. "Get a license plate?"

Bren shook his head.

"Then it can wait until morning." Just as the call she had to make to Roger and Cheryl could wait.

Miranda released her hold on Bren and, thanks to the warmth of the fire, shed her sweater. She no longer needed it. It wasn't as if her pajamas were so sexy and revealing she had to keep covered up. Besides, she'd seen him naked. Twice. A nudist probably wouldn't give a second thought to seeing a woman in her pj's.

Bren cursed when he saw her arms. He reached out and took her wrist, much as she had taken his, and rotated it gently to expose the worst of the scrapes on the underside of her arm. "We need to clean this so it doesn't get infected."

The flickering firelight did interesting things to his bare chest and muscled arms. Longish black hair fell forward and created shadows that hid a portion of his face from her, but she could see enough to know that he was concerned for her. He shouldn't be. They were strangers still. One kiss and a sizzling erotic dream didn't change that fact.

"In a minute," she said softly, her eyes pinned to his face. "I'd like to sit here for a little while, if you don't mind. I swear, I feel like I'm just now catching my breath."

He nodded and continued to hold on. She liked it. The sensation of his fingers around her wrist was steadying and comforting.

"Why are you being so nice to me?" she asked.

"Maybe I'm just a nice guy."

Miranda gave in to a small smile. She didn't believe that for a minute. "Whatever the reason, thank you." She wondered if she should tell him that his mother had been haunting her, trying to play matchmaker from the next life, helping Miranda with an unusual ghostly strength as she'd made her escape down from the deck.

Pushing her off the road.

No. She'd told Bren what she could do and he'd accepted it. That was enough for now. He didn't need details; details might be more than he could handle. Knowing that his mother was keeping an eye on him from beyond might be more than he wanted to know.

After a few moments he pulled at the hand he held and helped her to her feet. When she was steady he guided her out of the impressive main room and down a long hall to a bathroom that was nearly the size of her bedroom at the cabin down the hill. The room was done in tan and dark blue and forest green, very masculine and yet also decadently elegant. The shower was set in multicolored tiles shot with green and blue, and there were three large and sparkling-clean showerheads set at different angles.

This was no neglected bachelor pad, that was for sure. This was a home, a very fine home that had been lovingly designed and well taken care of.

While she admired the bathroom Bren collected anti-septic, soap and washcloths from the bathroom closet. He didn't hand everything over and leave the room, but dampened a cloth and, dark eyes intense, rough-looking hands more gentle than she'd imagined they could be, washed away the grime from her arms.

She had a flashback to the dream she'd been enjoying before the intruder had awakened her, and suddenly her body responded intensely to the gentle touch. Her breath came more raggedly; her heart pounded. She found herself staring at Bren's hands, mesmerized by the way they moved against her flesh. His hands had been darkened by the sun and weathered by hard physical labor; her arms were pale and slender. In her mind she could see those strong hands on other parts of her body. She could almost feel them.

His body moved closer to hers as he worked, seem-ingly intent on what he was doing as he cleaned away the dirt around her abraded flesh. Miranda found herself tilting her head so she could glimpse his fine neck, found herself studying his bare chest and the cut of the muscles just above his low-slung jeans. She wanted so badly to reach out and touch him just beneath the belly button. She wanted to let her fingers linger there and slip even lower. When he came across a splinter he stepped away from her for a moment to fetch a pair of tweezers from the bathroom closet, and then with steady hands he expertly removed the offender. When that was done he searched for others. The antiseptic wash came last, and while it stung a little bit Miranda found she didn't care.

All the while they drifted closer and closer, until her body was almost pressed against his. One small motion and she could rest her head against his chest, as she wanted to do. One step, and she could press her body to his. The spacious bathroom suddenly felt too small, as if the walls were closing in on her. She could barely breathe. Her skin was on fire. At this rate her heart would soon burst through her chest.

She had a choice, a very simple choice, to make. She could take a step back, thank Bren for his help and close off whatever this was between them. Or she could step forward, touch him and open herself to what might come. For most of her life she'd been a step-back kind of girl. Jessica had been the sister who'd enthusiastically grabbed what life had to offer. Miranda always wanted to study and analyze everything to death. She always looked closely before she leaped.

If she studied this situation too closely, she'd write off her strong reaction to this man to some weird hormonal fluctuation, or else to the effect of the adrenaline rush brought about by her narrow escape. She'd call Roger in the morning, tell him his plan for vacation had been a real bust and order him to come get her the hell out of here before she did something stupid. Like end up shot or in this man's bed.

But if she did that, what chances would she miss?

Fearless, Miranda moved forward. She leaned into Bren's chest and rested one hand against his side. She allowed her fingers to slip just barely beneath the denim of his jeans, to slide to the front where with the backs of those fingers she could caress the soft skin she had been fantasizing about moments earlier. Heaven above, he was warm. He was warm and hard, and his heart beat as rapidly as hers did. This man she barely knew was comfort and safety and pleasure in a world that had not always treated her kindly. He was a refuge, *her* refuge.

She lifted her head slightly and pressed her lips to his neck, which was salty and male and wonderful. His arms draped around her, gently and possessively, and she moved closer than before, pressing her body to his, feeling as if she could not get close enough. He could not mistake what she wanted; he couldn't deny that he wanted it, too, not with his body pressed to hers this way.

For a while they simply stood there, holding one another in silence and a strange sort of acceptance. Then Bren moved her hair aside and kissed her neck, and in an instant Miranda felt as if she was falling or flying, as if she was no longer earthbound. With his mouth on her she felt like the ravens that circled the cabin at night, soaring on air and gliding on silken black wings. Free. She felt wondrously free and not at all alone.

Bren slipped the strap of her pajama top aside and

kissed her shoulder, starting at the sensitive place where it curved from her neck and traveling slowly, wonderfully slowly, across to the top of her arm, each kiss small and lingering and arousing. Her body tingled from the place where he touched her to the tips of her toes. His kiss warmed her blood and set her heart to hammering. She felt that heartbeat low, an insistent thrum between her legs.

Bren returned his mouth to her throat, where he lingered for a while as if he were eating her up slowly and surely, as if he were dining on her. He could have her; he could have every inch of her.

"We should stop now," Bren whispered in her ear, while at the same time he slipped a large, warm hand up her pajama top and cupped a breast possessively, brushing his thumb across a hard nipple.

"We should, but I don't think we will," she said honestly, leaning into him and adjusting her body so they fit together more closely, more certainly.

"You don't understand," he said softly.

"I understand enough." She turned her head, cupped his face and planted her mouth on his. His lips parted and so did hers, and they came together with a fierceness that had not been present in this afternoon's more public kiss. A stranger? No. Perhaps she hadn't met Bren Korbinian very long ago, but she knew him to the pit of her soul. He was no stranger, not to her.

Physically she felt like she was being drawn into him in a whirlwind. She'd never experienced a raw desire so strong, had never wanted anything the way she wanted Bren now. No, *want* was the wrong word. Want indicated a wish, a *choice*, and what she experienced went far beyond any normal desire. She *needed* Bren desperately, as if he was a necessary part of her that had been missing for her entire life, as if he was already a part of her in a way she did not understand. She would only be whole when they were finally together in all ways.

Bren felt the need, too; she knew it when he pulled off her pajama top, being careful of her sore arms in spite of his urgency. He lifted her easily and placed her on the generous marble bathroom counter so that she perched on the edge and he fit between her legs. The tile was cold, but the man who held her was warm. Very warm. He placed his mouth on her breasts, lingering there as he had lingered at her neck and her shoulder, arousing her beyond any height she had ever imagined. She was wet. Her body trembled and she ached for him to come inside her. She literally hurt with wanting him, and she spiraled well beyond control. It was unexpectedly beautiful, this complete loss of control in Bren's arms.

At his urging she leaned back slightly and he kissed his way down her stomach with agonizing slowness. Her entire body trembled, she ached with wanting, but she did not urge Bren to rush. His pace was perfection, and every moment was a fine gift she would not give up. There was unexpected beauty here, a surprising tenderness. She closed her eyes against the bright lights above and allowed herself to simply feel without any thought beyond the occasional realization that this was good and right.

Finally Bren caught his fingers in her elastic waistband and slipped the pajama bottoms over her hips and down, discarding them and running his hands along her bare legs, up her thighs. She opened her eyes and watched Bren as he studied her intently, looking at her as if he had never before seen a naked woman. He touched her with reverence and awe and with an obvious need, like the one she felt for him. From above harsh, fluorescent lights lit their encounter fully and without shadow, but she did not feel ashamed or timid. She felt only need and beauty and urgency. She had never before felt such urgency, not in any way, in any situation.

She reached for the button at the waistband of Bren's strained jeans and unfastened it, then pushed the waistband down over lean hips to expose his erection. He was hard and thick and no shier than she was, apparently. Feeling bold, she touched him, caressed him, then guided him toward her as she scooted herself closer, closer to the end of this lightning encounter. Her body burned for this, for him.

"Miranda," Bren said, his voice strained.

The tip of his penis touched her, as it had in her dream. He was right there, almost inside her, and she didn't want to wait any longer for what she knew had to happen. Nothing existed beyond this moment, this need. "I want you," she whispered.

That was enough to end whatever doubts he might have. He pushed inside her, filled her, pumped into her fast and hard and then thrust deep and held himself there, completely and totally within her. Miranda held on to Bren, precariously balanced on the edge of the counter and clutching him tightly. She wanted more, she wanted this to last, but she could not control her response to having him inside her. She came so hard she cried out as she shuddered around him. Pleasure so intense she had not imagined it could be so rippled through her body. She threaded her fingers through Bren's hair and pulled his mouth to hers as the final waves of release rippled through her. She tasted his tongue, his lips and his own unfulfilled need.

He was still hard, still deep within her, and he moved slowly now, so slowly, so gently. Bren moved once, twice, each time with leisure and demand. He moaned and then he withdrew from her quickly and completely.

"You didn't…" she said breathlessly, and he set her farther back on the counter and stepped away from her.

"No, I didn't," he said. "Not yet." She could see the strain of stopping too soon in his dark eyes and in the set of his mouth, as well as in his body.

With her own need satisfied, a touch of sense returned. "Oh, do you have a condom?"

His eyebrows lifted slightly.

Her cheeks grew warm. It was long past time for blushing! "I know it's a little late, but it's not the right time for me to get pregnant, and…and…" She didn't know how to tell the man that he had stolen all reason from her. Miranda Lynch did not lose control; she didn't follow her instincts and forget reason. At least, not until now.

Bren snapped up her discarded pajamas and thrust them at her before turning away and reaching into the shower to start a hard spray of water. "My bedroom's at the end of the hallway," he said gruffly. "You can stay there tonight."

"What about you?" Miranda asked as she slipped down

from the counter. Her legs were weak, so she took a moment to find her balance. Heavens, her entire body was warm and trembling and satisfied in a way it had never before been. The question she asked had many possible meanings, but she didn't feel the need to elaborate.

"I'm going to have a very long, very *cold* shower," Bren said, glancing over his shoulder and pinning his dark gaze on her.

She might feel embarrassed, she might think Bren didn't want her at all if she didn't recognize the pain in his eyes. A part of her was relieved—perhaps even a bit joyful—to know that walking away from her wasn't easy for him.

Chapter 6

Bren took an icy-cold shower that didn't do a whole helluva lot of good, while he much too clearly imagined Miranda, satisfied and still ignorant of all their strong attraction meant, settling into his bed.

Had he really thought he could stay away from her? Had he truly believed that logic could win out over instinct? He'd found his Kademair, just as his father had, just as Korbinians for thousands of years had. The modern world might make the process more difficult than it had once been, but obviously it was not impossible, as he'd believed for so long.

His life was settled; he'd resigned himself long ago to living alone. He wasn't a gregarious person, no one would ever call him the life of the party, but he was satisfied with his life. He enjoyed his work, he'd done well financially, and it wasn't as if he lived like a monk. Was he willing to throw it all away because he'd discovered a woman who could give him children? A woman who invaded his dreams and so easily made him lose control? He'd known her one day. Perhaps in times and cultures where marriages were arranged and choice had nothing to do with the matter, that would've been acceptable, but in this day and age only a fool let his dick make his decisions for him.

Much as he wanted Miranda, it wasn't in his nature to follow the little head wherever it might lead.

Even if he did decide to pursue a future with his Kademair and bring the Korbinians back into the world in force, he wouldn't go any further until Miranda knew full well what she was getting herself into when she gave in to the instincts she didn't yet understand. Perhaps some of the old ways survived, perhaps they were drawn to one another more strongly than was explainable, but he did have a choice in the matter. So would she, even if it killed him.

There was so much more at stake here than sexual attraction and a drastic change of lifestyle.

It would be easy to dismiss what he knew and to let himself believe that he and Miranda would be somehow different from those who had gone before them. This was a new day, a changed landscape. The modern world was more accepting than the one his ancestors had lived in. He and his sons and grandsons, if they came to pass, would not be burned as witches or captured and tortured in order to release whatever "demon" ignorant simpletons believed made their transformation possible. If

their secret was discovered they would not be wor-
shipped *or* feared, and they would not be cut apart by
those more curious than afraid.

He was a man like any other, as this painful moment
proved. His ability was a product of simple genetics,
nothing more.

As was his attraction to Miranda.

It would be nice to believe that humanity had
changed enough to accept those who were truly different, but deep down he knew that was not the case. There
were still too many in this world who feared what they
did not understand, and the morbidly curious certainly
survived. What would become of him if his ability was
uncovered? What would become of his sons?

Some decisions had already been made, and he would
not veer from them, no matter what happened in the days
ahead. He would continue to live in isolation, whether
he took Miranda into his life or not. There was no other
choice, not for him. This was not a life he would thrust
upon her in a moment of need, when he could think of
almost nothing but being inside her. No, the decision was
hers, as well as his, and that decision could not be made
in ignorance. If he decided to make her his in all ways,
if he decided to risk this life he'd made for himself, how
best to tell his Kademair what she'd stumbled upon?

There was only one way to explain to Miranda what
he was, and that was to show her.

Miranda pulled on her pajamas and crawled into
Bren's mussed bed, determined to wait for him. They
still had a lot to discuss. They also had much to do that

would require no discussion at all. That thought made her smile; it made her feel warm all over, warm to her very bones. The pillow held a touch of his scent, and she pulled it to her face and breathed deeply.

She fell asleep clutching that pillow, listening to the distant and soothing sounds of the shower he stood beneath, her body unable to fight against the intense relaxation that followed the rush of adrenaline and the flush of pleasure. Boneless and warm, she slept without dreams, without fear. She could not remember a time when she'd slept so deeply.

Miranda awoke with a start to find Bren standing over the bed, morning sun breaking through the window behind him. He didn't wear a happy expression on his harsh face on this fine, sunny morning. His hands were clamped into tight fists, and he was dressed in worn jeans and a white T-shirt that had Korbinian Construction emblazoned across the front. She blinked twice. Was that a raven in the logo of his company? Yes, it was. Given the meaning of the name, that was not surprising, she supposed, but still the intricately drawn bird flying across his chest gave her a chill.

The clock on the bedside table told her in a luminous digital red that it was almost nine-thirty. Surprised that so much time had passed since she'd crawled into his bed, alone, Miranda sat up slowly, noting her stiff, sore muscles as she moved. She'd known she'd hurt today, and was grateful it was no worse.

"You should've gotten me up sooner," she said, pulling the covers over her breasts—though it didn't make sense to feel shy now because she didn't have on a bra and her nipples were poking against the thin fabric. Last night Bren had seen it all, he had touched and kissed and made her come…and then he'd walked away, unsatisfied. Was that why he looked so stern this morning? Didn't the man have a condom anywhere in this big house?

"The sheriff is at the cabin waiting for us." He tossed her the sweater she had worn last night.

She took the soft garment and gratefully, if carefully, pulled it over her scratched arms. The sweater was huge on her, warm and soft. Miranda looked down as she buttoned the cardigan, glad for a moment not to look directly at the man who continued to stand at the bedside, hard and tense and unhappy.

Miranda's heart, which had been so full moments earlier, sank. Bren was not pleased. Obviously he believed that what had happened last night had been a mistake. At least he'd been the smart one and had stopped before things had gone too far and they'd had to face the pos- sibility of pregnancy. Wrong time of the month or not, in this day and age she should know better! Sheer terror, as well as the fact that it had been a *long* time since she'd let a man touch her intimately, had driven her to the point where she'd lost control. Maybe it had been the excite- ment, the absolute gratitude that she was still alive, the fact that it had been years since she'd been that close to a man…hell, she didn't know what it was.

So, with all those thoughts racing through her head, why did she still want to grab Bren by that T-shirt and pull him into the bed with her? She'd lost her mind. That was the only explanation.

Miranda stood, and Bren took a step back from her, as if he didn't want to get too close. She took a step forward, drawn by a longing not to be too far away from him. If he would allow it, she'd fall into his arms as she had last night. He was obviously not so sure.

"I need to call Roger, too, and tell him what happened," she said.

"If you call he'll come and get you," Bren responded, sounding even unhappier than he looked. Those dark eyes were piercing; the jaw was taut. She longed to run her fingers along that jaw, to kiss him and make him smile.

"I suppose he will."

Bren took a deep breath. His fingers flexed. "Then don't call."

Miranda looked into his eyes, genuinely surprised. His body language told her he wanted her far, far away, but his words didn't match what his body told her. "I'd think you'd want me out of here as quickly as possible." It was obvious he didn't want her here. And why should he? She'd done nothing but turn his life upside down.

"I should," he said, "but I don't."

"Last night—"

He interrupted her harshly. "We can't talk about last night right now. The sheriff is waiting for us and he's not a patient man."

"Neither are you," Miranda countered.

Bren's lips twitched. "I think I've proved I have an abundance of patience."

What he'd displayed last night had not been patience: it had been incredible self-control—not that she wanted to extend this conversation by voicing that point. "We probably shouldn't leave the sheriff waiting any longer," she said, brushing past Bren and heading for the doorway with the oversize cardigan covering her thin pajamas and warming her chilled flesh. Whatever they'd started last night was not done; she felt it to her bones. She wanted Bren all over again, and if she got another chance she wouldn't let him go so soon.

Bren didn't like the way the interview was going. He didn't like it at all. Sheriff Wayne Lawrence had been friends with Joe Korbinian for many years, and as he paced in the driveway, thumbs hooked in his straining waistband, he made it clear that friendship was the only reason he'd made a personal appearance. If not for his ties with the Korbinian family, he would've just sent along the deputy, a smaller, younger man who today took notes for his boss. Neither of the lawmen believed that things had happened exactly as Miranda described them.

The older lawman's expression was condescending and pitying. The deputy just seemed annoyed. Last night's offender had been, in their minds, a druggie out looking for something he could sell fast to get his next fix. It was just bad luck that Miranda had been in the cabin at the time, and it was certainly understandable that her imagination had gotten the best of her.

Bren knew that Miranda wasn't lying about anything. She didn't exaggerate, not for attention or to make herself seem more important. She wasn't a hysterical woman. If anything, she preferred her life to be low-key and without any unnecessary excitement. He couldn't tell the lawmen how he knew these things, though he did tell the sheriff that he'd been out for a walk and had seen the car speeding away. A dark, two-door Toyota. Not much help, the sheriff had said as he'd looked suspiciously from Bren to Miranda and back again, coming to his own conclusion about why Bren had been out and about so late, and why Miranda might've embellished the tale to make her situation seem more dire. Even her scraped-up arms didn't impress the lawman, and all too soon the old man and his deputy were on their way down the mountain.

Neither Bren nor Miranda expected that there would be much help from local law enforcement. No crime-scene unit would be coming in to take prints or look for fibers. No one had been hurt, and that was all that mattered. Case closed.

One question in particular nagged at Bren. After Miranda had told the lawmen that she'd heard the intruder say her name, the deputy had asked, "Who knows you're here?" The sheriff hadn't given Miranda a chance to answer; he thought excitement had seeded her fertile imagination. He did everything but pat her on the head and call her "little lady."

But the question stayed with Bren. Who, indeed? Someone who could find the isolated cabin in the middle of the night, someone who knew her name, knew she was here…knew she was alone.

After the sheriff left, he followed Miranda into the cabin, even though she had not invited him in. With a rush of rage in his blood, he slammed the door behind him.

"Maybe if I'd ended up dead Sheriff Lawrence would've mustered up an iota or two of concern,"

Miranda said as she walked into the room, which was well lit, thanks to the sunlight streaming through the sliding glass door.

Bren's mind had taken another direction. "How well do you know Roger Talbot?"

"We've worked together for close to three years," Miranda answered casually, her eyes scanning the interior of the cabin as if it had somehow changed. The sunlight was not enough to wipe away her memory of last night's darkness.

"That doesn't answer my question!" Bren snapped. "Does Talbot have any reason to want you dead?"

Still barefoot and wrapped in the thick sweater that hid her shape from him, Miranda spun around to glare at him. "No!"

"You told me he all but insisted you take a vacation here. You could've gone to a resort, you could've holed up in a nice hotel somewhere, but he made sure you were smack-dab in the middle of nowhere, alone. You don't find that at all suspicious?"

"I've been overworked…"

"A handful of people know you're here, and he's one of them."

"Roger is my *friend*," she insisted.

It was very easy for Bren to make his annoying neighbor the bad guy in this scenario. "Maybe he just wants you to believe he's your friend. Maybe he's been planning this for years."

Miranda stalked toward him. "You don't like Roger because he won't sell you this place, so he's the first suspect that comes to your mind. How convenient."

"If not him, then who?"

"I don't know, but *not* Roger."

"You're quick to defend the man."

"He wouldn't hurt me!"

Bren felt an unexpected fear rise inside him; it was a terror unlike any he had ever known. The world was spinning out of control, tilting wildly, and there was nothing he could do to stop it. "I don't trust Talbot, not with your life."

The anger fled from Miranda's face; her lips softened. She was so vulnerable, so fragile. The very idea that someone might try to hurt her took Bren's breath away. He wasn't given to unnecessary fears; but then, he'd never before had anyone to protect. As far as he was concerned that was yet another reason to let her go.

"You don't have to watch over me, Bren. You're not responsible…"

"I do need to, and I am responsible." He could deny himself only so much and only for so long. He hurt with wanting her much more than he had hurt last night. The need to lose himself in her, to keep her, to protect her, was stronger than anything he had ever known. It pissed him off royally.

He didn't know how to tell her who he was and what he could do, if things progressed that far. He'd never had to do that before. Only his father and his mother had known the family secrets, and they were both gone. Maybe they were together in the next life, as Korbinian and Kademair were meant to be. Maybe their spirits were still entwined, still one. The kind of bond they'd found was the basis for a happiness Bren had never thought to know, and now here Miranda was, standing before him, ignorant of all that could come to them if they chose to claim it.

She wrapped her arms around him, and Bren closed his eyes and did the same, holding her, pulling her soft body against his. She had to feel his erection pressing against her, but she didn't react, didn't move away or shift her body or rub against him. She simply stood there, as if it was the only place she wanted to be.

Miranda thought a condom would solve all their problems, but he didn't think any sort of protection would keep her from conceiving, not for very long. No Pill, no patch, no cream or condom would stop what was meant to be. If they chose to be together, if they followed their instincts, eventually the next of the Korbinians would be created. He could lie with any other woman in the world and not have to worry about making a child, but with this one, with his Kademair, creation was inevitable.

His desire for her was unstoppable, as was hers for him. He shouldn't have followed her into the cabin, he thought as he unfastened the buttons of the sweater that covered her pajamas and gently drew it over her shoulders and down her arms before dropping it to the floor. He shouldn't have stayed with her after the sheriff had left. They shouldn't be alone like this, not until he was certain and she knew the truth. They were tempting fate, tossing away their chance to end this before it went too far.

But it was too late. Miranda's hands were on him. Her mouth brushed his throat, up and down, gently tasting. Her breath came fast and heavy, her heart beat in time with his, and when he looked into her eyes, he saw the depth of desire there, he saw in her the same driving need he felt to the pit of his soul.

Had she dreamed about him last night? Did a part of her already know what he was?

"I've never felt like this before," Miranda whispered. "I'm not…I don't…" She pressed her body more snuggly against his and moaned. "What have you done to me?"

What had *he* done to *her?* He'd laugh, but it wasn't funny. This woman had the ability to turn his well-ordered life upside down. There was so much to consider before he made that decision. Did he want the life he had accepted as impossible? Did he want the responsibility of siring, teaching and protecting the next wave of Korbinians? How could he think with Miranda so close, with her smell in his nostrils and her warmth melding with his?

Bren reached for reason. Even if he was sure this was what he wanted—and he wasn't at all sure—he couldn't tell her the truth here and now. That conversation, if it came, called for calm and control, for some semblance of logic. At the moment he could find no logic. To simply show her who he was, as he'd considered last night, wouldn't be wise. Not now, when she was shaken and uncertain. It would be too much of a shock to her already fragile system.

He needed more time, and he felt as if he had none.

She reached out and grasped his waistband, her thumb brushing the button there and then down the ridge beneath. He could try to tell her that he didn't want her, but she'd never believe him. He'd always been good at keeping the secrets he had to keep, at hiding his thoughts and feelings from those outside a very small circle. But what he felt was so strong, and Miranda was in the center of it all. Surely she knew; surely she could see.

He stilled her maddening caress with a hand on her wrist. He couldn't lose himself inside her and then stop, not again. He was too close to the edge. Too close to losing what little control he had left.

But before he put an end to this he could—and did— touch her. His fingers on her throat, his mouth on that sensitive spot beneath her ear, his palms on her slender hips. She responded to every touch, no matter how gentle. He could have her here and now if he chose to, and then the decision would be made for both of them. She would no longer have a choice, and neither would he.

Sunlight poured through the sliding glass door, and in this place where just last night Miranda had experienced terror she gave in to warmth and pleasure. She lost herself in his caress, melting in his arms and making his decision to wait all the more difficult.

"I want all of you," she whispered, boldly and firmly laying her hand over his erection.

"Not yet," he responded, his voice grating and more unsteady than it should be.

"Why?"

"It isn't time," he said.

Miranda seemed to accept the statement, even as her body fit warmly and welcomingly against his. These two bodies had been made for one another, and though this woman, his Kademair, did not yet know who he was—or who she was—she instinctively recognized the rightness, the inevitability, of their coming together.

Could he have her without claiming her? Could he somehow take what he wanted without creating a child that would change his entire world?

Her body trembled with need; so did his. He held her close and they stood there, without words, without demand. Finally Miranda's head fell back and she looked at him squarely.

"Is this love?" she asked, open and plainspoken.

"No, it's not," Bren responded honestly. Their attraction was physical; it was nature's demand that the species survive. It was sexual heat and the spiritual bond known only to his kind. That wasn't love.

"I've never wanted anything the way I want you. And I want all of you, Bren. Every inch, heart and soul and body. I will not be satisfied until you are entirely and completely mine, until we are together and you hold nothing back." She shook her head. "I can't figure out why I feel so strongly. In truth, I barely know you. Is it the isolation of this place? Is it a response to the fear I experienced last night? Or would I feel this way if I'd met you in the grocery store over the tomatoes?"

He could answer all her questions, but he wasn't ready to tell her everything, not here and now. Maybe it would be best if he sent her home and told her never to come back. Their lives could continue as they had before she'd come here…and he would forever want what he couldn't take.

Bren reluctantly pushed away from her. He hadn't decided to claim her; he hadn't decided to tell her the truth. But he did know one thing. While she was here, Miranda was his to protect. "Pack a bag. You're moving to my house."

Her eyebrows lifted slightly. She attempted to look defiant. "Don't you think you should invite me into your home rather than ordering me there?"

Biology or not, destiny or not, he did not play games. His life was not a sport and neither was hers. "The sheriff is an idiot. Someone broke into this cabin last night and tried to kill you. I don't like it. Pack a damn bag and make it snappy."

"Yes, sir," she said with a reluctant smile, snatching her sweater from the floor as she walked toward the bedroom.

"And put on some clothes," he called after her. "I have some errands to run and I'm not leaving you alone." He wasn't letting Miranda out of his sight until he knew who had tried to hurt her—and why.

Miranda dressed in comfortable blue jeans that fit her snugly and a teal blouse that was cut slightly lower than her other blouses. It wouldn't hurt to show just a hint of cleavage, such as it was. She didn't have much makeup with her and had brought along no perfume at all, but thank goodness her cupboard was not entirely bare. She put on some pale pink lip gloss and a touch of mascara. She brushed her hair vigorously before plopping her favorite porkpie hat on her head. Maybe she would never be gorgeous, but she could be attractive when she put forth a little effort.

Bren made her feel gorgeous. He looked at her as if

she was the most beautiful woman in the world, even when she wasn't at her best.

When she was prepared, she quickly gathered up anything she thought she might need and dumped it all in her purse, then she packed a small bag she could take to Bren's house. How odd, to be moving in with a man she'd just met and feeling so completely comfortable with the idea. She'd never lived with a man before, had never even considered it. True, this arrangement was just for the week, but it was still momentous.

Before leaving the bedroom with her things Miranda glanced around. "Well, Dee, are you happy now?"

There was no response.

Bren was waiting for her as she walked out of the room. He took her suitcase, looked her up and down, and mumbled something she didn't entirely catch. Something about trying to kill him, she thought. She snagged her laptop and exited right behind Bren, locking the cabin door. Maybe that was a waste of time, with the broken window so close by and obvious, but it didn't seem right to leave the cabin wide open. While they were out she'd make arrangements to get the window repaired and the wiring fixed. Surely Bren would know someone who could handle the job.

Driving down the hill with the trees seeming to close in on her and the shade of those trees ominously dark, Miranda felt a knot forming in her stomach. A knot and butterflies. She instinctively gripped the door handle.

Even though he barely glanced at her, Bren apparently realized something was wrong. "Are you okay?"

"Yes," Miranda said in a lowered voice. "I'm fine."

Last night's fear was finally catching up with her. Why hadn't she felt any warning before the intruder broke into the cabin? Why hadn't she instinctively known yesterday that something was wrong? Why *now?*

Bren reached across and laid his hand on her thigh. His fingers momentarily slipped between her thighs, lightly teasing, amazingly arousing, and in that instant Miranda knew why her instincts had failed her. Her inescapable desire for this man wiped away everything else. It was stronger, more potent, than any fear could possibly be.

"How long will these errands of yours take?" she asked.

"A couple of hours."

One of those errands needed to be a stop at a drugstore for condoms. She didn't want to get carried away again, and she knew if any man could make her forget all reason it was this one.

Was this love? Maybe. Lust? Absolutely, and in an all-consuming way she had not known was possible.

Duncan leaned against his car door as he peered through a pair of powerful binoculars. At Korbinian's present jobsite, the builder issued orders while Miranda Lynch waited in his truck, her eyes glued to the freakish thing as if she were physically incapable of looking at anything else.

Considering what he'd heard when he'd arrived in town early that morning after driving much of the night, he was not surprised when his cell rang and he saw a familiar number on the caller-ID display.

"Archard," he answered brusquely, continuing to

study his subjects through the binoculars, in case they decided to take flight while he was occupied with explanations. Not for the first time, he mentally groused that he'd joined the Order to do good and had ended up a freakin' birdwatcher.

"Was it you?" Quinn asked simply.

"It was not," Duncan replied honestly. "Even if I had been so inclined, there's no way I could've made it from your place to the cabin in time."

"You could've hired it done," the old man said. "You might've come here merely to establish your alibi with me and with the Order. You know we don't take kindly to rogue agents."

Duncan's jaw tightened. "Given the choice, I'd take out Korbinian, not Lynch. Freak or not, she does some good with what she's been given. It makes more sense to kill Korbinian."

"I thought you might've decided to go after the softer target."

"No, sir," Duncan replied, insulted and not afraid to reveal that reaction in his voice. "My only participation in the event was to call the sheriff when I heard the news and suggest strongly that Ms. Lynch is a bit unstable and given to exaggerating events. I thought it best that local law enforcement not spend too much time investigating her, as we do not know what the coming days will require."

The old man sighed into the phone. "All right, then, I suppose I have no choice but to believe you for the time being. Are you sure she's the one?" Quinn asked as he had too often last night.

"Positive."

"Have they…you know." A man of another genera-
tion, Quinn was sometimes strangely shy about intimate
matters.

"I don't believe they've had sex yet," Duncan said
plainly, "but I suspect it won't be long. Those two are
dancing around one another like they're walking on
needles, and they both jump at every sound. It looks to
me as if they're in the mating-dance stage, which won't
last long with them. They're skittish and wound up and
when the time comes you can be assured they won't be
showing themselves in public for a few days." No, they'd
be holed up at Korbinian's place, screwing their brains
out until Miranda Lynch was carrying an unnatural child
who could not be allowed to come into this world. "We
don't have a lot of time. What do you want me to do?"

"I have an idea." Judging by the lilt in his voice,
Quinn was quite pleased with himself. "It came to me
this morning as I was drinking my second cup of coffee.
Knowing what I do about Miranda Lynch, I believe the
plan will work perfectly. And best of all, no one has to
die. I understand that's not in line with your way of
thinking, but you must know by now that every elimi-
nation comes with a potential cost to the Order. It would
not do for you to be found out, Duncan. You're much
too valuable to risk."

That said, Quinn laid out his plan. Duncan watched
his prey and listened. He didn't agree with the old man,
but he was a good soldier who took orders and did as he
was told. He was also not oblivious to the veiled threat
in Quinn's words. If Duncan became a liability, he, too,

would be "at risk." The fact that the old man knew what had happened last night proved that not only was Duncan a watcher, he was among the watched, as well.

When Quinn finished laying out his plan, Duncan said, "If you insist, I'll give it a try. You're gambling on the girl's tender heart, and that's not exactly a given, not if she's strongly driven to reproduce by powers we don't entirely understand."

"I'm well aware of that. Still, I believe the plan is solid."

Duncan ended the call more agitated than he'd been when it had begun. The sheriff had made it clear to anyone who bothered to ask that whoever had broken into Miranda Lynch's place last night had been a burglar, probably an addict looking for something to sell so he could get his next fix. Nothing more. Pity, if that was true. If the man who'd scared Lynch into Korbinian's keeping had succeeded in taking out the pretty medium, Duncan's life here would get much easier. If there was no chance that Korbinian could ever reproduce, then all Duncan would have to do was watch and make sure the freak's abilities never became public.

It was even possible that if Lynch was out of the picture a new recruit could take this easy assignment and Duncan could move on to something more challenging. He'd heard there was a possible vampire sighting in Montana, and shape-shifters were a constant problem across the country and across the world. That was the type of work Duncan craved. He wanted action; he had joined the Order so he could kill the monsters that threatened the innocent.

Korbinian was a freak, but he was no monster. Lynch

was far from normal, but she wouldn't hurt a fly. And still, if Quinn's plan didn't work Duncan knew he would very likely have to kill them both.

Bren suffered few doubts about what the night would bring. They bought condoms, he touched Miranda when he could, and she looked at him as if she wanted to eat him up. He couldn't bear to let her out of his sight, so he didn't even consider leaving her in another safe place, with others he trusted. Instead, she stayed with him all morning and into the afternoon, so he could turn his head and see her there, safe and arousing and tempting. With every glance, every innocent and not so innocent touch, their coming together seemed more inevitable.

The day did not pass without doubts. This had happened too fast. His life and hers would be ruined if he followed his instincts and allowed Miranda to follow hers. He wanted her body, there was no doubt about that, but he wasn't sure he wanted what having her in his life promised. He'd almost convinced himself that he could have her in his bed for a night or two or three and then send her home, but deep down he knew that once he had Miranda completely, a night or two wouldn't satisfy him. Once they began he wouldn't let her out of his sight until she was carrying his child.

Even when he touched her, when he stole a kiss, he was aware of the uncertainties. Miranda talked to ghosts. What other secrets did she have? What if he let her into his life and when the strong sexual need was relieved, they found they didn't like each other much? Korbinians had always been promised that they and their Kademairs would bond and reproduce. Love and compatibility had never been mentioned. In the past couple of days they'd been thrown together, but in truth he didn't know Miranda Lynch. She sure as hell didn't know him.

Still, no matter what happened tonight, he intended to keep a close eye on Miranda and make sure she stayed safe. Someone had tried to kill her, and like it or not, he was responsible for her as long as she remained on his mountain.

Chapter 7

Bren's errands, which he had promised her would take no more than two hours, managed to eat up half the day. With every passing hour, every passing *minute,* Miranda felt more compelled to jump his lovely bones. There had been a fleeting but powerful moment when she'd actually considered attacking him while they were stopped at a red light.

He looked at her as if he wanted to eat her up. After they'd bought protection at the local drugstore, he'd seemed even more turned on. In the parking lot he'd touched her intimately, but then he'd moved away too quickly, and she'd seen a touch of uncertainty in his eyes and in the way his body tensed.

Bren wanted her physically, that much was evident. If she was reading his body language correctly, if her instincts hadn't *completely* deserted her, he also wasn't entirely sure about this relationship, which had blown up too fast. He'd been blindsided, she understood that. So had she.

Sometime after lunch Miranda reminded herself once again that the intensity with which she wanted Bren was not at all normal. Not for her, anyway. She didn't sleep with men she'd known two days. She didn't forget about protection, she didn't salivate over a man's body, no matter how fine it might be. Had he drugged her? Hypnotized her? Had she simply lost her mind in last night's terror and excitement? Was she having a nervous breakdown or some kind of weird hormonal attack?

Or was it something altogether different?

This morning she'd actually used the word *love,* and while Bren had not agreed with her that love was possible, had in fact said it was not, he hadn't run in horror, either. Maybe he should've, considering how long they'd known one another.

Every time she looked at Bren she felt a rush of adrenaline and desire. She could feel him as if he was still inside her, and she knew that when she had him there again she would not let him go so soon. Next time she would have all of him. She craved that; she had to have it. When they got to his house and were alone, when she could touch him properly, he'd set aside whatever doubts he was beginning to feel.

Was what she felt love or was it one of the more ordinary, less appealing possibilities that made her crave him to her bones? She really did prefer the possibility of love to mental instability or wacky hormones.

Finally all his work was done and they were going home. What would happen when they got there? Would he try to send her to his bed alone again? She didn't think so, but she also couldn't be certain. Miranda wasn't a woman who had any confidence in her ability to seduce a man, but where Bren was concerned she might have to give it a try.

The gas gauge on Bren's truck was sitting on empty; the red light on the dash came on, warning that he was dangerously low. Out of necessity, he stopped to fuel up before heading back up their mountain. In Miranda's mind there was no doubt that she'd be spending the night at Bren's house, no doubt at all. Whatever it was that attracted her to him remained as strong, perhaps stronger, than it had been last night. Her heart pounded, her mouth was dry. Heaven above, she had become so obsessed with what was to come she hadn't given the intruder and last night's narrow escape more than a passing thought or two as the day had worn on.

When he'd pulled up to the fuel tanks, Bren had lowered the truck's windows so she could enjoy the pleasant spring breeze while she waited. Yes, the air was slightly tainted with the smell of oil and gas, but it also held more than a hint of the crisp scent of mountain air. Why had she never accepted Roger's offer to come here to vacation before? Think of all the pleasant days she had missed; think of all the time she might've spent with Bren, time that was gone and could not be reclaimed.

A nice-looking and rather large man wearing worn jeans, a buttoned-up shirt and a baseball cap headed toward the truck as Bren went inside the gas station to pay. The big man had driven into the lot not long after Bren, and since getting out of his vehicle he'd been picking up litter that had been thoughtlessly tossed aside by earlier customers. He didn't look like a janitor of any sort, but she imagined maybe he worked here. Either that or he was a neat freak who didn't mind picking up other people's trash. Bren didn't seem to mind leaving her alone with the big guy, though she would never be out of his sight, so maybe this smiling man was a local Bren knew well and trusted.

"You must be Miranda Lynch," he said in a friendly tone as he approached the truck. "Name's Duncan Archard. Roger told me you'd be staying at his place for a while. Sorry to hear about your troubles last night."

"Thank you." There was no reason not to be at ease with this man, and yet something in Miranda's gut tightened. At this point her every response was suspect, since she could think of nothing but finishing what she and Bren had started last night. "Roger gave me your card and said you'd drive me around if I needed a lift anywhere."

Archard's eyes cut to the side as he said, "I see you've found yourself another ride." He glanced over his shoulder to watch Bren, who was talking to the cashier. When Archard looked back at her, his eyes were hard. His expression was no longer friendly, and she was suddenly aware that his size was due to muscle, not fat. "I have to make this quick, so listen up. This thing between you and Korbinian, it can't happen. It won't be allowed."

A shiver ran down her spine. "What are you—"

"You're a freak, Miranda Lynch," Archard said in a sharp voice. "The trouble is, Korbinian is a bigger freak than you are. He's unnatural. He can't be allowed to breed."

Miranda looked toward the glass-enclosed store. With the engine off she couldn't roll up the automatic windows. What she wouldn't give for an old-fashioned crank window right about now! To have a sheet of glass between her and the threatening man would surely ease her rapid heartbeat and the new rush of fear. Bren stepped out of the building, his easy gaze on her and on the man who leaned into her door. Archard's fingers wrapped over the window and into the truck, too near to Miranda. To Bren's eyes all would appear to be well, but it was not.

She doubted Bren would get here any faster if she screamed, and it was possible that such a response would cause Archard to move his large, too-near hand to her throat. Miranda held her breath and leaned away from the open window, wondering if this obviously crazy man had been the one to break into the cabin last night.

"Go home, Miranda," Archard said in a low voice. "Go home. Go back to Atlanta and forget you ever met Korbinian. Don't ever come back here. If you do as I say, I won't kill him."

She couldn't speak. Her heart pounded. Looking into this man's eyes, she could see that he was no sick trickster. He was serious.

"Tell him why you're leaving or warn him about me, and I—or someone else—will kill him. He'll never see it coming."

"I don't understand."

"I wish I had time to explain, but I don't." Again the

threatening man glanced toward Bren, who came closer to the truck with every long, too-slow step, and the flash of undisguised hatred in his narrowed eyes made Miranda shiver. "Ask your friend Talbot how long he's been watching you. Ask your keeper why monsters like Korbinian can't be allowed to flourish."

Miranda opened her mouth to ask Archard what the hell he was talking about. Keeper? But the hatred she'd seen in him disappeared as quickly and completely as it had appeared, and the man greeted Bren like an old friend, dismissing her.

Dee, who'd been absent since last night, popped into the back seat. "He'll do it, damn him," she said sadly. "Son of a bitch! I knew it was likely someone was watching, but I didn't know who, and I had no idea they'd go to such lengths to make sure the Korbinians become extinct."

"They?" Miranda asked weakly.

"He'll kill Bren without thinking twice, if he thinks it's necessary." Dee bit her ghostly lower lip. "And if he can't get to Bren, he'll kill you. Archard or one of the others," she added cryptically.

"Others?" Miranda said softly. She threw off her curiosity and attempted to think practically. That was not an easy task, as her mind was spinning and the fear was real and fresh. How could she stop the immediate danger? Was Archard the man who'd broken into the cabin with a gun in his hand and her name on his lips? "I'll tell Bren and he'll know what—"

"No!" the ghost said in a voice so loud and sharp Miranda wondered if those outside the truck might hear.

"If you tell Bren about the threats Archard will know. Bren's never been very good at hiding his thoughts, and if he knows that you've been threatened, he won't take it well. In that case, I have no doubt that Archard will do exactly as he said he would. If he doesn't do the killing himself, then another will."

Again with the *others.* "Who are these people you're talking about?" And was Roger really one of them, as Archard had suggested?

Dee waved off the question with a hand. "I need to think," she said, and then she was gone.

Bren opened his door and Archard called out, his voice and smile deceptively friendly. "I was just telling Ms. Lynch that I talked to Roger and he'll be here soon to collect her. He was quite distressed to hear about her troubles."

Bren's mouth thinned. "You called Talbot?"

Archard shook his head. "Nope. The sheriff called him and filled him in on what was going on. It's Roger's cabin and his guest, after all. Naturally he was quite upset."

"I can imagine," Bren said as he started the truck. Archard stepped away, and Bren steered his big truck toward the narrow road that would take him home. They hadn't gone far before he said, "You have Talbot's cell number, don't you? Call him and tell him you're going to stay. Maybe he's not too far from home and he can just turn around without wasting too much of the day."

Miranda stared out the passenger window. Archard's words replayed in her head. She didn't believe that Bren was a freak or a monster, but the man at the gas station knew too much, and she had no doubt that he would resort to violence if she didn't do as he ordered. Dee, who was in a position to see more than Miranda, knew it, too. She couldn't tell Bren, not without starting a confrontation that might very well lead to his death.

It was the "others" who worried her. Archard wasn't working alone. She might not believe *his* threats about others, but she couldn't dismiss Dee's. It would be a waste of time to tell the sheriff about the threats. Even if he did believe her, and that was unlikely given his treatment of her so far, there was nothing he could do. She had no proof.

Archard had called Roger her "keeper." Not her friend, not a coworker, but someone who was watching over her, or simply watching. He said Roger was the one who could answer the questions the threats roused.

"You'd better call before we hit the curve," Bren said. "Unless you'd rather wait until we get to my house and use the landline."

Miranda looked at Bren, not making a move toward her purse and her cell phone—which she hadn't even bothered to turn on today, even though off the mountain she got a decent signal. Had Roger been trying to call her since talking to the sheriff? Knowing him as she did, she was certain the answer to that question was a resounding "yes."

At the moment she had more pressing matters on her mind. Roger could wait. The word *love* had been tossed out as a very real possibility this morning. It was too early for her to know if it was love she felt or something strictly physical. Whatever it was, when she looked at Bren's face she knew the world was better off with him in it. If staying with him, even for a few days, meant that his life was in danger, then she had no choice.

She couldn't imagine why anyone would call this man a monster. Every instinct within her told her Bren was a good man.

"Maybe I shouldn't call," she said, her heart breaking a little. "Maybe I should just…go home."

Bren's dark eyes narrowed. "What about your vacation?"

Miranda stared out the side window because she couldn't look at Bren and lie to him. Could she make this dismissal light and frivolous, as if all that had happened to her since coming to the mountains meant nothing? She had to try. "It's been a crazy couple of days, huh? What a bust this so-called vacation has been. I'll go home with Roger and get back to work and maybe in a couple of months I'll take a real vacation. Jamaica. Hawaii. A resort with a spa and room service."

"I don't trust Roger Talbot," Bren said. He didn't attempt to make his voice and demeanor light or uncaring. There was a passion in his voice that she could not deny. "I'm not about to put you in a car with him and—"

"It's not your decision to make," Miranda said sharply. "It's mine. And I trust Roger. He's the only man in the world I do trust, to be honest."

Bren's face remained stoic. Eventually he said, "I thought you might trust me." They passed the curve where they lost cell service and the road turned sharply upward.

"I don't even know you," Miranda said softly, realizing as she spoke the words how true they were.

"I'd say you know me well enough," he responded, obviously unhappy with her decision. Just ahead the cabin came into view.

"Drop me here," she ordered, knowing that if she and Bren were alone in his house for any length of time they'd end up in his bed and she would change her mind. She'd been turned inside out and upside down. Her thoughts were jumbled, her emotions raw. This morning she'd used the word *love* in regards to a man she'd known for less than two days! In her current state she might very well end up choosing a little bit of pleasure over his life. She'd get carried away as she had last night and she'd take what she could get, damn the consequences no matter how dire they might be. Now, while she was thinking clearly, while her fear for his life overpowered her physical yearning, was the time to call an end to whatever strange thing this was.

"I don't want to leave you alone," Bren said as he turned into the little driveway.

Miranda drew her purse strap over her shoulder, then reached into the back seat for her small suitcase and the laptop. "And I don't want you here," she said, trying to sound cold and falling far short.

"Miranda…"

She opened the passenger door and dropped her suitcase to the ground. "Don't argue with me. I changed my mind, it's that simple. Women change their minds all the time. You know damn well this thing with us isn't normal. At least, it's not normal for me. I don't go home with guys I've known two days. I certainly don't move in with them, not even for a week." She stepped out of

the truck, laptop case in hand, without telling him that
she was not a girl who had sex on the bathroom counter
without even thinking of protection. She wasn't a
woman who lost control.

"After last night, I don't feel right leaving you here,"
Bren argued. "Let me stay until Talbot arrives."

Miranda turned and looked Bren in the eye. Upset as
she was, she wanted him still. Her heart broke at the pain
she saw in his eyes, and yet she couldn't tell him the
truth, not if the truth put him in danger. "No. I want to
be alone. I'll make you a deal," she said, fighting for a
lighter tone of voice. "You go home and leave me alone,
and I'll try to talk Roger into selling you the cabin.
That's what you've been after all along, right?"

Bren's jaw clenched. His eyes narrowed. Miranda
slammed the passenger door of the truck before he had
a chance to respond. She hated the idea of waiting alone
in this house where just last night her life had been
threatened. But she hated even more the thought of Bren
losing his life because she couldn't bear to let him go.

What had happened? One minute Miranda had been
smiling and anxious to get to his bed, and the next she'd
been cold and anxious in an entirely unpleasant way.
Had Duncan Archard said something to her? What could
he have said to make her change her mind about him?
Maybe she'd simply come to her senses, as he should've.

This thing with Miranda had happened too fast. He
didn't want a decision that would affect the rest of his
life to be made in the heat of the moment; he didn't want
to be led by baser instincts. He wasn't sure what

would've happened if he'd brought Miranda home with him as he'd planned.

That wasn't entirely true. In spite of his doubts, if he had Miranda here she'd end up in his bed and the decision would be made for both of them. It was better this way. As soon as Talbot took her home, Bren's life would return to normal. Without the physical proximity that had set his urges into motion, his life would once again be as he'd designed. Quiet, productive, satisfying and solitary.

No matter how glad he was to be rid of Miranda, no matter how anxious she was to go, he wasn't going to leave her alone, not when there was any chance that the intruder who'd frightened her last night might return. Miranda trusted Talbot completely, but Bren certainly didn't.

But dammit, he couldn't follow her around and watch over her for the rest of his life. If she trusted the man then there was nothing he could do about it; but nothing would happen to her while she was here on his mountain.

Bren stripped off his shirt and unfastened his jeans as he walked toward the deck and the sky, for the first time in a long while not waiting for the cover of night. He kicked off his shoes and threw open the French doors, not bothering to close them against the breeze that filled his home with cool spring air. He stepped out of his jeans and leaped toward the sky, bursting into a flock of seventy-seven ravens before his heavy human body even had a chance to begin dropping.

The ravens swooped toward the cabin below, their formation tight, their wings spread to catch the air. On one end of the formation three ravens dipped and twirled, the aerial acrobatics controlled in the same way a man might manipulate his fingers. There was little effort involved; to dance on air was as natural to Bren in his raven form as it was for him to breathe as a man.

Both man and bird were drawn to Miranda and he'd believed she was drawn to him just as strongly. And yet it seemed that she was ready to flee from him without a second thought. Was she truly Kademair? Was it possible that he'd been wrong all along? If she was truly Kademair she wouldn't leave him; if she was truly Kademair he would not let her go. Maybe she was simply a pretty woman and he'd been too long without a serious sexual relationship. Maybe the dreams and the strong attraction were perfectly normal.

Miranda stepped out onto the deck, as if drawn there by the approach of the large black birds. She stepped to the railing, grasping with pale, small hands and looking up into the sky as he swooped toward her.

Perfectly normal? No. Nothing about him, or her, was normal.

The ravens that approached the cabin were not small, sweet songbirds, but instead, large and magnificent creatures with sharp black eyes, deadly beaks, powerful wings and an eerily human-sounding series of caws. They came to the cabin so often and so easily Miranda could only assume that someone who'd stayed here had once fed them.

She knew enough about ravens to realize that they would not be drawn here by bread crumbs or birdseed. They were carrion eaters. If she wanted to call these birds to her to feed them she'd need to stock up on roadkill. Miranda shuddered but she didn't move away, not even when five of the birds perched on the railing and looked boldly at her as the others circled the cabin.

This close, the power of the ravens was impossible to deny. The beaks were sharp and deadly-looking, the eyes were somehow intelligent, and the wings were such a deep black they shimmered with iridescent streaks of blue and green. These were magnificent, powerful birds.

"Have you come to say goodbye?" she asked, preferring the company of the dangerous ravens to complete silence and loneliness. Maybe their presence, their antics, their beauty would take her mind off Bren for a while. She had no idea how long it would take Roger to get here, and since Bren had driven away from her the minutes had dragged by with agonizing slowness.

One of the ravens cawed a response that sounded like a mournful wail.

"I know how you feel." Miranda's gaze flicked up toward Bren's house at the top of the mountain. She couldn't afford to allow her thoughts to linger on the man there, because no matter how scared and confused she was, she still wanted him desperately.

Letting Bren go was right for many different reasons. Aside from the threat to his life, which would've been more than enough reason to walk away, he insisted what they had wasn't love. Whatever he felt for her was entirely physical, and the physical didn't last. Still, she didn't like how running away felt in her gut. She'd learned to trust her gut years ago, but at this moment she trusted nothing and no one. Not even herself.

On top of that confusion, she had so many questions
for Roger she didn't know where to start. Wait, yes, she
did know *exactly* where to start. Keeper? Explain that
one, if you please. When that was done, she wanted him
to explain to her why his friend would threaten to kill
Bren, why he called an ordinary man a "monster," and
she definitely wanted to know who these mysterious
"others" were.

Miranda leaned on the railing and looked down.
From here in the center of the deck it was a long drop
to the rough landscape. The back of the cabin jutted out
of the mountainside like an ugly red pimple. No wonder
Bren wanted it gone.

One of the ravens came closer, walking steadily
across the railing. Miranda didn't even think of shying
away. She didn't for one second consider moving to the
safety of the cabin, closing the sliding glass door to
separate her from these magnificent birds.

Instead, she slowly reached out a curious hand, expecting the bird to fly away long before her fingers
touched feathers. Surprisingly the bird did not flee, but
instead, stood very still while Miranda carefully stroked
one silky wing. That sharp beak was so close, and yet
she felt no fear. The piercing eyes seemed to scrutinize
her with intelligence, and she studied the bird in return.

"I have a ceramic raven at home," she set, allowing her
hand to fall. The bird did not back away, and neither did
she. "I found it at a garage sale, and I had to have it. It's
not very well made and there's a small chip on one wing,
but it called to me. In its own tacky way it's beautiful, but
next to you it pales. You've ruined me for it, I suppose. I

also have a book or two on ravens that I leave on my coffee table just so I can look at the pictures now and then, and there's a small painting I found in a furniture store that was going out of business." Again, she glanced up to the top of the mountain. "Bren would be horrified. He's not a fan of animals in decorating. Not that I would put my small collection of ravens in the same class as a dancing bear or a duck in a hat." For the first time since she'd met Duncan Archard, Miranda let herself smile. "Is that why you all come here to see me? Do you instinctively sense that I'm a fan?" Her smile died. "The paintings and the photos don't do you justice. You're much more impressive up close and all but in my hands."

A number of the ravens were perched in the dead tree just to the west of the cabin. Others sat on the railing while still more circled the cabin as if there was a tasty carcass on the roof. Or inside. Or maybe on the deck.

With a shudder Miranda stepped away from the railing and sat in the wooden rocking chair she'd claimed as her favorite. The chair was heavy and rustic, and it creaked when she rocked even a little bit. As she swayed back and forth she expected the ravens to leave, to break away from the cabin and fly across the skies. In the past couple of days they'd come here often, but they never stayed very long. This time they showed no sign of leaving her alone, not even when she went inside for a couple of minutes to grab an afghan from the couch.

When she returned to the deck she sat with the warm afghan pulled up to her shoulders. She looked beyond the railing, admiring the magnificent view. She'd never seen anything like it, and likely never would again. The world, which was crowded and noisy and often unkind, went away when she looked at those distant rolling mountains that were like a gigantic green wrinkle in the earth. She could be entirely alone in the world with the view before her. Yes, entirely alone.

Miranda studied the birds and wondered if she'd made the right decision in giving in to Archard's threats and giving up on Bren. Not the ravens or her worry about Roger could take her mind off the man she'd sent away without anything resembling a decent explanation.

What she and Bren had was nothing more than a freak chemistry that had taken them both by surprise. He wasn't her type; she wasn't his. If they'd followed their instincts they would've regretted it later. Not that she'd suffered any real regret last night. Bren had, though. He'd left her much too soon and then he hadn't joined her in his bed.

If she'd allowed Bren to stay with her, if she'd told him he could sit on the front porch until Roger arrived, she would've had a much tougher time letting him go. They'd be together right now. Naked, most likely, with him inside her. She shuddered. She'd never wanted anything so much; she'd certainly never wanted any *man* with such intensity. He stole her reason.

In order to get her mind off Bren and what she'd given up by sending him home, she pondered the coming conversation with Roger. How to start? *Who are you? Are you really my friend? Why did you insist on bringing me here?* Eventually she closed her eyes, took a few deep breaths and drifted into a restless sleep.

And she dreamed. Oh, did she dream! The image of

the flock of ravens joining her on the deck and in the rocking chair was vivid. Feathers brushed lovingly against her skin and in a strange kind of stereo they whispered her name. *Mir-an-da. Mir-an-da.* She should be afraid to have so many large birds resting on her lap and sitting on her shoulders. They perched on her body and flitted about her, coming dangerously close with claws and beaks but never hurting her. They sat at her feet and cawed, and she was not afraid.

In the way of dreams, the ravens turned into Bren in the blink of an eye. One heartbeat she was surrounded by large black birds with fluttering black wings, the next she was holding a naked man. "Don't leave me," he whispered into her ear where moments earlier a raven's wing had caressed her.

"I have no choice," Miranda whispered.

Since this was just a dream she did not fear for his life. She didn't send Bren away, and he didn't draw away from her. She didn't warn him that a man he considered his friend would kill him if he dared to love her. She allowed him to undress her, to press his warm body to hers, to spread her thighs and push inside her. Nothing had ever felt so right, so inevitable…

It wasn't fair. For a moment they'd been so close to all they wanted, and then a man's senseless threat had stolen it away. How could something so beautiful be a threat to anyone?

With slow, easy thrusts, Bren filled her again and again. Ripples of pleasure leading her to complete release teased, offered a hint of what was to come. She held on to Bren tightly because this time she would not let him go too soon. This time he would come with her, and her pleasure would be complete because it was shared. She clasped him to her with her body, with her arms, with her legs, and they began to move faster. He was everywhere…

"Dammit, Miranda!"

Roger's sharp shout from inside the cabin interrupted Miranda's dream. Her eyes flew open and for a split second she saw before her Bren as he had been in her dream, naked and wanting. She blinked and he was gone. Roger's voice frightened the ravens, and they all shot from the railing and the nearby tree as he threw open the sliding glass door and burst onto the deck.

He gave the birds a glance but didn't even pause before lighting into her. "A man breaks into the cabin and you don't even call me? You shimmy down a damn post in the middle of the night to escape, and when you get to a phone you don't even *think* about letting me know what's going on?"

Miranda didn't rise from the rocking chair. Instead, she looked up at her old friend and said one single word that stopped him cold.

"Keeper?"

The big man paled. She'd seen him study gruesome murder scenes, she'd watched as he kept his cool with suspects he could not yet confront with all he knew, and she'd been there when his youngest daughter had broken her leg. And she'd never seen him go white like this.

"Who have you been talking to?" Roger asked when he could find his voice. His eyes flicked momentarily to the top of the mountain.

"Not Bren, if that's what you're thinking." Miranda kept the afghan around her shoulders as she stood. "Though to be honest, I don't see that it matters where I got the information. Your reaction is enough to confirm that what I was told is the truth. Who do you work for?" She wanted very badly to know.

"That doesn't matter," Roger said, running his fingers through short strands of brown hair that responded by standing on end. "What matters is that—"

"You lied to me," Miranda interrupted. "That matters. You pretended to be my friend and I think that matters quite a lot."

"I never *pretended,*" Roger said.

"Oh, so you spy on all your friends?"

Roger's jaw clenched.

Miranda knew why she was being watched. She talked to ghosts. Why was Duncan Archard watching Bren? Why was Bren considered a monster? "What is Brennus Korbinian, and why would your friend Archard threaten to kill him if I don't leave?"

She knew Roger well enough to see that he was taken by surprise. "Duncan did *what?*"

"He threatened to kill Bren, or have him killed, if I don't leave. Something about breeding and extinction. Honestly, it was all too bizarre, but the man scared me half to death."

The ravens that had fled from the cabin when Roger had arrived were headed back in this direction, graceful and powerful, unerring in their fix on their destination. Roger glanced at the birds, took Miranda's arm and led her into the cabin. He even took the time to lock the sliding glass door behind them. It was almost as if he was afraid the ravens could hear and understand him. And Miranda began to wonder if maybe they could.

Chapter 8

As seventy-seven ravens, Bren circled overhead and watched as Miranda threw her luggage into the trunk of Talbot's car. The man who'd come to collect Miranda tried more than once to help her by taking her bags or offering a hand, but she refused his assistance in a manner that screamed of her displeasure. Why? Something had happened to scare her, and she wasn't happy with anyone at the moment.

She'd come to her senses, that was all. He was the cause of her foul mood. She'd found reason just in time to keep them from making a terrible mistake. If Miranda was not Kademair, then all they could've had was a volatile sexual relationship that would've burned out in a few days. If she was Kademair, then their coming together would have the power to change the world—

and his life. He'd tried to convince himself that times had changed, but in truth there was no place in the modern world for the Korbinians; he'd been well aware of that all his life. Best to let her go now, before they took a step they would never be able to undo.

The car that had collected Miranda headed down the curving road, and the flock of ravens flew toward the house at the top of the mountain. This mountain was entirely his once again. There was no need to share it with anyone, no need to hope for things that could never be his. He'd been a fool to think even for a few hours that he could share with a woman who he was and what he could do.

Miranda stared out the passenger window because she couldn't bear to look at Roger. He was cautious with his words and the story unfolded one horrifying word at a time. There wasn't much he could tell her, he explained, but he'd do his best, considering that his cover had been blown.

Roger started the tale with the day he'd met her. Their meeting had been no accident, as it turned out. He'd been assigned to her. Every smile, every warm word, the way he'd supported her when she spoke about the ghosts she saw, the way he'd made her a part of his family, it had all been false. He didn't say so, of course. He tried to convince her that their friendship was real, that he'd come to respect and admire and like her, but she didn't buy it. Why should she? He'd lied to her. Whether he'd admit it or not, he'd been *pretending* for as long as she'd known him.

"Who do you work for?" she asked, not even both-

ering to turn her head to look at him. She didn't want
him to see the tears she fought so hard to contain.

"I work for the FBI."

"Maybe you do," she said coolly, "but you also work
for someone else. You can tiptoe around it all you want,
but that doesn't make the truth go away. Your friend
Archard threatened to kill Bren if I didn't leave with
you. He also said if he didn't get the chance to do it,
someone else would. Someone like you."

The car remained steady on the road, but Roger's
voice was anything but. "He had no right to do that. As
soon as I get you to safety I plan to report him to…"

"To who?" Miranda prodded sharply when Roger
faltered.

He pursed his lips and said no more.

"The man you *hired* to watch me while I was on
vacation threatened to kill Bren in order to keep us
from…well, in order to keep us apart. Why? Please
explain to me in a way that makes some sense. Does
Archard scare away every woman Bren gets close to?
Is Bren not allowed to have any kind of a love life? I
seriously doubt he's a virgin." She wouldn't give
Roger the details, but a man with that kind of self-
control was no beginner. "Why are you people so
damned determined to keep us from…from…" there
were no words for what she felt, so she finally
decided on something ordinary and casual "…from
hooking up."

"I suppose it's true, then," Roger said softly. "At least
Archard has reason to believe it's true, otherwise he
never would've dared to threaten you."

"What's true?" Miranda asked, and her head snapped around so she could see Roger's traitorous face in the last light of the day. "Dammit, I've had enough of this dancing around the issue. I want the whole story!" she shouted. "In the past two days I've had to shimmy down a very long wooden post to escape from a man with a gun, I've been threatened, a friend has been threatened, and I've had my life turned upside down in more ways than I knew was possible. No more bits and pieces of the story. If you're telling the truth about being my friend, then you'll tell me all of it. Now."

For a long while Roger didn't respond. His expression was closed to her; it was cool and stoic. But he took the next exit off the interstate and headed for a yellow-signed Waffle House. "I need coffee and something to eat for this conversation," he grumbled.

Duncan had watched a very unhappy Miranda Lynch ride off with Roger Talbot. She'd given the gas station a brief and dismissive and almost forlorn glance as they passed. Quinn had been right, after all. Lynch was willing to leave in order to save Korbinian. She would deny the strong pull she felt to him in order to save his life. Too bad. In Duncan's opinion the world would be better off with the last of the Korbinians gone. All he needed was an excuse.

With any luck Lynch would make her way back here, inexorably drawn to the man she couldn't have. If she did, he'd be waiting, ready to finish the job Quinn hadn't allowed him to finish this time around.

Lynch and Talbot had been gone less than two hours

when Duncan's cell phone rang. He recognized the number. The old man was probably calling to gloat.

"Archard," Duncan answered.

"He's told her everything!" the old man snapped.

Duncan instinctively glanced to the nearby mountain road. "Korbinian?"

"No, you idiot, Talbot! I had a team on them in case Korbinian tried to pull a stunt to get the woman back. As we speak Talbot and Lynch are sitting in a public restaurant and he's telling her much more than anyone outside the Order should know."

Talbot was not the strongest or most dedicated member of the Order of Cahir, a fact Duncan had long been aware of. But he'd never imagined the man a turncoat. "What do you want me to do?"

There was a long moment of silence. "Can you take Korbinian?"

Duncan smiled. He'd planned and even dreamed of this scenario for years, hoping for the opportunity. "I can."

"I want him alive. Bring Korbinian to the farmhouse. I'll have Talbot bring Lynch." A long sigh echoed through the phone. "It's a shame, really. All these years and the boy's hurt no one. The girl has been a real asset. Separately they are merely oddities we can observe and study. But I'm afraid you're correct, Duncan. We can't allow them to join forces."

Miranda's mind was reeling as they left the Waffle House. Talbot had a hand on her arm, and she did not shake the support off, even though she was still furious with him.

The fact that there was a very large and well-organized group out there watching over those with what some would call supernatural abilities was hard enough to take, but what he'd told her about Bren and his abilities was even more shocking.

The ravens that had so often visited the cabin—they were Bren. They were Korbinian. Roger used the word as if it was more than a last name, and to hear him tell the tale, it was. Even though the story Roger had told her was fantastical it also made sense in a strange way. Bren didn't hike naked in the woods at night; he just didn't have clothes handy when he changed from raven to man. The piercing dark eyes, the silky black hair, the keen senses...

Over waffles and coffee Roger had told her how the Korbinians had lived in the Tennessee mountains for hundreds of years, their numbers declining until only Bren remained. There was more to the story, Roger had said as he'd glanced suspiciously around the restaurant, but the basics would do for now. Like her, Brennus Korbinian was very different. Like her, he was considered by some in the Order, an organization that had employed Roger to study her like a bug under a microscope, to be a menace to the world.

Bren was the last of his kind and the Order wanted to keep it that way. She still didn't understand what that had to do with her, but Roger insisted she had enough information to handle at the moment, and he was right. Her mind was spinning.

As Roger helped her into the car his cell phone rang. As soon as Miranda was situated, he snagged his fancy new cell and glanced at the caller ID. Tough man and liar that he was, his expression changed, softened a bit. "It's Cheryl," he said just before he closed Miranda's door and answered the call.

She watched Roger in the light that came from the restaurant windows, since while they'd been talking the sun had set and the parking lot was now dark, except for one lone streetlight. What a long day this had been! Dim light or not, she could see enough to know that something was wrong. Roger's eyes narrowed and his lips tightened, and he spat a few angry words Miranda couldn't hear. And then he stared at the phone as if it had turned into a snake, before dropping it into his pocket and slipping into the driver's seat.

"What's wrong?" Miranda asked.

"Nothing!" Roger snapped.

Something was most definitely wrong, but his unwillingness to answer her question only verified what she already knew. He could say whatever he wanted to, but he was not her friend. "Does Cheryl know?"

"Does she know what?"

"Who you are. What you do."

"Some," he responded distantly. "Not all. It's not safe for those outside the Order to know too much."

He pulled onto the service road and then onto an on-ramp. They were halfway to the interstate when Miranda realized that they were headed onto the northbound side of the highway. "Wrong way!" she said sharply.

"Are you sure?" he asked as he continued on the wrong path.

"Yes!"

"My sense of direction is lousy," he said absently. "We'll turn around at the next exit."

The next exit, as she remembered, was a few miles away—a few miles closer to Bren. Damned if she didn't feel like she was being pulled toward the raven-man. "I don't recall you ever having trouble with your sense of direction before."

"Get me a map out of the glove compartment, would you?" Roger said, his eyes on the road. "I might want to try a shortcut."

With a huff of disgust, Miranda leaned forward and opened the glove compartment. She rifled through papers and past an ice scraper and a car manual. There were a couple of pens and some change, but no maps. "I don't see any—"

She felt the sting in her arm before she realized that Roger had made a move. In shock, in spite of all she knew about this man, she glanced down and caught a glimpse of the syringe as he finished administering the shot. Almost immediately her head began to swim.

A syringe cap and a wrinkled plastic bag sat on the seat between them, and if she'd been able to do so Miranda would've laughed. She would've laughed and cried and screamed, but she could manage none of those simple actions. Her friend carried a syringe filled with some sort of fast-acting drug in a pocket or close at hand in his car in case he ever needed to put her out. The man who had just sworn that he cared for her was very well prepared to knock her senseless. Or had he just killed her because she knew too much?

Roger withdrew the needle from her arm and cursed

as she fell back against the seat. Already her body felt heavy; she could barely move a finger, much less an arm. She was defenseless, in the company of a man she'd never thought she'd have to defend herself against.

Her mind reeled, and silent tears slipped down her cheeks. She should've taken a bus home. She should've rented a car. Hell, hitchhiking would've been safer than getting in a car with the man who thought himself her keeper. Even after Roger had admitted that he'd been spying on her, she hadn't felt afraid. Now, too late, she was terrified.

"Am I dead?" she asked, her words slurring past thick and heavy lips. The lights on the dashboard blurred, as did the traitorous face of the driver.

"No. But you'll sleep for a while." Roger pressed the gas pedal to the floor and the other cars seemed to be standing still as he sped past them and past the next exit. He had no intention of turning around; that had been just another lie.

"Where are you taking me?" she asked while she could still form words. Already she felt as if she was being pulled into darkness.

"I'm sorry, Miranda," he said, sounding sincere as he avoided answering her simple question. "I don't have any choice."

She felt a flash of anger and would've lifted her head if she'd been able. She wanted to scream, but all she could do was murmur, "There's always a choice. Always."

By the greenish light of the dash she watched as his face hardened. Before she passed into complete darkness she heard Roger mumble, "They have Jackson."

GET FREE BOOKS & FREE GIFTS WHEN YOU PLAY THE... *Lucky 7*

SLOT MACHINE GAME

Just scratch off the gold box with a coin. Then check below to see the gifts you get!

YES! I have scratched off the gold box. Please send me the 2 free Silhouette® Nocturne™ books and 2 free gifts (gifts are worth about $10) for which I qualify. I understand I am under no obligation to purchase any books, as explained on the back of this card.

We want to make sure we offer you the best service suited to your needs. Please answer the following question:

About how many NEW paperback fiction books have you purchased in the past 3 months?

❏ 0-2

E4HQ

❏ 3-6

E4H2

❏ 7 or more

E4J3

238/338 SDL

FIRST NAME

LAST NAME

ADDRESS

APT.

CITY

STATE / PROV.

ZIP/POSTAL CODE

Visit us online at www.ReaderService.com

7	7	7

Worth TWO FREE BOOKS plus 2 BONUS Mystery Gifts!

Worth TWO FREE BOOKS!

TRY AGAIN!

* * *

Bren had been pacing the floor for hours. He didn't want to eat; he couldn't possibly sleep; he didn't even want to fly. The house felt strangely hot, so he wore nothing but an old pair of jeans as he stalked about the empty rooms, talking to himself and wondering if he should've handled the situation differently.

In a way he'd wanted Miranda gone; her presence brought too many changes to his life, no matter how strongly he was drawn to her. And now she was gone and he felt as if she'd taken a piece of him with her. He'd hoped distance from her would make his senses return, but at the moment he was positively senseless.

Kademair or not, Miranda was gone. Judging by the expression on her face as she'd jumped from his truck, she wouldn't be back. He was meant to be the last of his kind, as he had always known he would be. So why did this separation hurt so much? Why did he feel as if Miranda had taken a chunk of him in her suitcase when she'd left?

The sound of the doorbell surprised him. No one dropped by, not way up here. For a split second he thought maybe Miranda had returned, but he knew that wasn't true. If she was standing on the other side of his front door he'd feel it in that thrum he experienced only when she was near. In spite of his very real reservations he'd find himself running to the door, instead of walking.

Duncan Archard stood on the front porch, a strangely sappy smile on his face. "We had some news on that break-in at the Talbot cabin, and since you and the girl spent some time together I thought you'd like to know what was going on."

"Sure." Bren opened the door wider, and Archard stepped inside. "You didn't have to make the trip up the mountain in the dark. Why didn't you call?"

"I tried but your phone is out, and I didn't want to wait until morning to let you know what the sheriff found."

Bren headed for the closest telephone. Now and then there was an interruption in service, but not often. How long had he been without a phone? Had Miranda tried to call? The news must be important for Archard to make the trip, instead of waiting for the next time Bren had to gas up. "So what happened?" he asked as he reached for the phone, lifting the receiver to immediately hear a strong, steady dial tone. He turned to face Archard, who held a very large gun as if he knew how to use it.

Bren dropped the phone and dove to the floor, intending to roll to safety, but it was too late. Archard fired, and a dart with a long, thick needle punctured Bren's chest before he hit the floor. Pain radiated from the site of the wound through his entire body. He landed on the hardwood floor with a thud, and immediately the room began to go dark. From behind his back Archard produced a large net he tossed expertly so that it opened wide as it spun and drifted. Bren was unconscious before the net fell over him.

Miranda came to disoriented and with a killer headache. She no longer sat in the front seat of Roger's car, but was lying on a hard cot. Her hands were bound in front of her, though not too tightly. The sensation of being lost, of being disconnected, was overwhelming. She didn't know how many hours had passed since

Roger had drugged her, and she had no idea where she was. Soon enough she realized she was not alone. Whispering voices drifted to her from not far away, and she recognized one of those voices as Roger's.

Traitor.

Instead of sitting up and demanding answers, Miranda lay very still with her eyes closed, keeping her breathing slow and steady. Maybe if they thought she was still unconscious they'd say something that would give her a clue as to where she was—and why.

"Duncan should be here soon with Korbinian," a strange voice said.

"Why?" Roger asked. "This is a farce. Neither Miranda nor Korbinian have ever hurt anyone. Ask me to take out a vampire or a werewolf or snuff a demon and I'm there, but these two people—"

"They are not *people*," the strange voice interrupted. "That is your weakness, Talbot, you're too soft. Your father had the same failing."

"Humanity is not a failing."

The response was a long sigh. "This is why we had to detain your son—we had to make sure you did as you were told."

For a moment all was silent and then Roger said, "You still haven't told me why you're bringing Korbinian here. All you have to do is keep them apart. Let them continue as they have been. They don't know anything that can hurt us. Apart they're not a danger to anyone."

"Originally I had the same thoughts, but the truth of the matter is that their very awareness of one another changes everything. Now that they've met they won't be able to stay apart, no matter how determined they are to do so. Kademair and Korbinian. One of them will seek out the other, and then…well, you know what will happen."

"Yeah," Roger said darkly. "They fall in love. They have a family, and a species that is not meant to die out flourishes."

There was a long pause, and the other man said darkly, "You knew. Damn you, when you took Lynch up there you knew very well who she was!"

Knew *what?* How could Roger have suspected that she and Bren would hit it off so well? How could anyone have known? There was much more going on here than he'd told her.

"I suspected," Roger said in a lowered voice Miranda could barely hear.

If she ever got to talk to him again, he had some serious explaining to do.

A cold voice responded, "You suspected, and yet you did not bring those suspicions to me. Instead, you decided to perform your own little experiment."

"They found one another within a matter of hours."

Again, that sigh. "She knows too much now, about the Order, about Korbinian, about you, Talbot. It would be a disaster if she ever decided to seek Korbinian out and they joined forces. What if they disappeared? It might take us years to find them, if we ever did. No, she knows too much, and now we will likely have to kill them both, all because you had a suspicion and you acted on it rather than bringing those suspicions to me. If we'd moved her to the other side of the country and made sure they never met, none of this would be necessary."

Miranda found herself holding her breath.

"I believe one-half of your little experiment is awake," the strange voice muttered.

Miranda rolled over and opened her eyes. Solemn and pale, Roger remained on the other side of the gray, windowless room. He was still a traitor, since he'd lied to her all these years, but she understood why he'd done what he'd done—this time. The people who'd kidnapped her had Jackson, and Roger would do anything for his family.

Standing not too far from a narrow flight of metal stairs, the man who'd ordered her and Bren kidnapped, the man who said they would both have to die, looked like your average, slightly overweight grandfather. He had sparse gray hair and puffy eyes. He needed a shave; the white stubble on his face looked rough and unfriendly even as he smiled at her. He wore khaki slacks and a gray cardigan that was missing a button.

"Miss Lynch, what a pleasure to meet you at last," he said as he approached the cot. "I'm Ward Quinn, a compatriot of your friend Talbot. I've heard so much about your talents and experiences, and I have long yearned for a conversation about the afterlife and those who inhabit it. I do hate that we had to meet under such challenging circumstances." His grin widened, revealing crooked, yellow teeth. "You must be parched after such a long and difficult journey. Would you care for some tea?"

Bren came awake in an awkward position, as the vehicle transporting him hit a bump in the road and lurched. A large net covered him, and when he tried to move it aside, he discovered that the restraint was anchored in several places. As his eyes adjusted to the darkness he could make out the metal rings welded to the floor of the covered truck bed.

All this time he'd been protecting his secret, and it wasn't so much of a secret, after all. Archard knew. Otherwise he wouldn't have bothered with the net that would contain Bren even in his raven form. His hands were bound behind him, but not tightly. Maybe Archard had expected his tranquilizer dart to be longer lasting; maybe he was just sloppy. Bren easily slipped the bonds that held his wrists and then he tested the netting with his fingers, judging the thickness and the strength. He couldn't allow himself to be in this vulnerable position when the vehicle stopped and the rear doors opened. He would not remain here, helpless, at the mercy of the man who'd kidnapped him.

One thought spurred him on. If Duncan Archard knew Bren's secret, did he also know about Miranda? Had he taken her, as well?

It was nearly dawn when Duncan pulled into the familiar, deceptively serene driveway. Thanks to alarm sensors buried at the farm entrance, Quinn and the others would know that he'd arrived.

In years past many unnatural beings had been studied in the bunker that was so cleverly concealed beneath the typical, picturesque red barn beside the two-story white farmhouse with the massive front porch adorned with hanging pots filled with flowering plants. There were those in the Order who were more interested in studying monsters than in eliminating them. Duncan thought it would be best if they were all terminated, but only the deadliest of the unnatural beings they watched were taken out. When he was in charge that would change, Duncan thought as he parked the truck near the barn.

With the engine silent he listened carefully for movement from the truck bed. All remained silent. The tranquilizer should keep Korbinian out for another couple of hours, if his calculations were correct. At least here he'd have help moving the man. Getting Korbinian from the mountaintop house into the back of the truck had been a chore, and Duncan's muscles still ached from the exertion.

Quinn and a sour-faced Talbot stepped onto the porch. The old man must not have any faith in Duncan's abilities, since he cradled a shotgun in his arms.

Duncan nodded to the others as he unlocked the padlock and swung the metal doors open to reveal his prisoner. Before he had a chance to get the door fully open, the blackbirds exploded from the enclosed space into the open air.

Large black feathers blinded him, flapping in his face as one beak and then another pecked viciously at the exposed flesh of his neck. Duncan flailed his arms for a moment and then threw them across his face and neck, protecting his most vulnerable, uncovered flesh. He gasped for breath, and then he dropped to his knees. There were so many of the damned birds, and they kept coming in a cawing, fluttering flood of feathers and claws as they escaped the confines of their prison and took to the sky.

Duncan didn't like birds, natural or unnatural. They were dirty, ferocious creatures that might look harmless one minute and then peck out a man's eye the next. The ravens—that damned Korbinian—could've flown around him and made their escape, but they did not. Instead they purposely came at him, scratching and screaming in his ears, attacking him with ferocity.

The attack ceased, and after peeking around his folded arms to see that the birds were indeed gone, Duncan allowed those arms to fall. He stood and spun about to watch as Quinn calmly lifted his shotgun and took aim at the flock of birds that made its way almost peacefully across a gray morning sky. There would be buckshot in that weapon, Duncan imagined, since Quinn was always properly prepared. It would be difficult, if not impossible, to bring Korbinian down with a handgun, but with enough birdshot among those feathers he would surely no longer be able to fly.

"Do it," Duncan whispered as he placed a hand on his throbbing, bloody neck. "Kill the bastard."

Before Quinn could fire, Talbot surged forward and hit him in the back with his shoulder, sending an unsteady old man thrashing and fighting for balance. The shotgun dropped to the ground and the ravens made their escape, flying high and to the east, toward the thick woods that separated the farm from the nearby small town of Silvera.

Quinn regained his balance and turned to the traitor. "Why?" he asked Talbot in a low voice that sent chills down Duncan's spine.

"Why do you think I introduced Miranda to Korbinian?" Talbot said hotly. "Why do you think I went around you in order to make certain the species survives? Korbinian isn't a killer, not like some of the others we detain and execute. He has talents we could use. So does Miranda. If we could convince them to join us, think of the instances where their abilities could be put to good use in the name of the Order."

The old man walked toward Duncan, a scowl on his face. Talbot was right behind him, arguing his ridiculous point. Monsters in the Order? Unheard of. Impossible.

Duncan offered Talbot a glimpse of his bloody hand. "Not a killer? What do you call this?"

Talbot reached into the truck bed and drew out what remained of the net that had restrained Korbinian for a while. It was in shreds, the thick rope gnawed and unraveled, torn to pieces by beaks and claws. The net had been destroyed.

"If Korbinian had done to your face and neck what he did to this netting, you'd be dead now, or close to it. A couple of pecks in your tender flesh are merely a well-deserved reprimand for what you did to him." Talbot tossed the remains of the net to the ground.

Duncan studied the ruined net as he held one palm against a bloody wound, and in that moment he hated Korbinian more than ever. The thing was as unnatural as any vampire or out-of-control witch or loosed demon, and he had to die.

Chapter 9

Miranda sat on the cot butted up against one wall of the windowless room where she was being held, her legs drawn up beneath her, her arms and bound hands crossed over her stomach. If she could draw up into a tight, tiny ball and disappear she would; this was as close as she could get. Two armed young men stood near the metal staircase, watching her with open suspicion and vigilance. They'd joined her a couple of hours ago, when Roger and Ward Quinn had left. Was she so dangerous that they thought she needed two armed guards at all times? What did they think she was going to do? She talked to ghosts, which was hardly a dangerous ability.

At least they hadn't shackled her, though there were shackles nearby should they be needed. The metal restraints and short heavy chains made it very clear what this room was used for, as if she needed those obvious signs to understand what kind of nightmare prison this was.

There were stains on the gray walls here and there, stains someone had tried to scrub away but that would not entirely fade. Some of those stains were large, others were small, as if discolored droplets danced across the plain walls. There were four cots like the one Miranda sat on, all of them narrow and hard, and attached to the walls beside those cots were shackles of different sizes and strengths. Beside one cot there were four metal shackles attached to four chains, as if it was intended that a prisoner being held there be restrained hand and foot. What creature would require a chain of such a massive thickness?

This room was normally reserved for those who had unusual abilities that were, or could be, deadly. Miranda knew that because several lost spirits lurked in the corners, afraid to come near her. Afraid to speak. Even though they remained silent, not asking for help as most did when she saw them, she could *feel* the violence within them.

One poor soul was caught between man and some kind of large cat. He often covered his face with clawed hands, and he cried softly and constantly. There was a large man who even in spirit form bore the marks of torture, and though the chains he dragged behind him faded into nothing, he continued to wear the shackles that had bound him in life. Four of them. A female's dark soul watched Miranda from the center of the room, not afraid or confused but cautious. The woman was young and beautiful, with long dark hair, large green eyes and a pale and flawless face made more austere by what had been, in life, an excess of mascara and eyeliner. Colorless lips curved into a sad and still-evil smile.

Other less clear souls flitted in and out of Miranda's line of vision, weaker than the others or simply less present. All of them had suffered. Some of them had, perhaps, deserved that suffering; some had not.

Miranda wished fervently for Dee. Friendly, helpful, kind Dee, who had only appeared from the next world in order to help. Unfortunately she couldn't call ghosts to her. They came to her in panic or sorrow, usually in or near the site of their death.

A few hours ago Quinn had personally delivered a pot of tea and a very nice porcelain cup, along with anything Miranda might want for that beverage. Beside the teacup sat sliced lemons, cubed sugar, a small pitcher of whole milk and what appeared to be homemade blueberry scones. She tasted none of it, afraid the old man would happily poison her, smiling all the while. And Roger? Would he allow it to happen? Would he poison her himself? There had been a time when she'd trusted Roger entirely, but she didn't know about him anymore. She couldn't be sure of anything.

After a while the female spirit in the center of the room spoke. "They're going to torture and kill you just as they did me," she promised in a whisper. "All in the name of keeping peace, they say. Even when they cause great pain in trying to exact information, even when they take a life, quickly or slowly, they think themselves the good guys. Heroes of the world. Warriors of the freakin' Order."

"Who are you and what do you want?" Miranda asked.

The only way to get rid of a ghost was to see to its business and send it on to the other side, where it belonged.

"My name is Roxanna," the spirit said. "And all I want is to warn you." She looked to the two silent, stoic guards. "The blond one is afraid all the time." There was a touch of glee in the statement. "If you say boo, he'll probably piss his pants. The redhead is more experienced, more hardened, but he's also completely convinced that the world will be a better place if we are all like him. Dedicated. Untalented. Ordinary. Boring beyond belief." The spirit smiled. "He will drive a knife through your heart with the absolute certainty that the world is safer without you in it."

Roxanna opened her shirt and showed Miranda a pale, marred chest that still bore the marks of such a knife.

"Did he kill you?" Miranda whispered.

The spirit nodded silently and covered the wound that would not heal even in death.

"Why?" Miranda asked.

Roxanna shrugged and her form fluttered in and out of substance. She looked solid, then misty; she faded for a few minutes, then regained her form. "I killed a few men who did not deserve to live, that is all. I sought them out and I gave them what they wanted from me and then I fed on their souls. With each feeding I grew more powerful. Not powerful enough, apparently," she added bitterly.

As Roxanna spoke more spirits took form, perhaps heartened by the fact that Miranda could see and hear and speak to the dark ghost. All of them were tortured, all of them were different. Very different. They made

Miranda look like an ordinary girl next door, ghosts and all. Monsters, Archard would call them. Some were indeed evil, but others, like the half-human creature in the corner, had only committed the crime of being different. Like her. Like Bren.

Male and female, dark and light, the spirits began to take shape more clearly until many of them appeared solid to Miranda's eyes. Some, like the creature who cried, remained distant, but others were emboldened by the knowledge that they could be seen. They all spoke at once, shouting, whispering, begging. The very large man who dragged his chains behind him came closer. His eyes burned red.

The tortured spirits descended on Miranda, moving closer, talking more insistently. She begged them to leave her alone, and when that did not work she ordered them to back off. She told them this place was for the living, not the dead, and they must move on. They heard but they did not obey. Try as she might, she could not make the tortured spirits go away.

Bren alighted in the thickest part of the forest, and in a burst of energy he reclaimed his human form. For a moment he knelt amidst the trees, naked and alone, heart pounding. He had studied the area from the skies. Not too far away there was a small town, complete with a quaint steepled church, a general store, a gas station, a sprawling school, a small and neat collection of homes that spread out from the center of town and an old-fashioned main street. There he could steal or beg clothes, and when that was done he could make his escape. No one would catch him again. Realizing that there were men in the world who knew his secret, he would be sure to hide well. From now on he'd be on constant guard.

But instead of taking flight toward escape, he stood and turned to face the other direction, toward the farmhouse where his captors waited. Miranda was there, and she was not safe. He knew it. Felt it. Felt *her* as if she were screaming in his blood. If he had ever doubted that she was Kademair, those doubts were now gone.

All his life Bren had accepted that he was the last of his kind; he'd never doubted that truth. His father had warned him well and often, pointing out the decline in population over the years and the age difference between himself and his Kademair, as if Denise Brown's birth had been an afterthought or even a mistake. Bren's mother had been more optimistic about the future, but that was simply her way. She always saw the best, especially for those she loved. She very much wanted her son to know the bond of Kademair to Korbinian, and so she convinced herself that it would be so. Joe Korbinian had been more pragmatic and better informed about the history of his kind.

Believing his father, Bren had buried himself in work for as long as he'd been able. Work had become his life, filling the place within him that others might fill with family, with devotion for another. He'd come to like his life as it was; he'd been content. And now here he stood, the most important decision he'd ever have to make before him.

A new, lonely life and safety awaited him to the west, but to the east waited Miranda and an entirely different future. A part of him whispered that life without her was not life at all; it was simply existence. He had existed all these years, creating houses in the mountains he called home, flying alone, determined, destined, to live and die alone.

If he closed his eyes he could see and smell and taste Miranda. To claim her would mean an end to any ease in his life. He would have not only her to protect but the children they would make. It would take unending diligence to teach and protect a family, if he dared to take what this world now offered.

Bren burst once more into seventy-seven ravens and he flew.

Just when Miranda thought she could not take any more, when the voices and the pain of the spirits who lingered here reached the point where they overpowered her will, a strange sensation of peace fell over her. The voices dimmed, then stilled, and one by one the ghosts disappeared.

All but the spirit on the bed beside her, the one who wrapped her arms and her warm aura around Miranda in a protective manner.

"You should not be here," Miranda said, grateful but confused. Spirits remained near the site of their deaths. Always.

"All Kademair are gifted in some way," Dee said softly. "It just so happens that my special ability kicked in after death." She sighed. "I'm stronger than other spirits in many ways, as you well know. Perhaps that's no coincidence. Perhaps I was so gifted so I could assist the future mother of my grandsons now."

"What is a Kademair?" Miranda asked. The word Roger and the others had spoken was familiar to her, as if she'd heard it long ago, or in a dream.

Dee smiled kindly. Her aura grew brighter, more golden and warm. "No one has told you yet."

"Told me what?"

"You are Kademair. You are the mother of my grandsons."

Again with the grandsons. Miranda was in no mood for cryptic and incomplete answers, not even from this kind spirit who sheltered her and offered much needed peace.

"You're being very specific. What about grand-*daughters*?"

"Bren will only have sons," Dee said. "That is the way of his ancestors, the reality of what being a true Korbinian means. I would've loved to have a daughter, but it was not meant to be. You are the closest I have ever known to a daughter, my dear Miranda. I wish I had known you in life, but again, that was not meant to be. There's nothing to be gained by wishing."

The information Dee offered was too much to absorb. "I barely know Bren. What makes you think that if I ever get out of here there will be kids?"

"Kademair are the mothers of Korbinians," Dee said simply. "You are Kademair."

Dee's words didn't make any sense to Miranda. Kademair? She couldn't possibly be pregnant, and yet you'd think she was already carrying triplets! All boys, to hear Dee tell it. There were those who wanted to make sure Bren never fathered children, and then there was his mother, who apparently wanted to be a grand-

mother from beyond the grave. Miranda was pretty sure
Bren was no virgin, so why all the fuss now?

"I won't be the future mother of anyone's grandchil-
dren if I don't get out of here."

"He's coming," Dee whispered, as if the guards who
stood on the other side of the room, the guards who had
apparently become accustomed to their charge speaking to the ghosts that inhabited this prison, might hear
her voice.

"Bren?" Miranda responded as softly.

Dee nodded.

"No!" Miranda tried to touch the ghost but could
not. Her fingers penetrated Dee's misty form as if falling
through fog. "If he comes here they'll torture him just
because he's who he is." Man, raven, the last of his
kind. Archard used the word *monster* when he spoke of
Bren. No matter what abilities Bren might have, he was
no monster. "They'll kill him."

Dee's face remained solemn. "I imagine they will try."

"You must find him and tell him not to come here,"
Miranda said desperately.

Bren's mother shook her head. "Even if I wanted
to, I cannot. I've tried to talk to my son before, many
times. Abnormal spirit strength or not, he cannot see
or hear me. Among the living I have seen since death
only you have that ability, Miranda." The ghost once
again strengthened her aura and used it to wrap
Miranda in a warm blanket of serenity. "He's coming,"
Dee whispered once again, and Miranda was washed
in an echo of a protective fear she herself felt to her
bones.

* * *

Bren stood in the shadows of the forest and watched the farmhouse. Miranda was there somewhere, but where? How could he get to her when he had no idea where she was being held? The house was large, two stories with an attic and possibly a basement. The barn was massive, but should be easier to search than the house, if he could find a way in. He burst into his raven form and attempted something he had never before tried. Instead of moving as one, the ravens spread far and wide. Some remained in the forest, observing the larger scene before them. Still others flew to the farmhouse and to the barn, flying past windows and looking inside; more importantly, trying to capture and refine the invisible and undeniable lure that pulled him to Miranda.

It was dangerous, he realized that. These people knew who he was and what he could do. Would a single raven alarm them? Would that shotgun reappear? He had no idea what would happen to him if one of the ravens that made up the whole was injured or killed. It had never happened before. Would he be able to take human form again if the flock was incomplete? Would all of him die if one part was destroyed? He didn't know, but it didn't matter. Miranda was in there somewhere, and he had to get her out, no matter what the risk.

He didn't see her through any window in the house, though he did watch Archard and Talbot speaking with the old man who'd tried to shoot the ravens. He also spied on a gray-haired woman who busied herself mindlessly mending a man's shirt in another room. Bren found himself pulled more and more strongly toward the red

barn. There were no open windows there for him to peek
through. The structure was closed up tight, which was
unusual for an outbuilding. There weren't even any considerable gaps around the doors and shuttered windows.

Nor was there the sound of animals inside. Bren
strained to hear some noise from inside the structure, but
there was nothing, not even the rustle of a mouse. He
moved closer and listened more intently, calling on all
his senses. And then he knew; Miranda was there.

He'd not been circling long when the door to the
house opened and the three men stepped out—arguing,
as they had been doing for as long as Bren had been
watching. The raven perched atop the overhang
remained still and silent, watching. Waiting to hear
Miranda's name from their lips.

They walked to the barn, where the old man took a
key from his pocket and unlocked the sturdy padlock
there. Talbot was last to enter the barn, and before he
disappeared from view he glanced back. Bren remained
still, but he was certain Talbot saw him. Would they all
come rushing out? Would Bren have to flee from the
shotgun once more? Apparently Talbot wasn't alarmed
by the presence of one raven. He followed the others
inside and closed the barn door tight.

Miranda had almost fallen into an exhausted sleep,
but the appearance of the three men— Roger, Archard
and Quinn—scared and alarmed her. Through the ghosts
in this room she'd seen too clearly what these people
would do. Were they here to torture her as they had
tortured others? Would she soon haunt this prison as the

other sad souls did? Even Dee's protection wasn't enough to ease her now.

There were no windows, no door in her line of vision. There were only the stairs the men descended. Miranda tried to work past her fear and panic to think rationally. Could she run toward the stairs and the trap door above it? Five men stood between her and freedom, five men who all wished her dead. Her eyes fell on Roger. Even this man she considered her friend wanted her dead, if that meant saving his son.

"She's been talking to ghosts," the blond guard revealed in a lowered voice.

"Truly?" Quinn said. "How extraordinary. I had no idea the fiends we exterminated here had souls that lingered on."

Miranda saw no reason to hide what she knew. "Some of those you killed here were innocent."

"None of the creatures who were disposed of in this room were innocent, I assure you," he said.

Roger tried to step between them. "We don't need to address this—"

"But we do," Quinn said sharply. "It's too late to hide, too late for deception. If your girl had never learned our secrets, she might've been allowed to live out her life in peace and ignorance, but not only did you tell her more than she should know, she's been talking to the enemy and might've been corrupted by their lies. You have no one but yourself to blame for this situation, Talbot. *You* took Ms. Lynch into Korbinian's circle, *you* all but introduced them, *you* told her secrets that were not yours to share. And now here we are. Korbinian has escaped and your little medium has been speaking to the insignificant remains of the enemy."

Miranda's spine straightened, as three words played again in her head. *Korbinian has escaped.* They'd tried to take Bren and he got away!

"There's only one logical solution," Archard said bitterly. "Without her we won't have to worry about there being more Korbinian freaks." Miranda could not help but notice that his neck was thickly bandaged in two places. She could only hope that a raven or two had taken some chunks out of his hide. "Even if we don't catch up with Korbinian, the world will one day be safe from his kind."

"What if Korbinian comes back?" asked the red-headed guard Roxanna's spirit disliked.

"Oh, he's long gone," Quinn said with confidence. "I doubt we'll ever see him again. Survival is a strong instinct within the primitive brain. He will yearn for and mourn his Kademair, perhaps, but his need for survival will keep him far away. He'll start over elsewhere, I imagine, and live out his life in fear that he'll be found out. If he does decide to take his revenge by going public with what he can do, we'll know where he is and we'll have another opportunity to dispose of him before he does too much damage. We can easily dismiss any public displays as trickery and in time he will be forgotten. Of course, if she remains alive he will find her and this debacle will begin again." He gave a sigh. "Which means, yes, we must eliminate Ms. Lynch."

Like Bren couldn't find another woman to have his children? There was still something going on here that Miranda didn't understand. First Dee and now this…

"My suggestion—" Roger began.

"That we recruit her?" Quinn interrupted. "Perhaps if things had not progressed so far we might've done so. But she is more Kademair than woman, and we have taken her from her mate. She will never forgive us."

"No, I won't!" Miranda snapped.

Roger rolled his eyes at her.

Miranda glared at the man she thought was her friend. "What, do you expect me to play along? Yes, please, let me help you find and eliminate those who have powers that you don't approve of or understand. So what if a few innocent souls are destroyed along with the evil, is that not an acceptable price to pay?" Her voice rose higher and sharper with each word she spoke. Her eyes met Roger's. "I'd rather be dead than turn into what you've become."

Archard smiled. "Let's oblige her."

A wave of rage rushed through Miranda's body. "Before you five strong, armed men take on the chore of murdering one small defenseless woman, would someone please tell me what the hell a Kademair is?" *Kademair are the mother of Korbinians,* Dee had said. "I'd like to die fully informed, if you don't mind."

It was clear that the two bodyguards weren't going to answer. In fact, they looked as if they had no idea themselves. Archard looked angry, as usual, and Roger appeared to be chastened. It was the old man who took a step forward. "The Kademair are—or *were* I should say, since you are the last of them—those rare females who are genetically capable of giving birth to Korbinians. One Kademair for each Korbinian born, that is the way of it. That is the way it has always been."

Miranda swallowed hard. "Are you saying that I was literally *born* for Bren?"

"Mated, some would say. Destined to find one another. You are the only woman in existence who can catch his child."

"I don't believe in that kind of nonsense," Miranda said softly, drawing in her knees, curling up in a ball on the hard cot. No, she did not believe, but it made some sense. The dreams, the unnaturally strong attraction to Bren…even her fascination with ravens. All explained in one fell swoop.

"Believe or not," Archard said sharply. "It's the truth."

"So you can see why we must deal with this situation with the most drastic of measures," Quinn said almost logically. "The Korbinian breed is dying, and we can't allow you to save it."

With that, Duncan Archard pulled a long, wicked-looking knife from a sheath at his waist. Miranda instinctively backed up until she was against the wall, realizing too late that her head was very near one of the disturbing stains on the gray wall. She had nowhere to run; no one would save her. Dee said Bren was coming, but she hoped that wasn't true. He wouldn't stand a chance against these horrible, violent men.

"Wait!" Roger moved forward, placing himself between Miranda and the knife. "You can't dispose of her the way you did the others. She's well-known. Too many people will miss her and ask questions if she simply disappears. A professor from Arizona has been trying to set up a time to test her paranormal abilities. He calls at least once a month. There's a local TV reporter who does the occasional piece on her. Miranda isn't like the monsters that have hidden themselves from the public eye and can be taken out without causing a ripple. She's a part of the world we claim to protect. She has friends and clients and neighbors who will raise a stink if she doesn't come home. Hell, I was the last one to be seen with her. You think that won't raise questions if she just vanishes?"

A wave of relief washed through Miranda. Someone would fight for her. In spite of all her doubts about his motives, Roger would protect her. And then he said, "It would be best to make her death look like an accident.

Miranda's mouth went dry and she fought against a gagging sensation. This man who had claimed to be her friend to the end was no one's friend.

"How?" Quinn asked.

Roger took a deep breath. "A fall, perhaps. I could take her back to the cabin and—"

"No, we'll do it here," the old man said. "A fall from the hayloft should do the trick. I'll rest easier tonight if I see her death with my own eyes. Not that I don't trust you, Roger. You've always been a fine, dedicated warrior of the Order. You will do what's best for all of us." He cleared his throat. "Cheryl is doing fairly well, by the way. She's followed our instructions and remained silent about Jackson's detainment. Your son is quite the impatient one, however. I had great hopes that he might follow in your footsteps, but now I'm not so sure he's suited to the calling. I'm not even sure that you're entirely suited."

Roger's jaw clenched. "Can we just get this over with?"

"Certainly," Quinn replied with glee in his voice and thunder in his eyes.

It was Roger who grabbed Miranda's bound arms and assisted her to her feet. When he started to untie her hands, Quinn stopped him with a sharp order.

"Let's not take any chances. We'll remove those ties after she's dead."

Roger all but growled. "Yeah, because a five-foot-two, 110-pound girl might reveal her hidden superpowers and take five men out between here and the hayloft."

"Stranger things have happened," Quinn said.

In defiance, Roger finished untying Miranda's hands. No one bothered to rush forward and bind her once more, because they all knew that Roger was right. There was nothing she could do against them, no way she could defend herself.

It was Roger who accompanied her up the narrow metal stairs and into a large, hay-littered, oddly clean barn. A little bit of light shot through cracks in the wood and around the door, but for the most part the barn was shut tight. No animals lived here; no farm equipment was stored in the vast space. The barn was just for show.

The man she had long considered her friend led her to a frighteningly tall wooden ladder that was propped against the hayloft, and he urged her up, one slow, easy step at a time. Quinn remained below with the two young guards, but Archard followed Roger and his prisoner up the ladder as if he did not trust either of them. As soon as they were all in the hayloft, Miranda glanced down. It was a long drop from the hayloft to the barn floor, and a fall from this height would likely do the trick. At the very least, she'd be severely injured, and faking the rest would be easy for men like these.

Roger didn't push her over, though. Instead, he took her arm and together they walked toward the large closed door at the front of the barn, where, if this were a real working farm, bales of hay might be dropped into the yard. Light broke in around the doors, falling onto and around them. A metal rail on a rusted track was built above the door, making Miranda think that perhaps this had once been a working farm, before Quinn and his sick army had taken it over.

Roger threw the latch that held the double doors shut and pushed them open to reveal an oddly bright spring day. There was not a cloud to be seen in the bright blue sky above the thick forest to the west. Her old friend maintained a tight grip on her arm, as if he was afraid she'd try to escape. Where did he think she would go if she did escape from his grip? Behind them stood an armed Archard. Before her… Miranda glanced out of the hayloft door to the ground below and her stomach twirled and dropped. It was a very long way down.

Miranda looked at the ground, listening to the men below as they unlocked the barn doors and opened one side with a creak and a *swoosh*. Quinn and the two armed guards shuffled out of the barn doors below and into the yard.

A stiff breeze caught Miranda's hair, and she prepared herself to embark on that trip everyone had to make to the other side, to death and the spirit world. She'd always known she, like everyone else, would go there someday, but she hadn't imagined it would be like this, betrayed by a man she called a friend. Would she haunt this earth or would she easily move on to peace? She closed her eyes and waited for a shove that would send her into the air and to the ground below.

Roger whispered in her ear. "He's out there. Call him."

Miranda's eyes snapped open. "What?"

Behind them, Archard grew impatient. "What are you two talking about?"

"I'm saying goodbye to a friend," Roger said. "Do you mind?"

"Yeah, I do. Make it snappy!"

"Call him," Roger whispered. "Speak to Korbinian, do whatever it is you can to call him here."

"Why?"

"Just this once, Miranda, listen to me. Trust me."

While she didn't trust Roger, not anymore, she saw no harm in closing her eyes and thinking of Bren. She saw no harm in whispering his name, in telling him in a silent voice she hoped he could hear that she loved him. She wanted him to know. What she felt for him was more than physical. More than a need for what pleasures he could offer her. Their bond went to the soul, she knew that now. If that was not love, then what was?

Fantastic as it was, yes, she believed to the pit of her soul that she'd been born for one man, for Bren.

"Tell Cheryl I…" she began, but Archard lost his patience and ran toward the hayloft door, pushing Miranda forward so that the tips of her toes, her face, her arms, were on air. A cool breeze wafted over her, almost as if the air could catch her as she swayed there. Her toes were barely perched on the hayloft floor. Far below watchers had gathered to witness her death, but they stood well back so as not to be sullied by her blood. They wanted to see her death, just not too closely.

Roger continued to hold on to Miranda's arm, but Archard was working against him, trying forcefully to peel those strong fingers from her arm. The two men struggled and even though they were upon her and fought about her, Miranda could almost manage to dismiss them from her mind. In the middle of the fight Roger managed to give the rail above a push, and with a creak the rusty metal pole swung out of the doors.

And in the near distance Miranda heard a sound that she now realized was for her ears alone. Black wings fought and floated against the air, and out of the corner of her eye she saw the dark wave of seventy-seven ravens shooting over the farmhouse.

Roger's hand was yanked away, Archard pushed once more, and Miranda fell.

Chapter 10

Miranda reached up and snagged the rail. She didn't have a good grip, but she held on as best she could. Her fingers began to slip from the metal, and no matter how desperately she tried to hold on, she couldn't. The ravens swarmed around and under her as she dropped, and for a split second—and a split second was all she had—Miranda panicked. Claws and sharp beaks caught her clothing as she was instantly surrounded by the flock of birds in a tight formation that banded and wrapped around her, almost becoming a part of her, they were so close. The ravens descended upon her so quickly and completely that she could see nothing but midnight-black feathers as they joined together to hold her—to catch her.

Miranda didn't hit the ground as she'd expected to.

The ravens surrounding her slowed her descent, and then, amazingly, they lifted her. She had no control of her body, none at all, but floated on a cushion of feathers. It was the oddest sensation, to hover in air amidst the ravens. Below her men shouted; Roger's voice remained silent. Miranda tried to twist her head to get a look at the man who had all but thrown her out of a barn, insisting that Bren would be there to catch her. He'd been right, but how could he have known? She could see nothing for the ravens that held her, and the sensation of flight was so disorienting Miranda found herself instinctively fighting to regain some semblance of control over her own body. For a moment she wasn't sure which direction was up and what was down. There was no ground to orient her, nothing solid to hold on to.

Relax. The word came to her mind as a whisper.

"Easy for you to say," Miranda muttered.

A few of the ravens cawed as if in response, and she did her best to relax, to let the big birds—to let Bren—carry her away. Though she could not see anything but black feathers, a few beaks and a couple of ravens' eyes, she felt a change of direction. Between the swaying movement and the lack of control and the way her head and arms floated up and down as the ravens carried her, Miranda began to feel ill. Seasick, almost. Her stomach roiled and her head swam. Not one claw or beak touched her skin, and her hair flowed freely around her, but almost every inch of her clothing was caught in a bird's grasp, and beneath her they offered the support of their backs and their wings. She was oddly secure as she floated across the sky, away from the men who would kill her without a second thought or a hint of remorse.

Gunshots fired, the report loud and alarming, but the sounds seemed far away. A handful of ravens shrieked in response, and Miranda gasped in horror. Were those weapons aiming for the ravens? Had Bren been hurt?

Or had Roger just paid a high price for helping her escape?

She closed her eyes against the motion sickness; she relaxed and allowed the ravens to carry her. The sensation of moving very quickly was dreamlike and at the same time very real. She had to tell herself to breathe, to relax, to trust Bren as she had never trusted anyone else.

When they began to descend she felt the change in altitude in the waves that undulated through her stomach. Birds working as one realigned, and she was shifted from horizontal to standing on air. The queasiness was lessened in this position, and the ravens had repositioned themselves so she could see the forest around them. Having her sight back helped her to reorient herself. Ancient trees grew close together, which made the birds' movements crucial and precise, as they lowered Miranda to her feet in a clearing. When she was standing on her own they freed her, releasing their hold on her clothing, breaking away in a burst of black feathers as if she were at the center of an explosion of ravens.

After the excitement and the flight and the motion sickness, her knees would not hold her. She sank to the ground, landing on those traitorous knees and instinctively digging her hands into the earth. The solid ground beneath her seemed to spin for a moment, and then it was finally and wondrously still.

The ravens swarmed in concert, coming together, swooping up and then down again, and finally, in the blink of an eye, drawing into one another and transforming, taking the form of the man she had known them—him—to be.

"Are you hurt?" Bren asked as he stalked toward her, ignoring the uneven and less-than-kind ground beneath his bare feet, and Miranda wondered why she'd never seen it before. The dark eyes, the grace, the power... She should've known all along that he and the ravens were the same.

She shook her head and he gently helped her to her feet. When she was standing he gathered her into his arms, holding her as if he would never let her go.

Duncan swore as his shot, fired from the same hayloft door from which Miranda Lynch had fallen, went wide. The ravens flew quickly and soared high, even though they carried the weight of a woman within them.

Below, the old man and his newest recruits watched in awe, not moving or speaking or reacting at all. You'd think they'd never seen anything unexpected and unnatural before this moment.

Talbot remained still, too, watching the cloud of black birds and the woman within it.

"You knew, didn't you?" Duncan asked as he turned his weapon on Talbot. "When you suggested this method of disposal, you knew if Lynch fell, Korbinian would swoop in and save her."

"How could I have known?" Talbot asked, but there was little conviction in his voice. He ignored the muzzle that was pressed into his side. If Talbot was smart he was already expecting his own death. Yet apparently it wasn't enough to frighten him into submission.

"Quinn still has your son, you know," Duncan reminded the traitor. "He'll be here soon, I imagine. For his sake you'd better hope the old man believes you." He leaned in closer, taking an even more threatening stance as he whispered, "I don't."

Bren couldn't hold Miranda tightly enough. She was a part of him and always had been. Before they'd met, when he'd foolishly tried to let her go, when he'd convinced himself that to take her or not was a choice…she had forever been a part of him.

She held him just as tightly as she assured him again that she was unharmed, and then they stood there in the middle of the thick forest, holding on, breathing deeply. The sounds of the forest were muted and natural. No one was upon them; no one was near. Even if the men they'd left behind at the farmhouse had run after them without hesitation, they'd be far away, still. He'd flown far and fast with Miranda in his grip, over a rushing stream, beyond a sheer rock cliff, into the heart of the forest. They were safe, for now.

The strong sense of relief soon gave way to the primitive desire he always experienced when he touched Miranda. Naked as he was, Bren could not hide his physical reaction to having her in his arms—not that he wanted to hide anything from his Kademair. Her response was much the same. He felt it in the way her heart beat, in the way her fingers caressed him, in the way she melted into him. Soon her soft lips pressed a kiss to his chest, one and then another, and her hands settled possessively on his hips. He cupped her head in his hand and tilted it back so he could kiss her fully and rightly, taking her mouth without reservation or caution.

"I thought I'd lost you," he whispered as he slipped his hand beneath her blouse and caressed her skin.

"Never."

"I was willing to let you go," he said, and then he gently slipped her blouse up and over her head. "Just yesterday I was willing to let you walk out of my crazy life, but no more. You're mine, Miranda, no matter what comes."

"I'm yours."

He unfastened her bra and slipped it off her arms, turning his attention to nicely rounded, firm breasts and sensitive nipples. She was a miracle and he found himself entranced by her womanly beauty, her softness, her giving. Miranda threaded her fingers into his hair and pulled him closer, urged him to pull the flesh he tasted deeper into his mouth. She was warm and soft, sweet in the way only a woman could be.

Bren had known desire in the past, but he had never ex-perienced anything like this. There was undeniable power in their coming together; there was nature and heart and the force of the universe in the way they touched.

In a perfect world he would lay her in a soft bed covered in crisp sheets, but they didn't live in a perfect world. They had here and now, with no promises of tomorrow, no guarantee beyond this moment. He had almost let Miranda go once; he wouldn't make that mistake again.

She kicked off her shoes and he shucked her trousers down and away. They worked together almost frantically until she was as naked as he was. For a few moments he held her close and still, skin to skin. She was so soft, and the part of him that had been able to send her away from him once was overpowered by the fear that had assaulted him when he'd seen her pushed to what might've been her death, when he'd seen her hanging from a rail that he knew she could not hold on to for very long. He'd seen her fingers slipping away, and the sight had terrified him.

But that frightening moment was gone, it was in the past, and now they faced another life-changing moment more powerful than any other. Motionless and grateful, they shared heat, their hearts thudded in rhythm, and the need that had brought them together grew stronger.

Bren bent his head and kissed Miranda's bare shoulder, allowing his lips to linger, to taste. From there he kissed his way down her body—arm, breasts, soft belly, gently curved hip—until he knelt before her and delved his tongue between her thighs, arousing her, teasing and then pulling away, making her tremble. Her hips swayed gently, in rhythm with his tongue, and she gave a soft, satisfied sigh.

Perhaps this was the way their coming together was meant to be. This deserted forest, so deep and forsaken, was not a part of the civilized world they lived in. They might as well be living thousands of years ago, one of the first Korbinians and Kademairs, bonding without worry that danger awaited. There was nothing else but this, nothing else that mattered. He tasted her, he caressed her thighs and her hips, and he kissed the bruise on her thigh, angry to the pit of his soul that she had been harmed in any way. He knew without doubt that she was his.

He spread her thighs slightly and tasted her more deeply than before. Miranda gasped, she moaned and shuddered, and then she grabbed his head and gently moved away from him. "I want all of you this time," she whispered huskily. "All of you, Bren."

He didn't have the will to fight her. It was time.

The forest seemed right for this, but he wouldn't make the ground Miranda's bed, wouldn't ask her to lie on dead leaves and pebbles and sticks that would mark and irritate her tender skin. He would be her bed. Bren took Miranda's hand and lay back. She followed, as he had known she would, kneeling over him, straddling him with her wet center so close to his erection he caught his breath. She didn't immediately take him inside but leaned forward and kissed him deeply, her tongue exploring, her warm, soft breasts pressing against his hard chest. She teased him, circling her gentle fingers around his length and guiding him to her entrance, then taking the tip of his penis into her body— nothing more as she rocked against him, mouths and bodies together as they were meant to be.

Her kisses became lighter, their lips barely touching, as she continued to rock in a slow, maddening rhythm. "I don't want this to end," she whispered against his mouth as they were barely joined and she shifted her hips to take him a half inch deeper before drawing away again. "I am driven toward the end, I crave the end, and yet I don't want it to end because then it will be over. I feel like I'm flying, like the pleasure that awaits is more than my body and soul will be able to withstand." Again she swayed, and again she took him a little bit deeper. Her eyes closed. She moaned and her body shuddered.

And then she lost control. Perhaps a part of her wanted this encounter to be prolonged, but her body commanded that she take more of him, that she drive faster and harder toward the pleasure of release. Eyes closed, fair hair swaying, she rose to straddle him and take the entire length of him into her body. One last long, complete, demanding stroke was all it took. Miranda cried out. She shuddered hard and gasped. The release her body demanded could not wait. Bren came with her, giving himself over to his own pleasure while Miranda's inner muscles quivered around him.

What he experienced was more than physical release, more than the comfort and satisfaction of man and woman. Miranda had what she'd asked for, what she'd demanded. She had all of him.

Bren had not chosen this portion of the forest by chance, Miranda discovered. There was a low but deep cave a short walk from where they'd landed, and hand in hand, he led her there.

Her body was still warm and content, inside and out she was content, in spite of the horrors that had led her to this moment. "I didn't know you could catch me in the air that way," she said, her eyes on Bren's back and then on his ass. Since he had to walk around naked so often, it was a good thing that his body was hard and lean and gorgeous. In spite of everything, she found herself smiling. She'd put her clothing and more importantly her shoes on before they started the walk, but Bren had nothing. Heaven above, he was gorgeous!

"I wasn't sure that I could," he confessed. "But when I saw you and realized what Talbot had planned, I knew I had to try."

Miranda's smile was short-lived. "He told me you would come. How could he know if you weren't sure yourself?"

"There's no way he could've known. I'm going to kill the bastard," Bren said darkly. "I never did like him, and now this—"

"No," Miranda said sharply. "He's not like the others, not like Archard and Quinn. Roger's intentions—"

"The road to hell is paved with good intentions," Bren interjected as he stopped outside the cave. "Isn't that what they say?"

"They kidnapped his son," she argued.

"If he wasn't involved with them in the first place, that never would've happened." Bren turned to her, his face set in stone. "I won't risk my ass, or yours, to save him."

"So what comes next?" she asked, some of her intense satisfaction fading in the face of reality. "From what Roger told me, it seems that this Order is large and quite powerful. A lot of people will be looking for us, and we won't be able to trust anyone."

"You can trust me," Bren said, taking her in his arms once more. "You can always trust me."

Miranda sighed. That was the truth; she felt it to the depths of her being. "I do," she said simply. The cave before her was small and rough, as was the ground she walked on. She and Bren were entirely alone here, they were safe, at least for now, but they couldn't live this way forever. They needed food, proper shelter, clothes… a decent bathroom with all the facilities, including a hot shower.

Bren kissed her all too briefly and told her to wait there for him. He promised not to be gone long, and then he backed away from her. In the blink of an eye he burst from the man she loved into the flock of large ravens she'd come to know so well. The birds circled upward in a formation that resembled a thick column of spiraling dark smoke, and then they shot across the sky. Miranda watched as they disappeared from view, abruptly and entirely alone.

The forest that had seemed so friendly moments earlier took on a darker, more sinister tone, and Miranda sat before the cave and pulled her knees to her chest, dropping her head on those knees. She picked at her blouse and her pants, which had been ruined while in the ravens' grasp. Claws and beaks had picked at the fabric. Not that she was complaining. It was a miracle that the ravens had managed to carry her without putting a single mark on her skin. The only evidence of violence on her body was what remained of Sunday night's fall at Roger's cabin— a couple of bruises and a few minor scrapes.

"Do not be afraid."

Miranda's head snapped up at the sound of that gruff voice. Directly before her stood the creature she'd seen in the prison cellar, a half-man, half-cat being who radiated sadness and fear. He looked frightening, like a monster out of a horror movie, and yet he told her very gently not to be afraid.

Despite his seeming lack of power, the creature must possess strength to travel so far from the place where he'd died. There was so much about the afterlife Miranda still didn't know. Some spirits came to her, others did not. She hadn't seen Jessica since that day in the hospital, and she'd never seen her parents. Some ghosts never left the precise site of their death, while others could apparently travel quite a distance. First Dee and now this ghostly thing. What else did she not know about her gift? She suspected she still had much to learn—if she got the chance.

"My name is Miranda," she said gently, hoping not to scare him away. Deformed and seemingly monstrous as he was, she did not sense any evil within his spirit. There was no darkness around him; in fact, he was infused with a bright white light.

"I know your name, Miranda. They are very upset that you and your friend escaped." The expression on his face was twisted, as if he was trying to smile but could not.

"What's your name?" Miranda asked, since he had not offered the information on his own.

"Pete," he said. "My name is Pete." The spirit creature gave her a gentlemanly bow. "I am pleased to meet you. I haven't spoken to anyone for a very long time, at least not anyone who could hear me. Certainly no one has seen me for a very long time, either. I'm pleased that you are not offended by my grotesque appearance."

She wouldn't lie to Pete and tell him that he was not grotesque. Ghosts sensed lies acutely, and did not care for being deceived. "I can see the kindness within you, as well as the oddness without."

"Others did not," he said, his voice lowered.

While she waited for Bren to return, perhaps she could help Pete. No matter what he'd been in life, his kind spirit should've moved on after death. He should've released the physical deformity that twisted his features even in death. Torture kept him here and in this form, she imagined. Torture, physical and mental and spiritual. Had Roger had a hand in destroying Pete? Heaven above, she hoped not.

"Have you seen the light?" she asked.

Pete shook his head.

"It's there for you," Miranda said. She stood slowly, hoping that she would not scare Pete away if she moved closer to him. He'd come to her for a reason. Did he want her help? "On the other side there is—"

He shook his head. "I cannot go there, I cannot. I'm not the man I was supposed to be. I've been tainted with evil that runs through my blood still. And I can't leave…" He dropped his head and looked to the ground, so he wouldn't have to look at her. "I'm not here to ask for assistance for myself. I'm lost, and you cannot help me. I'm here to tell you that you must go back to the farm."

Miranda shook her head. She didn't bother to tell him that Bren had already refused to help the men who'd kidnapped them in order to end the existence of the Korbinians. "What could we do against armed men? Bren and I aren't soldiers, we aren't…"

"They will kill the good man and his son, because they helped you. That's not right." The creature shook his head in abject sadness. "It's not fair. Will you fight for fairness? Someone must. I thought it would be you."

Miranda's mouth went dry. "Jackson is only fifteen years old. They won't hurt him!"

"I was seventeen when my father slit my throat," Pete said.

"Your father?"

The creature continued. "During my first mission I was bitten by a werecat. Scientists working for the Order had come up with what they thought was a cure, and my father insisted that I take it before I turned into a monster like those he had trained me to fight. This is the result. Not a man, not a were, not a wild creature, but something caught horribly in between. I thought we would try other cures, but one night my father came in and offered me tea. I was sitting on a cot, trying to understand why they would not release me. These men knew me. I was one of them! My father asked me what kind of tea I wanted, and he began to list them all. Chamomile. Green. Black. Peppermint." Pete's breath hitched. "While I was trying to decide he slit my throat. He did the task very quickly, perhaps hoping that I would die instantly, but I lingered a few minutes. I lingered long enough to look him in the eye and see that he felt sorrow but not regret." The creature shuddered. "He told my mother that I ran away from home and forbade her to ever ask about me."

"Tea?" Miranda whispered. "Was your father…"

"My name is—*was*—Peter Quinn," the creature said.

"I grew up in that farmhouse. I was once one of *them*." His spirit eyes met Miranda's, and she felt a rush of heartbreaking pain. "Please save the boy, at least. Save him, as no one saved me."

Chapter 11

As a flock of ravens, Bren headed toward the town to the west with practical matters on his mind. In the past he'd flown in this form as release, as entertainment, for nothing but the joy of flight and complete freedom. Transporting Miranda had shown him that he could do more if it was necessary.

The ravens circled the small town, spotted what was needed, then swooped down with specific targets in mind. A clothesline, an outdoor market, a charity bin, he raided them all in a matter of seconds before lifting up again. Below men and women shouted, laughed or scurried away from the bold ravens. Some of them searched out the safety of a sturdy building, sheltering their children as they ran from him, as if he would next try to snatch up one of them.

He returned to the forest more slowly than he'd left it, tired and weighted down with the things he carried. And still, he moved quickly across the sky, carried by the wind and his wings and the power of the Korbinians.

Bren had never spent such a long period of time in this form, and until today he'd never carried anything more than a twig or a pebble. As he dropped what he'd stolen to the ground near a waiting Miranda, he experienced a wave of exhaustion that was new to him. Still he wasn't done. Not yet.

Miranda tried to call him to her as he lifted to the skies once more, headed east this time. Her voice carried across the wind to him, and he also heard that call inside, where no one else could touch him. He longed to turn about, swoop down and become a man again so he could hold her. But he couldn't, not yet. He'd told Miranda that he had no intention of risking his skin or hers for Roger Talbot, but her insistence that the man's son was also in danger was a concern.

He'd seen the younger Talbot out and about when the family had stayed in their cabin and invaded Bren's mountain. The kid had an affinity for the mountains, an innocence that shone through the attempts at manliness. Jackson Talbot was a tall, gangly child who had no business in the hands of those like Duncan Archard.

The ravens flew at the tops of the trees, staying low, moving fast. Most of the trees were leafed in the lush, new green of spring. Wild dogwoods were in bloom, dotting the forest with their delicate white flowers. As the birds drew closer to their destination they dipped down and flew between and among the trees, hidden from any who might be watching for his return.

Near the farmhouse seventy-five of the ravens perched on tree limbs while two continued on to the buildings. If Talbot had helped Miranda as she'd insisted he had, then he was likely already dead. Bren didn't entirely understand who these people were or what they wanted, but they knew too much, and they were willing to do anything to get what they wanted. He wouldn't put Miranda in danger, wouldn't allow her to be held by these people ever again, but he had to know. Maybe he could tell her that Jackson was nowhere near the farmhouse, and Talbot was having a good laugh—or making nefarious plans—with his buddies.

If that was the case then he had no obligation to anyone but Miranda.

The barn door stood open and there was no one inside, not that he could see. Through a window of the large farmhouse he saw the plump, white-haired woman in the kitchen cooking supper, stirring a big pot of something that smelled savory and hearty. Through yet another window he spotted Archard and the old man talking in low voices about what might come next. They were clearly not happy.

Talbot wasn't present. Maybe the man had escaped or been killed. Bren would like to think that perhaps Miranda's so-called friend had simply left the farmhouse, but his car was still here. Was Talbot being held as Miranda had been? Is that why the two younger men, the armed guards, were not with the old man and Duncan?

The ravens heard the car before they saw it, and though it was too far away for those in the house to hear the engine, there was an alarm that sounded, alerting them to the fact that someone had turned onto the long driveway.

The men left the house. Two ravens perched on the roof behind the metal gutters, listening and watching as Duncan and the other met the approaching car they'd obviously been expecting.

The older man was in the lead, clearly in charge. He looked harmless enough, but from all Bren had witnessed he was anything but harmless. The driver that stepped out of the dark sedan nodded with respect, and then he opened the rear door and reached inside.

Bren immediately recognized Jackson Talbot. His longish brown hair fell over his eyes, his skin was sallower than usual, and he was dressed as always, in jeans and a too-large T-shirt.

And his hands were bound behind his back.

The kid tried to present himself with attitude, but he was obviously and rightfully scared. He was too young and too honest to manufacture bravado. Shit. Miranda had been right.

So, where was Talbot? Bren didn't have to wait long to find out. The old man greeted Jackson with a smile and then, leading him toward the barn, said, "I'm sure you'd like to see your father. He's waiting for you."

With Jackson in tow the three men entered the barn, and the driver, who was the last to go inside, closed the barn doors behind them.

Miranda, after gathering up all that the ravens had dropped as they'd passed over and swooped down, took inventory: one pair of khaki pants that looked to be too large for Bren, a tattered blanket, a bag of chips and a bag of peanuts, cheese crackers, five juice boxes, a couple of handfuls of strawberries, a length of rope. She almost laughed. She'd heard that ravens were winged thieves, and now she knew it to be true.

It heartened her somewhat to realize that even though Bren had sworn they would not go back to help Roger, he was at least surveying the situation. He must be a little concerned, otherwise he'd be here with her now, resting or talking or making love.

She didn't have long to wait. The sun was low in the sky when she saw and felt the ravens returning to her.

Bren didn't realize what the men at the farmhouse were, what lengths they would go to—why they wanted him. Why they wanted her. He didn't know what had happened to Pete Quinn, what a monster the innocent-looking Ward Quinn was. If he knew, then he would agree with her that something had to be done.

Though she had seen the transformation before, it still took her breath away. The change was so quick the actual shift was invisible to the eye. One moment the flock of birds circled into itself, and then in the blink of an eye a naked Bren appeared where they had once been.

"Naturalist, eh?" she said as he began to walk toward her. She could see the exhaustion in his dark eyes, but his step was strong and steady.

"It was the first excuse that came to mind," he said solemnly, and then he took her in his arms and pulled her close, without words, without explanation.

It would soon be dark. The sky was gray and the cover of trees made the forest dim. Nightfall would come quickly here. While Bren had been gone Miranda had made a bed of sorts inside the cave, with dead leaves for cushioning between the ground and the blanket, and the food he'd collected sitting nearby. She didn't think he would've collected those things if he didn't plan to spend the night here.

"What did you see at the farmhouse?" she asked as she rested her head against his chest.

He hesitated. "You were right. They have the kid."

Miranda sighed. "We have to do something."

"I won't put you in danger, not even to save your friend and that child," Bren said sharply.

"Because I'm Kademair?"

"You're not a fighter, and even if you were I would not allow you to do battle with those men."

"But—"

"We'll rest here for a while," Bren continued. "When I can fly again I'll go back to the town and tell the police that a young man is being held prisoner at the farm. The law can handle the situation."

"So could we," Miranda argued.

Bren shook his head. "I refuse to risk your life, even for the boy. Talbot is the cause of the situation, and he can damn well save his own kid. I'll send the police to help, but that's it. It's Talbot's job to protect his family, just as it is my job now to protect you."

Her hands pressed to his bare skin. She couldn't walk away and leave Jackson in the hands of those horrible men! Some Order—they were nothing but a bunch of thugs. What was she going to do? Bren seemed adamant in his refusal.

She loved him. It was true that she didn't know nearly enough about Bren, his ancestors, what would happen to her in years to come if they remained together—if they both survived. He didn't understand how her ability called to her and drained her, how she lived with ghosts and the grief or horrors they left behind.

When he touched her she could think of little else. She was drawn to him with an incredible power she could not deny. Kademair and Korbinian, according to the Order, and to Dee. They were drawn together without will, without choice, their attraction as powerful and unstoppable as a river rushing into the ocean.

Was it love or was it obsession? What she felt was surely more than her body calling to his thanks to genetics or some weird folklore. At this moment Bren needed to know about Pete and what had happened to him so he'd realize how serious the situation at the farm-house was, or could be. Maybe she could reason with him; maybe she could change his mind.

She told Bren what the tortured spirit had shared with her, all the while holding on to him for strength and warmth and the love she felt but had not confessed. She told him what she'd learned in the bunker below the barn, how they were determined to make sure Bren was the last of his kind.

He listened, nodding now and then. She felt the tension in his body, as well as sensed it within him the way she often sensed emotion in a ghost. In all her life, she'd never been this close to another human being. It was wonderful and frightening, both at once.

But he didn't suggest that his plans change. At the

moment he cared only for protecting her. It was an urge as primal and undeniable as the sexual attraction that tugged at them. Would he regret his decision later if something horrible happened to Jackson? She would, she knew it, and she told him so.

Bren's hand settled over her stomach, low and arousing. "The next Korbinian might already be right here inside you. You will be the mother that saves an entire race." His lips rested on her neck. "Even if I were willing to risk you, which I am not, it wouldn't make sense to risk all that remains of us."

"I don't care about the future," she said. "I can't. Not when the three men I love most in the world are in danger."

He pulled away and looked her in the eye. There was such dark power there she trembled. "You love Talbot?" he asked.

She nodded. "I'm angry with Roger. I hate what's he's done. But he's like an older brother to me, and Jackson…I've watched Jackson grow from an annoying kid to a fine young man. They are my family, the only family I had for years before I met you."

The sky was growing darker, and in the distance critters scurried. Bren stepped toward the shelter of the cave, leading her as if they were dancing, as if he was afraid to let her go. "I'm your family now."

"Fine," she said, unhappy with his decision but knowing by his stern expression and fathomless black eyes that there was no use in arguing. "Get your rest, and then when you're able, fly to town to alert the police."

"And then you and I will disappear," Bren said. "We'll find a place where no one will ever again bother us. No one will threaten you or our sons, I'll see to it. I promise you that."

The cave was low and tight, and as they settled onto the blanket their bodies were entangled, closer than close. Even though they did not agree on how to handle the situation, she couldn't be this near to Bren and not want him. She couldn't lie with him and not think of taking all of him. His response was the same apparently, since, exhausted or not, he began to undress her, dragging her jeans over her hips and down, pulling her blouse over her head, arousing her with long, talented fingers that already knew her body well and warm lips that tasted her throat and breasts as if he was hungry only for her.

Her hands skimmed his long, hard body, and she kissed his throat, which tasted of salty, warm maleness, and when his mouth settled over hers she felt as if he was drawing her very soul out of her, as she was drawing his.

And then he was on top of her and her legs wrapped around his hips. She urged him to push inside her, she drew him deeper, more completely into her aching, needful body, and he filled her. Long and hard, he plunged deep, buried himself inside her, and ribbons of pleasure began to grow.

They moved in a slow rhythm that wiped out memories of danger and uncertainty, memories of a time when they had not known the other existed. Their dance pushed away all past loneliness, all fears. This coming together began without the pulsing demand of their past encounters, without so many plaguing questions.

Soon there were no thoughts at all, no awareness

beyond the physical as their dance grew faster and more demanding, as they reached for the intense pleasure that began and grew and burst upon them as their bodies shuddered together, and once again their movements slowed and the world returned.

Bren's body remained above hers, warm and sheltering. A part of her wanted to take him and what they'd found and run, just as he planned. She didn't want the man she loved to put himself in danger, not even for Roger and Jackson. Yet deep down she knew neither of them could walk away and live happily knowing what they'd left behind.

She also knew she couldn't change Bren's mind. She was discovering that he was stubborn to a fault.

"Quinn told me what Kademair means," she said gently, running her fingers through Bren's hair because she couldn't bear not to touch him. "Not just that I have the ability to carry your child, but…" In this day and age it sounded so outrageous she had a hard time saying the words aloud. But she managed. "He said I was born for you."

Bren hesitated a moment and then said, "Perhaps you were."

"You're not sure?"

He gave a low, gruff laugh. "At the moment I'm sure of nothing. Nothing at all."

"If it's true, if I was literally born to be yours, how amazing is it that in a world so large we found one another?"

"I can't explain it, but here we are. I've been hiding all my life, and still you found me."

"With help from Roger."

At that, Bren snorted. "I refuse to give him any credit. He brought you to me and then he damn near killed you."

"I told you, Roger said you would save me."

Bren's voice was dark and angry as he responded. "He took a risk with your life, and that's unforgivable."

No, she could not possibly change his mind.

Bren sighed, and she could hear the exhaustion within him. He rolled to the side, keeping her in his arms, where she wanted to be always.

"I love you," she said easily. "I love you so much that it's insanely easy to accept the preposterous idea that I was literally born to be yours."

She longed to hear Bren say the same words to her; she wanted him to accept that their strong physical attraction could come laced with love. But he didn't repeat her words, not tonight. His eyes closed and he slipped into a deep sleep. The day's events had exhausted him. How long before he was able to fly again? He said it would be a few hours, but how many hours would pass before he could alert the authorities so Talbot and Jackson could be saved? Did they have hours?

Miranda kissed Bren's shoulder as he slept. She rested her hand on his chest, feeling the comforting beat of his heart and the steady rise and fall of his chest. When she was certain he was sound asleep she whispered, "Don't be angry. I can't sit here and wait, and I can't run away when the people I love need me. I wish we could do this together, but if I have to I'll do it alone." She only hoped he was not too horribly late getting to the police.

Miranda quietly grabbed her clothes, a juice box, a bag of crackers and Bren's newly stolen pants, then slipped soundlessly from the cave into darkness.

The woods were ominous without the sunlight or Bren to show her the way. She faced the direction she thought led to the farmhouse as she stood outside the cave and put on her snagged and wrinkled clothes, second-guessing her decision a hundred times in a matter of minutes. Dressed, her few provisions stored in the legs of the stolen pants, which she'd tied so they resembled a large tote bag she could sling over one shoulder, she took a few uncertain steps. Her right foot almost immediately landed in a small hole in the ground. She stumbled and caught herself, thankful she hadn't twisted her ankle or fallen.

"A little help would be nice," she muttered.

And then the help arrived, in the form of a solemn Dee and a deformed Pete, who together led the way with ghostly steps that illuminated the path like a smattering of fireflies.

It would be a long trip; exactly how long she wasn't certain. With Bren carrying her, she'd flown over the landscape at a frightening speed. On foot, the pace would be much different. She concentrated on putting one foot in front of the other, on watching her step on the uneven ground, on telling herself again and again that Roger and Jackson were still alive, very likely in that horrible room where so many had died. All was silent for a long while, and then Dee said, "Bren will be so angry with you for taking off like this."

"I know," Miranda said, and then she smiled. "But I

think he loves me enough to understand. When this is all over he'll forgive me."

Dee cast a glance over her shoulder, and her expression made it quite clear that she was not so sure.

For a change Bren slept hard. He dreamed not of Miranda but of Talbot's kid, and before he began to come awake he knew what he had to do. Like it or not, he couldn't fly away with his Kademair until he knew Jackson—and yes, even that bastard Talbot—was all right.

He rolled over, expecting his body to meet Miranda's. The leaves beneath the rough blanket crinkled beneath his weight as he found nothing where she should be. He was instantly awake, and it didn't take him even ten seconds to realize where Miranda had gone.

Had she not listened to a word he'd said? Didn't she realize how important she was?

Bren cursed as he left the cave, stepping into the deep darkness of night in this thick forest. These woods were not so very different than those he called his own, and since his night vision was quite good, as was his hearing, he had no problem surveying the deserted landscape. Miranda was long gone—she'd left here hours ago.

Anger, fear and worry boiled up in him. Until meeting Miranda he'd rarely felt any of those emotions, and now they seemed to be daily experiences. He'd told her she was to keep herself safe. He'd decided to help her friends, even though all he wanted was to take Miranda and escape to a part of the world where they could start over fresh and together.

This war of deep emotions was new to him, and he

didn't like it at all. Was she worth it? The sex was incredible, but the intense connection and the needs it awakened weakened him. Survival instincts insisted that he take flight and escape from those who would gladly kill him and those like him who were unfortunate enough, or blessed enough, to be different. Everything else within him commanded that he follow Miranda, even to the ends of the earth, even to death and beyond.

Kademair and Korbinian were said to be connected in ways that were impossible for others. The shared dreams, the call for help, the way he'd been drawn to her from first sight…all went beyond the physical.

Bren reached out for Miranda now, not certain that his call would reach her, not sure that she would hear. He thought of her. He pictured her blue eyes, her soft lips, the curve of her cheek. He remembered the wonder of her body and his together until he could almost feel her tight and hot around him, until her scent filled his nostrils, and then he whispered to the night.

"Don't take another step. Wait for me."

Chapter 12

Miranda stumbled when Bren's voice echoed in her head so loudly and clearly it was as if he was physically there, standing beside her and speaking into her ear. *Wait for me.*

"Don't be mad," she whispered, sensing his displeasure, as well as hearing the words he spoke.

Either he didn't hear her or else he simply didn't bother to respond.

She'd been walking for hours, trudging forward because she had no other choice. In so many ways it would've been easier to do things Bren's way and let armed lawmen handle the problem, but she couldn't let that happen. This was her responsibility. No matter how angry she was at Roger, he and Jackson were her family—a family by choice. She didn't see how that could continue once they got out of this situation—if they did—but she wouldn't abandon them to Ward Quinn and Duncan Archard, not without a fight.

Bren said she was important and could not risk her life; Miranda knew she couldn't ever feel right again if she didn't do all she could to see that an innocent boy was safe.

She returned her attention to the uneven ground, to the faint unnatural light Dee and Pete created for her, to the sparkling trail that would lead her to Roger and Jackson. She had to be close to her destination, if her calculations were correct. Her feet had gotten wet a while back when she'd crossed the shallowest part of a narrow stream, but she didn't stop to lament the cold that had seeped into her shoes. Her toes were icy cold; her steps sometimes squished.

The spirits who were with her could lead, but they couldn't help her with the physical challenges. When it came time to climb a jagged stone wall or fight past an overgrown section of the forest in the dark of night, she was on her own. Her arms ached, she was cold and wet and miserably alone, and when she had to climb she wondered if Dee would be able to help her if she fell. Bren was nowhere nearby to catch her, she knew that without question.

Dee's voice was soft in the night. "You didn't tell Bren about seeing me, talking to me." She didn't sound censuring, just…curious.

"Everything has happened so fast. The time just hasn't been right."

"You're worried about what he'll think."

Of course she was worried! "I love you, I'm hot for

your body, and oh, by the way, your mother is around here somewhere."

Dee laughed gently. "I can see where that might be an awkward conversation."

"I'll tell him one day. Promise."

Dee's answer was a graceful nod.

Miranda had grown accustomed to the fact that she was almost never truly alone. Others sometimes had a hard time with that. Would Bren?

More than once in the long night it would've been easier to turn back than to go on, but she didn't retreat, not even to glance into the darkness she'd already passed. There was no time to look back. Did Bren's "Wait for me" mean he was going to join her to help? Would she reach the farmhouse too late? Would she arrive to find the men she loved the most in this world dead? She pressed on, aching and scared and wondering with every step if she'd made the right decision. Thanks to her, Bren was once more in danger.

And then she thought of Jackson. Roger could take care of himself. If he went down as a victim of his own Order, then it had been his choice, perhaps even his destiny. Bren had escaped from the Order, had flown into their midst to save her, and he'd gotten away without a scratch. He could do so again. But Jackson...Jackson had not chosen his father's life. He hadn't asked to be involved in this madness. His was a ghost she could not bear to face, and she would not sit in a cave and wait, or worse, run away while events unfolded.

Miranda pushed onward, even though she wasn't sure how she could help once she got to the farmhouse.

She had no weapons. Even if she'd had a gun it wouldn't have done her any good. She'd never held a firearm and had no idea how to use one. So how could she get her friends out of there?

Doubts assailed her as she trudged through the forest, and still she was driven onward. What if Bren was so angry she'd disobeyed his instructions that he refused to help? He hadn't exactly allowed her to argue last night, and he might be one of those men who insisted on doing everything his way. She loved him, she felt love from him, but he'd never said the words. He'd never admitted that he needed her in any way beyond the physical. Though she knew she was his—as he was hers—she wondered if the Lynch love curse could strike even a destiny like theirs.

Her feet hurt, she was cold, and she felt lonelier than she ever had. Even after the accident and Jessica's death, she hadn't suffered such isolation. She'd discovered what it was like to be a part of something bigger and finer than she'd ever imagined, and she'd walked away from the man who was at the center of these new feelings.

What if she was too late?

What if she did more harm than good?

What if she was recaptured and they used her against Bren?

The sky turned gray, and dim light seeped through the trees. As day broke Miranda could see farther ahead, could see more than looming darkness and the closest tree or bush or rock illuminated by ghostlight. Now that daylight was coming she looked through the tree trunks, past undergrowth and dipping limbs, hoping to catch a glimpse of the farmhouse or the barn ahead, but still she saw nothing. She'd walked all night and now that daylight had come she was breathless and exhausted and aching, and she seriously doubted Bren's intentions. And though she felt she was close, believed her night's journey was almost done, in truth she had no idea how much farther she had to go. Had she misjudged the distance so horribly? Or was the farmhouse going to come into view at any moment?

When Pete stopped beside a misshapen, wild dogwood tree, she thought perhaps he was allowing her a moment of rest. But the way he stared at the ground, the way he went stone still, made her realize that something else was going on here.

She and Dee both stood behind him. "What is it?"

"My father buried me here," the spirit said. "With no ceremony, no goodbye, no marker. He told my mother we'd had an argument and I'd left. He was afraid if she knew that I was dead she wouldn't be able to hide her sorrow, and questions he didn't want to answer, questions from an outside world where he doesn't have complete control, would be asked. Then he dumped my body in this shallow grave and walked away. He didn't even look back. I know because I watched him walk away. I stood over my grave and *screamed* at him, but he didn't hear me."

Miranda wanted to lay a comforting hand on Pete's shoulder, but she couldn't. She could see him, hear him, feel his pain. But she couldn't touch him. This was not the first time he'd mentioned his mother, and she decided the woman could be a significant factor in sending him on to peace. "I'll find a way to tell your mother that you didn't run away."

Pete seemed not to hear her words. "Sometimes still, on Mother's Day or her birthday or at Christmas, she'll watch for the mail or sit by the phone thinking maybe this is the year I'll call. Sixteen years since my father buried me here, and still she waits. To watch her hope breaks my heart, as her heart is broken. I try to reach her, to touch or speak to her, but she doesn't have your gift. We are in agony together, but she doesn't know I'm there."

Perhaps Miranda couldn't touch Pete, but Dee apparently could. The spirit of Bren's mother laid her hand on the malformed spirit's twisted shoulder. "Before this day is done, your mother will know the truth," Dee said.

Pete nodded and turned away from his unmarked grave, continuing toward the farmhouse.

"How much farther?" Miranda asked.

"Not far," Pete said. "Not far at all."

Miranda glanced up at the gray sky above the trees. Since setting out, she had not seen or heard a single raven, much less a flock of them. If she got to the farmhouse and Bren wasn't there, if she had to battle the Order without him, she didn't have a chance. "Where are you?" she whispered. Though her last steps had seemed to drag, it hadn't been all that long since she'd heard him in the depths of her mind. If he'd flown straight to her he'd be here by now. Without Bren, it was likely she and Jackson and Roger would all end up like Pete, buried in the woods, lost and forgotten.

With that thought, the spirits of others who'd been

buried here appeared, each of them standing over his or her grave, ghostly markers of an Order's violent calling. Men, women, creatures that were not entirely human, so many had been disposed of here. So many had died in the bunker where Miranda had been held. All she had to do was glance at the ghosts to know if they were evil or simply unlucky, if they'd chosen to be so monstrous that the Order felt they had to stop them, or if they'd simply been different and therefore a threat to the world orderliness as a handful of men saw it.

They had died in horrible ways, killed with as much hatred and evil as the Order claimed to fight against. Would she and her family be next?

Duncan paced impatiently, ragged with lack of sleep, annoyed that the thing he'd observed for so many years had gotten away. In the underground room, which was more bunker than cellar, Roger Talbot sat on the cot Miranda Lynch had once occupied. The former warrior of the Order was shackled, restrained by sturdy chains while his son lay beside him, drugged into a senseless state.

The old man had interrogated Talbot all night, trying to break him, trying to get him to veer from his story of ignorance. Talbot claimed he'd had no idea that Korbinian might swoop in and save Miranda at the last minute. Yes, he'd come to consider the medium a friend, but that didn't mean he'd forgotten who he was and what he'd been charged to do. Fear for his son was evident in the way he did his best to protect the unconscious boy with his body, even though he was all but helpless himself.

Quinn was tiring of Talbot's professions of innocence, but he didn't give up. Lack of sleep and fear for his child would make the traitor tell all. Eventually.

Even though Duncan had studied the freak he was assigned to watch, he was well aware that no one knew more about the Korbinians than Roger Talbot, whose father had not only watched over Joseph Korbinian for nearly forty years, but had researched the dying breed incessantly, collecting volumes of information and lore. If anyone knew how to track and kill Brennus Korbinian, it was this man. For that reason alone, Duncan had not yet suggested that they kill Talbot and his son and move on.

Miranda reached the edge of the forest exhausted and certain that the whole Korbinian Kademair thing was nothing more than a fairy tale. No one was born for another person; no two people were destined for one another. If Bren wanted to procreate, she was certainly not the only woman on earth who could help him out. That was just a part of the fairy tale the Order had bought into.

Yep, the Lynch love curse was in full effect.

She couldn't blame Bren for taking off. This was her family in danger, not his. They weren't blood, but she'd made them family and had thought of them as such for the past two years. They were all she had in this world. Bren had wisely avoided close attachments that could lead to moments like this one, where the choices to be made were not choices at all but compulsions. Requirements.

He'd given her a choice. She could've made her escape with him and maybe they would've lived happily ever after. Maybe not. Now she'd never know. The cowardly thought was spurred by fear and uncertainty, and didn't last very long. She had to be here.

Pete and Dee stood behind her, waiting for her next move. They'd done their part in leading her here, and what came next was up to her. Straight ahead sat the quaint and sturdy farmhouse. To the right rose the barn. Her eyes were drawn to the closed hayloft door, and her mouth went dry. She could almost feel her stomach roiling at the sensation of height.

Where was Ward Quinn? The two armed guards? Duncan Archard? More important, where were Roger and Jackson?

The scent of bacon and coffee reached Miranda, faint but unmistakable. Inside that house her only possible living ally in this battle was busy making breakfast.

"Will she listen to me?" Miranda whispered.

"Mom's a good woman," Pete responded. "She doesn't know the whole story where my father's affairs are concerned. She knows some, probably more than he realizes, but she doesn't understand that he's a bad man."

Miranda dropped her supplies to the ground and left the shade of the forest, walking directly toward the front door of the farmhouse. Her hammering heart seemed to be stuck in her throat. At any moment a gun could fire; she was an easy target in the open space between the woods and the picturesque porch, which looked peaceful and wonderfully ordinary. Halfway there she began to run. Exhausted or not, running seemed to be a good idea.

Dee and Pete flanked her, floating at her speed, whatever that speed might be. They were great moral support, but when it came time to fight they wouldn't do her any good at all. They couldn't stop a bullet if one was fired in her direction. They could throw themselves between her and any weapon used against her, but they didn't have the physical form to stop a mosquito from alighting on her skin. Dee *might* be able gather the strength to push one opponent or another aside, but that wasn't going to help much. So Miranda had moral support, but physically she was on her own.

She all but leaped onto the front porch. Before she could change her mind about what had to be done, she rushed forward and knocked soundly on the front door. If the old man answered, she was sunk. If it was Pete's mother who came to the door she *might* have a chance. The footsteps that approached were steady and even, and it was impossible to tell if the approaching resident was male or female. Miranda held her breath as the doorknob turned.

The door swung open on a gray-haired older woman who was the very picture of a farm wife. Mrs. Quinn was slightly plump, her bosom was considerable, and her face was not as lined as it might've been, given her age. There were sad lines around her mouth, and having listened to Pete, Miranda understood why. But for the most part the woman appeared pleasant and friendly and normal. Miranda craved normalcy at this moment when nothing was as it should be.

Miranda said simply, "I need your help."

The woman wiped her hands on a dishtowel and leaned out of the doorway to look at the driveway. "Have you had car trouble? Out on the road? I can call the gas station in town. Len's quite good with all sorts of mechanical problems."

"I walked through the woods," Miranda said.

Mrs. Quinn studied Miranda up and down, her eyes and her expression critical. An overnight hike through the forest couldn't look pretty on any woman. "Have a seat on the porch. When my husband comes in for breakfast perhaps he can—"

"Your husband tried to kill me yesterday," Miranda blurted. "Right now he's holding two of my friends hostage in a secret room under the barn, and I'm afraid he's going to hurt them."

"Don't be ridiculous," Mrs. Quinn whispered. "My husband has a hobby room in the cellar under the barn, and he often has his buddies over, that's true. They're playing cards. Why you would tell such a tale I never—"

"One of my friends is only fifteen," Miranda interrupted. "Please, call the local police. Call the sheriff's office. I can see that you don't believe me, but dial 911 and have them send everything they have. If I'm crazy, the police will take me away with them and you'll never see me again. If I'm right, then you've just saved the life of an innocent young man."

Mrs. Quinn stepped inside the house and reached behind the door, coming out with a shotgun in her hands. She held the weapon as if she knew how to use it. It was pointed at Miranda.

Not the expected response.

"I know a bit more about my husband's hobby than he realizes, though I do try to play innocent when I can. I watch. I listen. If Ward tried to kill you, then he had good reason, but I can't let you call the police. They would never understand. My husband searches out the wickedness of the world and disposes of it. If he's holding a young man in the barn, then that young man is anything but innocent."

Miranda's heart fell. She'd risked everything to come here and ask for help, and this is what it got her. Pete's mother was not as guiltless as he seemed to believe.

Still, she had to present some kind of argument. She had to believe that Pete was right about his mother. The alternative was not at all acceptable; she refused to accept death or a return to the bunker under the barn.

"I imagine some of the men and women your husband disposes of are indeed anything but innocent, but sadly, that isn't always true," Miranda said. "I talk to ghosts. Where's the harm in that? I've never hurt a living being. All I've done is try to help lost souls and lock away the very human monsters that killed them. Maybe I made the mistake of falling in love with the wrong man. I don't see anything horribly wrong in that." She tried to ignore the weapon that was trained on her, but it wasn't easy. She didn't know anything about weapons, but she assumed that a little weight on the trigger, and this would be done. If it came to that point, then Roger and Jackson would be lost, too, she imagined. "One of your husband's associates, Duncan Archard, broke into a cabin where I was on vacation and tried to kill me. I've never hurt anyone, and yet they want to be rid of me because I have a gift they don't understand."

She hadn't wanted to share the news this way, but it looked as if she had no choice. "Your husband took Pete's life when he was injured. Was Pete wicked?"

Mrs. Quinn's response was to pump the shotgun, which didn't make Miranda feel any better. "You don't speak my son's name. He ran away from home years ago…"

"He didn't get far!" Miranda snapped. "Pete's buried in those woods behind me, buried beside a dogwood tree because he was injured doing your husband's business and the father could not allow the son to live."

"Liar." Mrs. Quinn stepped onto the porch, and Miranda stepped back. The muzzle of that shotgun was much too close to Miranda's face. She couldn't help but look directly at it and wonder if Pete's mother would actually pull the trigger.

"Tell her I'm here," Pete said.

Miranda took a deep breath and pulled her eyes away from the weapon, looking into Mrs. Quinn's eyes, instead. "Pete is here now. He brought me here. He led me through the woods to your door."

Mrs. Quinn went pale. "My son ran away…"

"He tells me it breaks his heart to see you sit here on holidays and special occasions and wait to hear from him when he has no way to reach you."

"You can't use my son this way," Mrs. Quinn said angrily. "It's cruel. Why would you torture me? Why would you remind me of the son who ran away from me without a word or a letter or a…"

Pete stood behind his mother, but he spoke to Miranda.

Miranda stared into the older woman's sad eyes. "Pete says you used to make him pancakes every Saturday morning. Not ordinary pancakes, but blueberry or chocolate chip or banana. Whatever he wanted."

"Lots of people knew that," the woman said. She tried to remain unmoved, but her voice shook a little. "Peter's friends. My husband's associates who sometimes stay here for days. They all knew."

Miranda continued to listen to the spirit who now touched his mother's hand. "That's true enough," she said, "but who else knows that when your husband forbade you to speak of your son again, you closed yourself in the bathroom and cried? Who knows that you cried almost every day for two years?"

The weapon began to tremble. Mrs. Quinn took another step toward Miranda, and Miranda backed away. She had nowhere to go. She couldn't run faster than the pellets expelled from a shotgun, and even if she made it into the woods, then what? Bren wasn't here; he wasn't coming.

"I imagine no one else knows that you went into Pete's room shortly after he was murdered and took a small toy that was one of his favorites when he was a child. It was a figurine of some sort, a small soldier holding a sword. He tells me it's still in your bedside drawer, hidden beneath a stack of handkerchiefs where your husband won't easily stumble across it. You know he wouldn't approve of the fact that you keep that toy so close to you, not forgetting Pete as you were told to do, never letting go."

Something miraculous began to happen as Miranda spoke. Pete's malformed spirit began to change. Where once there had been a half-man half-beast monstrosity, there now stood a handsome young man with intelligent blue eyes and fine blond hair. Oh, he was so young!

"Pete has your nose," Miranda said gently. "He also has your gentle heart and did not want to join his father in hunting down the wicked and those whose only crime was to be gifted with some power that's not yet understood."

"You're a con artist of some kind," Mrs. Quinn whispered. "You're cruel to remind me of the son who ran away."

"Your son didn't run away," Miranda insisted once more. "His father offered him tea and then he slit his throat. Call the police and I'll show them where Pete was buried. If I'm wrong, then you can shoot me." The woman's questioning eyes met hers. "I'm not wrong," Miranda added kindly. "Help me, please."

But it was too late. It had taken her too long to convince Pete's mother of the truth. While they'd been talking, Ward Quinn and Duncan Archard had left the barn and positioned themselves between Miranda and the forest. They were both armed. She couldn't convince herself that they would be as hesitant as this woman to pull the trigger.

Miranda prepared herself for the shot that was coming; she imagined both men were accomplished marksmen, and now she was their target. It was over. Her gamble in racing here had failed.

But Mrs. Quinn nudged Miranda to the side and stepped around her, effectively shielding Miranda with her broad body. "Ward, you have some explaining to do."

"Now, honey, this is my business and you have no—"

"Did you kill Peter?" the woman asked outright, her voice almost steady.

Miranda expected the old man to lie to his wife, but surprisingly, he did not.

"There was an accident and Pete was wounded. He got very sick within hours, and soon I could see that he was turning into one of the creatures he worked so hard to fight. He was tainted by bad blood and he ceased to be the boy we both loved…"

"So, you did kill him. Slit his throat and buried him in the woods, to hear this girl tell it."

Quinn took a step toward the porch and his armed wife, while Archard moved to the side, no doubt trying to line up a clear shot at Miranda.

"I made Pete's passing as quick and painless as I could, and then I protected you from the ugly truth."

Pete sighed. "I was not a monster on the inside."

Miranda repeated his words in a soft voice for Mrs. Quinn alone, and as she did she heard the sounds of birds, of ravens, approaching. Her heart reacted and her stomach flipped. Bren was coming. He hadn't forgotten her.

"I didn't have a chance to fight for my life, or say goodbye."

Again Miranda told Pete's mother what he said.

Without warning, Mrs. Quinn fired on her husband. The blast was deafening, the effects of the shot on a man so close was gruesome. Miranda turned her head to see that Archard had not been fazed by the violence. He took aim. At her.

The ravens dove, the man with the gun their target. Seventy-seven ravens diving at full speed was an awesome sight, one that took Miranda's breath away. Once before the birds had attacked Archard, but this time their intent was much more deadly. Claws found and tore skin; sharp beaks stabbed. They forced his arms out and away from his sides, and they snatched the gun from his hand and dropped it to the ground several feet away. When that was done, the attack lessened, but did not stop. Duncan Archard was surrounded by flapping wings that covered his face and surrounded his body, pecking, scratching, disorienting him. Ravens dove in and out, wave after wave moving in to attack and then winging away, making room for another.

When Miranda had been surrounded by the ravens, she'd been protected. Archard was under full assault, and he didn't know how to defend himself.

In the distance Miranda heard approaching sirens. Lots of them. Bren hadn't abandoned that part of his plan, after all. Help was on the way. The birds that had attacked Archard dispersed as a line of sheriff's cars entered the driveway, lights flashing. Archard lay on the ground, bleeding and shaking, incapable of speech or movement.

The officer in the lead car leaped out, armed and alert as he surveyed the situation. Mrs. Quinn held a shotgun, and her husband was very dead, obviously killed by the weapon she held. Archard was alive but badly injured. His injuries were not so easily identifiable to those who had not seen the ravens' vicious attack.

Those birds flew into the forest, disappearing into the trees as the gruesome scene was surrounded by armed lawmen. Only Miranda watched them go.

Mrs. Quinn wisely and calmly put her shotgun down. "He murdered my son," she said simply. "Peter's body is buried in the woods and this girl can show you where." With that she turned away, showing her back to the armed lawmen. "My biscuits are burning, dammit."

Chapter 13

In the years since Jessica's death and the awakening of her abilities, Miranda had been in some strange situations. Nothing topped this one.

The sheriff and his deputies raided Quinn's bunker and arrested the two young guards. Poor boys, they were confused. All along they'd thought they were the good guys. The lawmen believed differently. Roger and Jackson were freed. Roger desperately needed sleep and Jackson suffered from a kind of hangover, thanks to the drugs he'd been given. They were both taken to the local clinic for treatment and observation.

The sheriff decided the shotgun blast that had killed Ward Quinn had been an accident, and none of the deputies said a word to hint otherwise. Mrs. Quinn gave a brief statement but was not detained. Miranda suspected the local lawmen knew more than they let on. How could they not? There had to have been years of strange comings and goings from this farm where no traditional farm work was done, and no one who spent much time with Ward Quinn could possibly think him an entirely innocent man.

The fact that Archard was raving like a madman and also that an FBI agent and his son were being held captive didn't hurt Mrs. Quinn's case at all.

Miranda declined to make a trip to the clinic where Roger and Jackson were being treated, instead accepting Mrs. Quinn's invitation to rest in Pete's room until she felt like traveling. No one had slept in his bed for sixteen years, but unknown to Ward Quinn, his wife had laundered the sheets at least once a month, preparing for their son's eventual return. What Quinn had done to his wife was almost as cruel as cutting his own son's throat. He'd let her believe that Pete had run away; he'd allowed her to grieve and to hope all these years. He had taken from her the right to tell her son goodbye.

After the majority of the lawmen had cleared out, Miranda had accepted the loan of a nightgown much too large for her and had crawled gratefully into Peter Quinn's bed. She'd gone to sleep with her window wide open and the sheriff's words echoing in her brain.

A naked fella showed up at the station before the crack of dawn with the most outrageous tale I've ever heard. Ran in and out in a matter of seconds, telling the deputy at the desk that a couple of fellas were being held captive in Ward Quinn's barn. The deputy on duty tried to detain him. It's against the law to run around town with no clothes on. But the guy ran around a corner and was gone, just like that. 'Course, Jim's been known to take a drink or two on a slow night, so there's no tellin' where that naked fella actually took off to.

Miranda was relieved to know that Bren hadn't been late arriving because he'd had second thoughts about her. About *them*. He'd gone to Silvera for help, and then he'd flown to her. If she'd done as he'd instructed and waited for him in the woods, she never would've been in danger. Not that she regretted forging onward. Still, if she had known what he'd planned . . .

With her head resting on Pete's pillow Miranda fell asleep quickly, exhausted and shaken, yet certain that somehow everything was going to be all right. Bren had not deserted her.

She didn't dream of ravens or men. In fact, she didn't dream at all, not that she recalled. The bed was like warm, welcoming quicksand that sucked her in and allowed her to claim the rest she so badly needed. When her eyes opened, the sky beyond the open window was dark and Bren sat on the side of the bed. She'd thought he might come to her, which was why she'd left the windows open when she'd gone to sleep.

He was not entirely naked, having found and donned the trousers she'd left in the woods. His expression was not one of sweetness and love, nor was it of relief. No, he was furious with her and didn't mind at all that she so easily saw his displeasure.

"I told you to wait. Didn't you hear me?"

"Hello to you, too," she said. "I'm fine, really. Not hurt at all. I ache everywhere, but that's thanks to the hike through the forest, not anything Quinn or his twisted allies did."

Bren pulled her up and into his arms, so that her head rested against his bare chest. He held her close, his warm, hard body telling her what he refused to admit aloud. He'd been scared, not angry, and fearing for someone else's safety was new to him.

"Right now I just want a hot bath and some clean clothes," she said, resting her cheek against his chest and loving the way he felt. After that...she didn't know what would happen after. She was Bren's Kademair, his life mate; she'd easily accepted that fact in the heat of the moment. But was that true or was it only desire that made him think there was more to their feelings than sexual attraction? Would Duncan Archard have kidnapped any woman Bren expressed a quick and intense interest in? Maybe the whole Kademair Korbinian thing was just what it sounded like. A fairy tale.

"You'll get your bath, and I have clean clothes for you."

She tilted her head back to look at him. This close she could see the stubble on his untended chin, the pulse at his throat, the lips she longed to kiss again. "Did you steal them off someone's clothesline?"

"I borrowed them from Mrs. Quinn."

Miranda tried to imagine what the much larger woman might have that would be suitable, thinking that she'd end up in something like the nightgown that now swallowed her whole, when Bren added, "The clothes are not exactly in style, but they should fit you well enough to do until I get you home." He sighed deeply. "The woman apparently never throws anything away. She also offered me some of Pete's clothes if I should need them."

"Are we leaving tonight?"

Bren shook his head. "Tomorrow morning you're going to show some of Roger Talbot's associates—associates of the FBI type, I'm happy to say—where the bodies are buried. Literally. He says these will be men you've worked with before, so we don't have to worry about hiding what you're doing or convincing unbelievers. When that's done we can go home."

Miranda sighed. She wanted to go home, and she so wanted that home to be in Bren's mountain house. She waited for him to say something to that effect, but he didn't. In the cave where they'd made love he'd talked about disappearing, but now he talked easily about home. His? Hers? Theirs?

Bren drew the oversize nightgown over her head and tossed it aside. He touched her, caressed her body as if she was precious and fragile. She liked the feel of his hands on her body—she always had. Relaxing in his arms, giving in to the sensations that the simplest touch aroused, was the most natural thing in the world. Apparently he wasn't *too* angry with her.

She wanted Bren inside her, again and again, but he didn't go that far. Instead, he stopped far short, snatching up the gown he'd tossed aside and pulling it over her head, gently tugging it down so it covered her body, loosely and completely. When that was done he gathered her in his arms and lay down beside her, holding her close, keeping her safe. She didn't question why he'd stopped, why he didn't make love to her.

"You came for me," she said softly, content to cuddle in his arms for now.

"Of course I did. Did you doubt me?" he asked.

Miranda didn't answer that question. She didn't want to admit to Bren that she had doubted very much.

Bren stood in the hallway outside the bathroom while Miranda took her shower. He listened to the spray of the water and imagined her there, tired and shaken but thankfully whole and alive. He could've waited downstairs or in the room where he'd found her asleep, but he didn't want to be that far away.

Because she was his, a group of nuts had tried to kill her. Some of them might've been well-meaning nuts, but the rest were simply killers who found a way to rationalize their violence and hatred. They would've taken her life without hesitation, thrown her to her death just because she had the power to give birth to a Korbinian.

Ward Quinn was dead and Duncan Archard was under constant guard at the local clinic, where he occasionally raved about birds attacking him, flapping his arms as if he was surrounded by ravens pecking at his flesh. When he was lucid, the badly wounded Archard steadfastly denied breaking into Talbot's cabin and making an attempt on Miranda's life there, but he did admit to kidnapping Bren on Quinn's orders. Naturally he wouldn't say anything to the local lawmen about why he'd been given such a command.

Bren didn't think for a moment that because those

two were out of the picture, it meant the Order was done. No, there were others like Quinn and Archard, including some who were probably worse. They would return one day to finish what the others had started. All too soon other men would take their places and the quiet war would continue.

How could he take Miranda home, marry her and give her children when he knew there were those in the world who would take drastic measures to end the Korbinians? How could he make her a part of his life not knowing when someone would come for them? He'd thought they could hide, but could they? In a world so small was it possible to disappear?

All his life he'd known he was meant to live and die alone. For a few days Miranda had jostled that certainty, made him think he could have more. And now he was going to have to give her up, for her own good and for his.

The shower was turned off, and he listened to her movements on the other side of the door. It was possible that she was already pregnant, but it wasn't a given, not by a long shot. His parents had been married for months, almost a year, before he was conceived. He'd have to keep an eye on her for a while just to be sure, but that didn't mean he couldn't let her go.

If she did have a baby, it would be years before the Korbinian abilities kicked in. Until then, he could stay away from both of them; he could watch from a distance and do what he could to keep her safe. If there was a child. If not, then he could simply cut all ties with Miranda Lynch. That would be for the best, for both of them.

She opened the bathroom door and stepped into the

hallway with an unexpected smile on her face. "Very cool, eh?" she said, twirling to show off her brightly colored striped halter top and the lime-green bellbottom pants that hugged her hips and dragged on the floor. She was several inches shorter than Mrs. Quinn had been when she'd been small enough to wear this particular outfit.

"It'll do," he said, trying to ignore the blatant fact that she wore no bra, resisting the urge to fold her in his arms again. "Hope you saved me some hot water." He walked past her carrying the clothing Mrs. Quinn had given him. The worn blue jeans and *KISS* T-shirt were not quite as dated as Miranda's borrowed clothes. "Roger and Jackson are downstairs," he said coolly. "They're anxious to see you." With that he closed the bathroom door behind him. He stood there without moving until he heard Miranda move away.

Miranda was still leery of Roger. Yes, he'd helped her and had almost paid a high price for that help, but he was not the man she'd thought she knew. He'd lied to her for years. As far as she was concerned, there had been an ulterior motive behind every kind word he'd ever spoken.

She had no reservations about giving Jackson a long, tight, heartfelt hug, before she sat down at the dining-room table across from Roger. He was wise enough not to rise and make a move toward her. There would be no hugging for him, probably not ever again.

Mrs. Quinn had apparently passed the day cooking. Maybe it was her way of relieving stress. Maybe she didn't know what else to do with herself. Heavenly aromas drifted from the kitchen, and the table was laden with homemade cookies, biscuits, casseroles, a chocolate cake and a loaf of freshly baked raisin bread. A bowl of steaming stew sat in front of Roger, and Miranda hadn't been in her seat more than a few minutes before the older woman delivered a similar bowl and a soup spoon.

Miranda reached out and took Mrs. Quinn's hand. "You don't have to do all this," she said kindly. "Sit. Rest."

Mrs. Quinn held on to Miranda's hand for a long moment, and then she squeezed it tightly. "I need to keep busy," she responded. "It's best to keep my mind off what happened this morning as best I can." She sighed and removed her hand. "I suppose I always knew deep down Ward's business was no good, but his intentions seemed to be noble ones. I had no idea how far he would go. I didn't know innocent people would get hurt. And Peter…" She shook off the thought and returned to the kitchen to lose herself in pots and pans and flour.

Miranda looked Roger in the eye. "Now what?"

"A team of FBI agents will be here in the morning…"

"I'm not talking about that!" she snapped. "This Order you belong to, the men who are so damn determined to see that anyone who has an ability they don't understand is wiped out, what will *they* do next?"

Roger's jaw tightened. "It's not like that."

"Isn't it?"

Roger looked at a wide-eyed Jackson. "Go see if you can help Mrs. Quinn in the kitchen."

"But, Dad…"

"That's not a request."

Jackson rose slowly and with that boneless grace

only the very young possess, and with a decided lack of speed, he made his way into the kitchen.

"The Order of Cahir has existed for thousands of years, and their purpose has always been a noble one," Roger said in a lowered voice. "Yes, now and then someone gets carried away, but that's not the norm. We serve a purpose, Miranda. We stop monsters."

"Monsters like me and Bren?" she asked.

Roger's eyes flashed. "We also observe and study those who have nonthreatening paranormal abilities. There's a great store of knowledge in the Order, and scientists are always trying to find out why some among us have such abilities while others do not."

"You've been studying me," Miranda said softly. "Like a bug under a microscope. I'm sure you had great fun pretending to be my friend." She remained stoic. "So what's the skinny on Miranda Lynch? What exactly have you learned about me?"

Roger leaned over the table and lowered his voice once more. "You had nothing beyond a relatively normal level of intuition before the accident, when something within you was jarred to life. Whether that jarring was physical or emotional or spiritual, we cannot say. You seem to be getting stronger, or else you're simply learning to control the capabilities you've had all along. Your ability to converse with the dead and to clearly observe past life replay has been most helpful in catching murderers who might otherwise go on to kill again."

"If I'm so useful, why did Archard try to kill me Sunday night?"

Roger's eyes narrowed. "He believes that you're

Kademair, and that to allow you and Korbinian to get together would be too dangerous. In his opinion, it would be best to let the species die out. Besides, he says he didn't try to kill you Sunday night."

"And of course we believe him," Miranda said dryly.

"He says he was here, meeting with Ward Quinn."

Miranda glanced toward the kitchen. "What does Mrs. Quinn say?"

"Someone was in the house meeting with her husband, but it was late and she didn't come downstairs, so she doesn't know who was here."

"No one else has any reason to kill me, unless there's someone else in your blasted Order that decided to take me out before anyone had to worry about the possibility of a little Korbinian making an appearance in nine months."

She hadn't heard Bren come down the stairs, but suddenly he was there, standing directly behind her. "That's not possible," he said. "Miranda is not Kademair."

Bren sat down at the end of the table as far from the other two occupants as possible, and casually poured himself a glass of tea from the pitcher. Miranda and Talbot were both staring at him, waiting for him to say more. "I'll admit," Bren said as he set the pitcher aside, "there was a time when I thought maybe she was Kademair, but it was just great sex and wishful thinking. Nothing more."

"How can you be sure?" Talbot asked sharply.

Bren took a plate and scooped up a large spoonful of what looked to be tuna casserole. He grabbed a biscuit and dropped it beside the noodles, sauce and fish concoction. "How can I explain the depth of emotion connected with Kademair and Korbinian to someone who will never know it or anything like it? The bond goes well beyond sexual attraction." He made himself look at Miranda, and her expression showed such distress, such hurt, he almost wished he could take back what he'd said.

But this was the only way, and he couldn't let her in on the secret because she was so open, so honest, she would be unable to play her part.

"She's a beautiful woman and we were both lonely and unattached." Unable to look into Miranda's hurt eyes anymore, Bren turned to Talbot. "I told her a pretty story, and yeah, maybe for a little while I actually bought into it myself. That's the beginning and the end of this story, or would've been if you bastards hadn't gotten involved." He took a deep breath. "Some days I may wish it isn't true, but I *am* the last of my kind. There is no Kademair, not for me."

"But—" Miranda began softly.

Bren interrupted her. "So, Talbot, tell your asshole buddies to leave Miranda the hell alone. She poses no threat to them or to anyone else, and she never did. From what I can tell she does a lot of good with her gift, so whoever takes Quinn's place should be told to lay off. You be sure to tell the next guy that Miranda Lynch got laid on vacation and damn near got herself killed for it, and that's not fair in anyone's book. If they're so determined to see the last of the Korbinians they only have one place to look, and that's at me."

Talbot went so still and calm, Bren wondered if the

man didn't somehow realize what was going on. If so, he wouldn't tell. In his own twisted way, he did care for Miranda.

"That's too bad," Talbot finally said. "I'm not the only man in the Order who thinks it wouldn't be a bad thing if the Korbinians flourished as they did so long ago. Maybe that's why I convinced myself that Miranda might be Kademair. Not only can she speak to ghosts, which is most definitely a Kademair-worthy gift, she has the most bizarre collection of raven doodads you've ever seen. Books, pictures, figurines… And once when we were on a case a flock of blackbirds passed overhead, and she stared at them as if they'd hypnotized her, as if they were speaking to her in a way only she could hear. I thought it wouldn't hurt to put you two in the same general vicinity and see what might happen." He shrugged. "You're remarkable, Korbinian, as was your father and all those who came before you. It's a sad thing to see the end of something so special."

Bren pushed the food around on his plate. Compliments from Talbot made him uncomfortable. "At least I finally know why you've always refused to sell that cabin. You spied on me from there."

"On occasion," Talbot admitted. "Now that you know, I suppose it doesn't matter so much anymore. The cabin is yours. I'll have the papers drawn up immediately."

"I'll pay you a fair price," Bren said, wanting no charity from this man or any other.

"Seems only—" Talbot began.

"Hold it!" Miranda said sharply. "Before you go giving that cabin away, I'll ask you to remember that I

haven't finished my vacation." She looked at Talbot, blatantly ignoring Bren. Her cheeks were flushed, her lips
soft. There were no tears in her blue eyes, no pleading
on her fine lips. "Another week," she said, the soft words
more a command than a request. "One more week, and
then you can do whatever you want with it."

Chapter 14

After a restless and horribly lonely night, Miranda walked into the woods a short distance from the Quinn farm and began to watch and listen, as she had learned to do over the past few years. Roger stuck close to her, and the other FBI agents behind her remained silent, not even talking to one another. The only sound was the constant crunching of old dried leaves and pine needles beneath their feet and the whisper of tortured spirits calling to her. Bren trailed behind them all, though his presence here was not at all necessary.

She couldn't figure the man out. He can't keep his hands off her, he risks his life to save her—again—and then the next thing you know she's just another convenient woman who can easily be set aside when he's finished with her. One minute she was born to be his and only his, and the next she's nothing to him but an easy lay. He'd been so cold as he'd delivered the words that marked her as nothing but a bed buddy. She didn't believe him. That or she simply didn't *want* to believe him.

She'd given him her heart. What they'd found felt like so much more than a vacation romance or a quick, easy sexual experience. At least, it certainly felt like more to her. Was the love she'd been so sure was in his heart nothing but a fabrication on her part? Had she made herself believe there was more so she could justify taking what she wanted from him?

Ghosts began to claim her attention, and Miranda put her personal problems aside to see to the job she'd come here to do. When the remains were found and properly buried, maybe these spirits could move on, as they should. Some were indeed dark, some had made terrible mistakes they could not take back, but most were merely tragic or gifted and different. Like her.

She walked through the forest by broken morning light, pointing out old and relatively new gravesites Roger marked with red flags for later disinterment. Standing over her unmarked grave, Roxanne's spirit didn't look so fierce or scary anymore. The ghost that had haunted Miranda in the bunker looked like a lost little girl who'd made a few very bad decisions and had paid for them with her life.

There were many spirits like Pete who were not quite human and yet not animal or monster. Some of these ghosts, she knew from talking with them as Roger marked their graves, were like Pete—injured and infected by a beast Miranda had always thought to be myth and killed so they would not become like the monsters they fought. Werewolves. Werecats. Shifters much like Bren, but with a taste for violence and blood.

She finally came to Pete's grave, and there he stood, not in his deformed state but as the young man his mother had waited for all these years. Blond and handsome and smiling and much too young to have passed, he nodded to Miranda in thanks for all she had done.

"Dee asked me to tell you that she's moved on," the spirit said to her.

Miranda felt a rush of sadness, as if a flesh-and-blood friend had left without saying goodbye.

"For a long time she waited for you to come, waited to see that you and her son found one another. Now, she says, what comes next is up to you." Pete gave an oddly archaic nod of his head, almost like a half bow. "She's joined her mate in death as they were joined in life, Korbinian and Kademair. If you ever need her, all you have to do is call and she will come."

Miranda smiled. She would not call Dee back from her well-earned peace. She wouldn't drag the spirit from a place she had waited so long to enter. Not even to ask the question that nagged at her as she did what she had to do. If she was not Bren's Kademair, then why would Dee have gone to so much trouble to make sure they met? If she was not meant for him, then *why?*

She had a few days of vacation left, and she intended to find out.

Bren stood on his deck and looked down on the cabin below, the cabin that would soon be his. When Miranda left, Roger would sign the cabin over to him and it would finally be done. This mountain would be his, and he would have the absolute privacy he'd always craved above all else.

It was best that Miranda never have to struggle with what he knew. That they were meant to be together, but could not. That they could start a family that would herald the return of the Korbinians, but would not. If she didn't know, maybe eventually the pain of separation would go away and she could find someone else. She could have a good life.

He couldn't. He would always know that his Kademair was out there and yet he couldn't claim her without putting her and any children they created in constant danger. Men like Quinn and Archard would always exist.

In the three days since they'd returned from North Carolina, he'd dreamed of her every night. She'd dreamed of him, too, for they were the same dreams. In their dreams there was no danger. In their dreams there was only love and laughter and pleasure.

But life was not a dream. Reality was much harsher.

Perhaps the dreams would cease when she wasn't so damned close. She said she did not intend to stay in the cabin for very long. Just a few days, and then she would call Talbot to come and fetch her.

And she'd be gone, finally and completely.

Miranda sat on the couch and pretended to read, but the words on the page were a blur. As she had since returning to the cabin she listened for the sound of ravens' wings. She occasionally glanced out the sliding glass door hoping to see a formation of large blackbirds that flew as one, that cawed in a way that seemed to call her name.

As always, there was nothing. Bren was staying away from her, as man and as raven. Once darkness fell, glancing out that window revealed nothing at all, but she did it, anyway, more often than she should. More hopeful than she should be.

She couldn't believe that all they'd ever had was sex. There was more, she knew it! The dreams she had of Bren were so real that when she awoke, she could still taste and feel and smell him for a long, wonderful moment. She was Kademair, he was Korbinian, and they knew a bond like no other.

And then she found herself alone, and she knew her moment of bliss had been just a dream.

The past couple of days had been what a vacation should be, she supposed. She slept and read. She ate junk food. She answered some of her personal e-mail and let the business matters wait. Autumn's e-mails had been mostly about the murder in her neighborhood and the progression of the investigation. Everyone suspected the husband, as was usual in these cases, and there was no evidence to point to any other suspect. That would be her first stop when she returned to Atlanta. She could put Autumn's mind to rest, make sure she knew there was no murderer roaming the neighborhood.

It was just after dark when Miranda heard the vehicle on the road outside the cabin. Roger wasn't supposed to come until she called him, but she wasn't sure he'd obey her orders, even though he owed her big time. The purr of the engine wasn't powerful enough to be Bren's truck. No one else came up this way. The engine went silent, a car door slammed, and in a matter of seconds there was a knock on the door.

Had Roger sent someone up the mountain to check on her?

Had Archard?

Miranda leaped from the couch and grabbed the baseball bat she'd kept close at hand since coming back to the cabin. Jackson's initials were written in black ink on the end of the bat; he'd left it here after one of their family vacations, she supposed. She gripped the smooth wood securely as she walked to the door. "Who's there?" she called, making her voice as strong and steady as was possible.

There was no hesitation as a familiar voice answered, "It's me, Jared."

Miranda sighed in relief and set the baseball bat aside, leaning it beside the front door. Her heart continued to hammer, but she managed a smile as she opened the door and greeted her friend's husband. "What on earth are you doing here?"

Jared gave her a sheepish smile. "Autumn asked me to check on you. Your e-mails have worried her. She's quite sure you're not telling her everything." He lazily shooed away the moths that had been drawn to the porch light. "She knew I was going to be in the general area, calling on a client near Pigeon Forge, so she asked me if I'd stop by and make sure you're really okay."

Miranda stepped back and invited Jared inside, and as she did she glanced at the car that was parked in the short driveway. She couldn't tell the exact color, not without more light, but Jared was driving a dark, two-door Toyota. Her smile died slowly. Her stomach flipped over. "That's not your car."

"It's a rental," Jared said as he closed the door behind him and swatted at one stray moth.

Miranda's instincts, instincts that had rarely led her wrong, screamed at her. *Get out! Get out!* Something was very wrong with her friend's husband. Jared did frequently travel on business, but none of his appointments took him anywhere near this part of Tennessee, and he rarely had to work on weekends. It didn't help matters any that he planted himself directly in front of the door—which was the only safe way out. She glanced over her shoulder to the sliding glass door and the deck.

Jared sighed and moved in closer, taking a threatening step in her direction. "You already know something's wrong, I suppose. That face of yours gives away every thought in your pretty head." Smoothly he drew a gun from inside his jacket, and Miranda had a flashback to the night an intruder had broken in and whispered her name.

Where are you, Miranda Lynch?

"Why?" she asked, taking another step back toward the sliding glass door.

Jared shrugged. "I always thought the whole thing about you talking to ghosts was creepy and more than weird, but I didn't know it would be so damned inconvenient until I had to kill a woman. When you get back home, *if* you were going to ever get back, Autumn would insist that you poke around our neighbor's house to see if the ghost is still hanging around. That would be it for me. If anyone knows where to look and looks hard enough, the connection can be made. Right now her husband is the number-one suspect and that suits me just fine."

"Your neighbor," Miranda whispered, backing slowly toward the deck and her only chance at escape.

"Yeah. Pam and I had a good thing going, but she was having trouble with her marriage and decided it was time to tell Autumn what had been going on so we could make our relationship official and open. Like I ever wanted that! Bitch," he mumbled. "I couldn't let her tell. Autumn has all the money and unless she dies—or perhaps I should say *until* she dies—I can't rightfully call it mine. A divorce would ruin everything. I had to string Pam along for a while until you left town, and then I did what had to be done. Then I came here to tend to you, but you weren't where you were supposed to be." He smiled. "Lucky for me you're here now."

"You won't get away with this," Miranda said as she backed up against the sliding glass door and felt behind her for the handle.

"I will, actually," Jared said confidently. "Everyone knows you and the nut job who lives up the hill have been carrying on and that it hasn't ended well. The whole town, if you can call that collection of misfits down the hill a town, is talking about it. You get shot, the cops go straight to him, and I'm long gone, with nothing to connect me to your death." His eyes were blank, his smile continued. "Who will you talk to when you're a ghost?"

Miranda pushed the sliding glass door open and ran

outside, embracing the darkness. Even though she felt freer here, even though she could finally manage to take a deep breath, there was nowhere to go. She wouldn't reach the post and make a quick and frightening descent this time. Jared was too close. He was holding his gun on her. Even if she managed to make it over the deck railing, all he had to do was point down and pull the trigger.

"Is there anything I can do to change your mind?" she asked.

Jared shook his head. "Sorry. Even if I could convince you to lie to Autumn, it wouldn't work. You've got that face that tells it all. Besides, I've never kidded myself into thinking I could bring you over to my side. You might promise anything to save your life, but we both know you'd go straight to my wife—or to the police— if you got the chance. Now, let's go back inside. The gunshot will be too loud out here. Someone might hear."

Miranda looked up to the mountainside house above. "I don't want Bren involved in this."

"Too bad."

She gathered the courage she could and looked Jared in the eye. How had she misjudged him so badly? Why had her instincts failed her? And then she saw it. He wasn't evil; he wasn't good. He was nothing. His eyes were empty, and so was his soul.

"I'm going to die, I accept that," she said. "If I jump they'll think it's suicide and Bren won't be a suspect."

Jared's eyebrows arched in surprise. "You'd kill yourself to keep Korbinian out of trouble?"

"I love him," she said softly and honestly.

"Okay, whatever." Jared motioned with the gun. "We'll

do this your way. But I'm not going to stand here all night waiting for you to get up the nerve. Jump or I'll drag you inside the cabin and put a bullet in your head. Your choice."

He didn't put the weapon aside, not even as Miranda hefted herself up to sit on the wooden railing. She looked down and her stomach roiled. It was a long drop to the rocky ground below, she knew that, but in the darkness she could see nothing. Clouds obscured the moon, and the shadows below were deep. Her head swam.

She turned her face up so her eyes were trained on Bren's dark house, and she silently called to him.

If you're right and I'm nothing to you, if you only saved me at Quinn's farm because you were there and I was in trouble and it was convenient to do so, then I'll likely die now. But if I'm right and I'm yours to the pit of my soul, then come to me now, Bren. Save me. Catch me.

She thought she saw a shadow of movement around Bren's house, a flicker of black on black, but it was so dark she couldn't be sure.

And Jared was growing impatient. "Need some assistance?" he asked, jabbing the cold hard muzzle of his weapon into her chest. "Maybe I should help you along with a good, hard push." He did push, using his weapon as he leaned into her. Miranda found herself leaning back and holding on to the railing with all her might. She didn't see or hear the ravens she'd tried to call to her.

Maybe Bren was right and all they'd ever had was sex. She was drawn to him, she dreamed of him because she was starved for emotion and friendship and sex. If that's all they had, she'd soon be dead.

Miranda didn't fear death. She knew life continued

on; she knew she would see her parents and her sister once again, and she would be happy. But she also knew to the pit of her soul that this life was not finished. She had more to do. Love, children, justice—perhaps even forgiveness for a friend who had lied to her. There were spirits to send on, a man to love, a life to make. She wanted to break the Lynch love curse—which had never been a curse at all, just bad luck, or destiny making sure she waited for Bren to come along—once and for all. Facing the dark abyss, she didn't want to die with those things undone.

But Jared was impatient. He gave her a final hefty push and pried her fingers from the railing. He shoved her and she fell backward. Miranda instinctively reached for the railing, grasping for support, finding it with a jerk as her body fell for a moment and then stopped. For a too-short moment she held on with one hand and grasped for a hold with the other, but it wasn't enough. She flailed for a moment, then her fingers slipped and she dropped.

She tumbled, and the fall stole her breath. Her head tipped back and in the darkness she saw a flock of birds jetting toward her. She heard the fluttering wings of ravens over the rush of air as she fell, and within a fraction of a second those wings were clustered around her, a cushion of muscle and cartilage and feathers. The ravens held her on air, as they had once before.

All was not soft in her cushion. Claws and beaks snatched at her clothing. Countless ravens positioned themselves beneath her, slowing her descent. This drop was longer and more dangerous than the one she'd taken at the farm, and her speed was greater than it had been from a hayloft. Not too far below were trees whose sturdy limbs would stop her long before her body found the ground. Such a landing would not be pleasant, she imagined. No, it would kill her, just as Jared had intended.

Before that happened the ravens took control of their movements and the sense of falling ceased. They carried her, as they had before, in a manner that made her suffer motion sickness and a surreal sense of floating across the skies without even the tiniest bit of control. She closed her eyes and relaxed, trusting herself into Bren's care. He'd come to her; he'd heard her call.

The ravens carried Miranda to a clearing in the valley and gently, but not too gently, dropped her there. She was prepared to watch Bren transform; she was ready to answer all his questions about what had happened, but he didn't give her the chance.

The ravens that had rescued her rose into the night sky, leaving her alone on the side of a dark, deserted mountain.

Bren had never experienced such all-consuming anger in this form, which usually brought him only peace. First Archard and now this. Why had the Order sent someone to kill Miranda so soon after her rescue? Hadn't he convinced them that there was no risk of the two of them restoring the Korbinian legacy? Didn't they recognize the sacrifice he'd made in order to keep her safe?

He would return to Miranda as soon as he could, but the man who'd tried to kill her would not get away. Not this time.

The intruder had apparently seen no reason to rush

from the cabin after Miranda had gone over the side of the deck, and he was just exiting the front door as the ravens shot over the top of the house. The man looked up, alerted by the noise of the flock, and the ravens dove, taking him by surprise.

The man who'd tried to kill Miranda was made of soft and vulnerable flesh, and he cried out in surprise and horror as the first beak found its target. While a handful of the ravens attacked the man, others attacked his car—the same car Bren had seen the intruder driving on Sunday night. Tires were slashed, windows shattered. The man screamed hysterically and reached for his gun, a weapon three ravens quickly snatched away.

The attack was vicious and unrelenting.

The man dropped to his knees and began to cry. Occasionally he screamed and flailed his arms, but his screams were weak and reached no ears other than his own. His frantic defensive movements did not dissuade the ravens in the least. His clothing was soon ripped and bloody, and his heart raced so fast it seemed to be on the verge of exploding. The ravens listened to that heartbeat, and to the ragged breathing, and to the constant moans as they attacked. Blood, black in the night, ran down the man's face and arms and neck.

In a few more minutes the man could be dead, and heaven knows Bren wanted the bastard killed. But he was not the monster Archard and his kind thought him to be, and he wouldn't allow them to turn him into one. He wasn't going to take this man's life in anger and revenge. In his condition he wasn't going anywhere.

The ravens broke away from the cabin as quickly as

they had come, leaving a sobbing, bleeding man and an all but destroyed car sitting in front of the Talbot cabin.

It was so dark that Miranda heard the returning ravens long before she saw them. Without words, she understood what Bren wanted her to do. She closed her eyes and opened her arms wide, and without stopping, without further preparation, the ravens gathered around her and grasped her tightly, before taking off again with her body caught in the midst of black feathers and deadly beaks.

This time she didn't experience motion sickness and disorientation. She relaxed completely; she trusted herself body and soul into Bren's care. His cold dismissal had been intended to keep her safe, she knew that now. Deep down she'd known it all along. She had been born for him; she was Kademair. Cool air washed over her body, and in spite of the terror she had just experienced, she laughed. She was flying. Flying! The mountain she had come to love rose before her; the green valley below sped past quickly, hinting at the speed at which she traveled.

The ravens carried her onto the deck of the mountain-top house, where they gently set her down before withdrawing and, in the blink of an eye, transforming into the man she loved.

Bren didn't say a word, just took her in his arms and held her close for a long while. Eventually he set her back, kissed her quickly and led the way into the darkened house, turning on a lamp as he neared the telephone. He quickly tapped out three numbers: 911.

Bren gave the dispatcher his name and told a quick and plausible story. He'd been headed down the mountain when he'd run into Miranda Lynch running up, having just escaped an attempt on her life. Together they saw the oddest thing. The man who'd tried to kill her was attacked by a flock of birds. He and Miranda didn't stick around to see what happened, Bren said, but rushed back up the hill to call for help.

When he hung up the phone, Miranda asked, "Is he dead?"

Bren shook his head. "No, but he's not going anywhere on his own, either. Not for a while."

She walked into his arms and rested her head on his chest. "He tried to kill me because of what I can do."

"I know."

"You *don't* know. The attempt on my life had nothing to do with you. Jared is not a member of any so-called Order that claims to keep peace. He had not even the tiniest bit of nobility in his intentions. He wanted to kill me so I couldn't tell his wife, my best friend, that her husband is a murderer."

Bren's hand rested in her hair.

"I dread telling Autumn who her husband really is," Miranda whispered.

"Maybe deep down she already knows," Bren said.

"Maybe." She tipped her head back so she could look into his face. "You heard me," she said softly. "When I called for help, when I screamed in my mind that I needed you, you heard me."

"I did," he admitted simply.

"You can't tell me what we have is just sex. You can't tell me we found one another because we were both lonely and horny."

That got a half smile out of him. "No, I don't suppose I can. But the truth isn't easy. Stay with me and you'll have to fight for survival against those like Quinn who would gladly kill to make sure I'm the last of my kind. Stay with me and if we're lucky enough to survive, your teenage sons will have the power to turn into ravens and fly away. I love you, I don't want to live without you, but stay with me and our life will be filled with secrets and responsibilities and—"

"Stay with me," Miranda interrupted, "and I will love you no matter what comes. Stay with me, and neither one of us will ever be alone again." She kissed him, then, with her heart open and ready to take any risk. Bren kissed her back, and she had no doubt about what was to come. "Get dressed," she said as she took her mouth from his. "We should meet the sheriff at the cabin so I can tell him who Jared is and why he tried to kill me. He'll have to believe me this time."

"And after that's done we'll come back here together and you'll stay," Bren said, not moving away from her to do what needed to be done.

"Yes, I will. I can't imagine living my life anywhere else," she said honestly.

In the distance sirens wailed. The noise was obscene on this beautiful, normally peaceful mountain. It did not belong here.

She did.

Chapter 15

Five Months Later

Miranda had wondered, in the months since she and Bren had married, if things between them would change once she conceived. Most especially, she wondered if the sex would change. Was their strong attraction simply a biological urge to see that the Korbinians survived? When she was carrying his child, would their fierce and passionate draw to one another diminish?

Apparently not.

They lay in bed at the end of the day, tangled and warm and aroused. Bren placed one hand over Miranda's very slightly rounded belly. She had not begun to show right away, but these days she definitely had a little baby bump.

"Are you sure I don't have to worry about wings and beaks and claws until he's a teenager?" she asked.

"Positive," Bren said, kissing the slight swell.

"I feel like the old nursery rhyme. 'Four and twenty blackbirds, baked in a pie.'"

He ignored her, which was just as well, and moved his mouth lower, kissing his way down her body. Miranda closed her eyes and said no more as she lost herself in the physical sensations her husband roused in her. Such warmth, such pleasure. Heaven above, such need had the power to drive her around the bend. In a good way, in a marvelous way.

She urged him on with hands and mouth and moans she could not control. There was no rush, not in this coming together or any other. She tasted him, touched him, marveled in him, and when they finally came together, the relief and the pleasure of having him inside her was sharp and all-encompassing. They made love, they had sex, they bonded, they got lost in one another in every way—physical and spiritual. And they found release together, sweating and grasping.

No, their desire had not changed just because the next of the Korbinans was growing inside her.

For a long while they lay together in the bed, satisfied and more than satisfied. Content. Happy.

"I got a phone call from an FBI agent I used to work with," she said, cuddling against Bren.

"Talbot?" Bren asked, only a hint of displeasure in his voice.

"No. Another agent I worked with a couple of times." She hadn't talked to Roger in a long while. He had done as he'd promised and signed over the cabin down the hill. Bren had tried to pay him for the place, but Roger insisted on calling it a wedding present. Between infrequent trips out of town to do what she did and making her home here with Bren, Miranda had redecorated the cabin. The roof was now a dull green that blended more pleasantly with the landscape, and the interior had been completely redone. The cabin down the hill was now a quaint, duck-free zone where her friends came on occasion to visit.

Autumn in particular got a lot of use out of the cabin. She escaped there to get away from reporters and curious neighbors and well-meaning friends. Finding out that her husband was a cheat and a murderer had been a shock, but she was finally finding her footing again, or at least beginning to. Their divorce was final— and Jared Sidwell was never going to get out of prison.

"This job of yours might be the last one, you know," Bren said. "Once you start to show we'll have to leave."

Not only leave, but disappear. They'd have to change their names, hide, make an entirely new life. She certainly couldn't let anyone know what she could do. If that knowledge became public she'd be too easy to find and identify.

Sad as all that was, it would be worth it to know their child—their children—would be safe. She just hated that Bren had to give up this mountain he'd worked for so long to call his own. It was finally entirely his, and he couldn't stay.

"I don't mind," he said softly, all but reading her mind. "I don't need a mountain. I have you, and you, Miranda Korbinian, are the entire world to me."

* * *

They had each packed a small bag, and for the past couple of months Bren had been taking money out of his accounts. They had enough cash to keep them comfortable for a while, more than enough to get settled.

He didn't know how long the cash would last, but it would give them a good start. If eventually he had to roof houses and Miranda told fortunes at a local carnival, they'd get by. They would find a way.

Bren had thought he'd hate to leave this house he'd worked so hard to build, but strangely enough he was more excited about what lay ahead than he was worried about what he was leaving behind. He loved his wife; he craved the sons he'd never thought he would know.

Miranda was more worried than he was. She looked cute as hell in her black pants, long and loose green shirt, and porkpie hat. No one could tell yet that she was pregnant, but he could see the changes in her. Her face glowed, her body was slightly more rounded, and she was as content as he was with whatever might come.

They were packed and ready to go, and Miranda was taking one last look around the place she'd called home for such a short time. She ran her fingers over the bar he'd built himself as if she'd come to love this house as much as he did. Almost lovingly she touched the raven figurine she'd placed there when she'd moved in. But she smiled, and he knew that like him, she realized the sacrifice was worthwhile.

The sound of the doorbell made her jump.

Bren was closest to the door, so he answered, confused about who might be on the front porch. It was the middle of the day. No one was staying at the cabin. Callers up here were rare.

Bren never expected to see Roger Talbot standing on the porch. Tempted as he was to slam the door in the man's face, he didn't. He grudgingly invited Talbot into the house.

Miranda kept her distance. She'd forgiven Talbot, for the most part, but she had not forgotten the years of lying and betrayal. She'd once trusted him entirely, and now she couldn't trust him at all. Maybe this surprise visit was a good thing. She might feel better if she had a chance to say goodbye—even if Talbot didn't know it was a final goodbye.

Talbot wasted no time. "I won't stay. Just dropped by to tell you that there's no need to run because Miranda's pregnant. She's not in any danger and neither is the child."

Bren instinctively stepped closer to his wife, compelled to protect her. The Order couldn't possibly know about the baby. They'd been so careful. She hadn't even told Autumn!

Miranda lifted her chin and said, "I don't know what you're talking about." She didn't lie well. Never had.

Talbot didn't move closer. "Please," he said, sounding thoroughly disgusted. "You bought chocolate ice cream and pickles at the grocery store last week. You've taken to wearing those long, baggy shirts, and you—" he turned to glare at Bren "—you've been taking cash out of your accounts for two months."

"Maybe we're just tired of being watched all the damn time," Bren said.

Roger conceded that possibility with a shrug. "Whatever. I just wanted you two to know that the man who took Quinn's place has issued instructions that you're not to be touched. Neither of you. If the Korbinians are meant to survive, then it's not our place to interfere."

"You're still with them?" Miranda shouted. "After everything that's happened, you're still working for the Order that damn near killed us both, the Order that kidnapped Jackson, the Order that condoned the killing of countless people?"

Talbot calmly said, "The only way to change wrongs like those is from the inside."

"You took Quinn's place, didn't you?" Bren asked.

Talbot looked him in the eye. "If I did I couldn't tell you. You don't want to know any more than you already do, trust me. Let's just say that decrees have been issued that end all study and observation of both of you. You're to be left alone. There are enough real monsters in the world to keep us busy." He looked only slightly chagrined. "You two are no longer being watched. Baby boy or no baby boy, you're off the radar."

"Why should we trust you?" Miranda asked. "Why should we believe a word you say?"

"That's up to you," Talbot said. "I've done everything I could to make up for being a part of the mess that nearly killed you both. I can't do any more. I just wanted to let you know." He turned to leave, but Miranda was obviously not ready to let him go.

"Roger Talbot, if you're not watching anymore, then how did you know about…about ice cream and pickles, and baggy shirts, and bank accounts?"

Talbot smiled tiredly. "That all came from local

gossip Autumn picked up on when she was here a couple of weeks ago. She told Cheryl, Cheryl told me. Simple community chitchat, Miranda, nothing more." He turned to Bren, resigned. "Whatever happens, take good care of her."

"I intend to."

The FBI agent opened the front door to exit, but stopped in the doorway and turned around, glancing from Bren to Miranda. "Believe it or not, the Order was formed to do good and necessary work, and as long as decent men are in charge, that's what happens. *Good* and *necessary* work. If you decide to stick around, your talents would be greatly appreciated."

"You've got to be kidding me," Miranda said sharply. "What makes you think we would ever work with men like Archard and Quinn and *you* again?"

Talbot shrugged. "Quinn is dead. Archard's locked away. That just leaves me."

"I can't believe you're still with them," Miranda said, disappointment clear in her soft voice. "After everything that happened…"

"Everything that happened is all the more reason for me to stay, to make sure the Order functions as it was intended to. Do you think you two are the only extraordinary people in the world? Do you think no one else has gifts they hide? The difference is, some of them get their kicks by killing innocents or stealing souls or turning ordinary people into monsters with a bite or a dark spell. Should I sit back and let them continue? Should no one fight against them?" He pointed an accusing finger to Miranda. "If a dark thing came after your son with the intention of tearing him apart or stealing his soul, would you not kill to stop it?"

Miranda instinctively laid a protective hand over her stomach.

"So, are you taking over that damned farmhouse?"

"No," Talbot said abruptly. "There was too much excitement at the farmhouse a few months ago, as you well know, and the local cops are watching the place too closely. Besides, it's been tainted."

"I would say so," Bren said darkly.

"We're going to be neighbors," Talbot said. "I bought a house on the next mountain over."

"What does Cheryl think about that?" Miranda asked.

Again, Talbot shrugged. "One minute she's furious. The next she's in tears. A few minutes later she's planning trips to the outlet malls and scouting out local restaurants and dancing schools for the girls. And then she starts the process all over again." He nodded. "The transition would be easier for her if she had a friend nearby."

With that statement Roger Talbot left, not giving Miranda a chance to respond.

Miranda blew out the candles on the huge birthday cake. It was another lovely spring day, another birthday, another gathering of friends. A new life.

This year Bren was cooking hamburgers on the grill, which was sitting on the deck that overlooked the lush green valley. The crowd that milled in and out of the house was large, but not too large. She adored them all. Autumn was attending the celebration with her new boyfriend, one of the real estate agents who worked at

Bren's company. She was happy again, and it was obvious that this new man adored her. Maybe something would come of it, maybe not. The important thing was Autumn's happiness, and her recovery from the betrayal of her low-life husband.

Jackson, a handsome sixteen and already a touch taller than his dad, had brought along his pretty girlfriend. They'd met and clicked instantly when school had started last fall. His old childish crush on Miranda was history—and thank heavens, he remembered almost nothing of his kidnapping, thanks to the drugs they'd given him.

Cheryl had adjusted to her new life pretty quickly, thanks to outlet malls and having Miranda nearby. The girls were resilient, the way children are.

Roger stayed busy, but apparently not too busy. Cheryl was four months pregnant. They hadn't planned to have more kids, and now and then Cheryl swore she was too old to go through the baby thing again. But she and Roger were both thrilled more often than they were annoyed by the "surprise."

It had taken some time, but Miranda had forgiven Roger. Considering that she—and Bren—had started working for him now and then, it seemed the thing to do. Besides, how could she hold on to anger when her life was so good?

After Miranda had blown out the candles on her cake, Bren handed her the baby. Joseph Jesse Korbinian was wrapped tight in a blue baby blanket, oblivious to the excitement around him.

There was one other guest at her birthday party, one Miranda had not expected to see again.

Jessica's spirit cooed over the baby. Joey must've seen his aunt, because his eyes—eyes that were blue at the moment but would one day be as dark as his daddy's—were fixed on the ghost. Jessica made faces at him and he smiled and kicked his feet.

"Happy birthday, little sister," Jessica said when she managed to take her eyes off the baby. "Nice work, by the way. That is probably the cutest kid I've ever seen, now that he's past the wrinkled, little-old-man stage."

How could she have ever doubted that her sister was around? "You've been visiting without showing yourself."

Jessica gave a nonchalant lift of her shoulders. "Now and then. It's not easy to visit once the move forward has been made, but if I want it badly enough and I work very hard, I can drop in for a moment or two."

Miranda wanted to have her sister here often, not now and then, not when she made a great effort just to appear. But if it wasn't meant to be, then it wasn't. "I miss you," she said honestly.

"I'm fine, really," Jessica said. "More than fine." She smiled as if she knew something Miranda did not—and she probably did. "I came today to give you a message."

Messages from the other side were rarely of the pleasant sort. Still, Jessica's smile eased Miranda's initial worry.

"It took a lot of work to get you and Korbinian together," Jessica said. "I just wanted you to know that things will be easier for Joey. He will know his Kademair almost all his life. He will never have a memory without her in it."

"What are you talking about?"

Jessica nodded in Cheryl's direction. "Their baby is a girl."

Miranda held her breath for a moment, and then she let that breath out slowly and smiled. In good times and bad, these people had been her family for years. One day their children would make it official.

Bren walked up behind her and wrapped his arms around her and Joey. For a long moment they stood there, looking over the valley together while the others talked and laughed and filled their plates. Her bond with Bren had only gotten stronger in the months since they'd married. He could get into her head so easily, and she always knew what he was feeling.

"Tonight?" she asked after listening to the rhythms of his body for a few precious moments.

"Yeah. After everyone leaves. Roger said a creature was spotted near Pigeon Forge. I'm going to do some recon after dark."

There was a place in the world for the Korbinians and the talents they hid from the world. As in the old days, Bren had become a warrior. He was a messenger and a fighter, as well as a builder of fine homes, a father and a husband.

Miranda had actually done some work for the Order herself, as well as her continuing consultations with the FBI. Talking to the ghosts of those killed by dark fiends had helped her to accept that the Order was a necessary evil. With Roger head of this division, injustices of men like Ward Quinn had been abandoned.

"If there's something over that way Roger had better take care of it ASAP. Cheryl will be royally pissed if a

were or a vamp messes with her favorite outlet mall."
Miranda leaned into Bren's chest, melting there.

Bren dropped a casual kiss on her neck, and Miranda smiled as she gazed at the majestic mountains in the distance. Those mountains were a wrinkle in the world, a soft fold of earth and green trees, and they were home. Her son rested in her arms; her husband held her close. Behind Miranda the sounds of friends and family filled the once lonely house, and before her stretched forever.

Don't miss Linda Winstead Jones's next title—
Coming in spring 2010 from
Silhouette Romantic Suspense
COME TO ME

"Aren't you going to say 'Fly me' or at least 'Welcome Aboard'?"

Amanda Bauer didn't. The softly muttered word that actually came out of her mouth was a lot less welcoming. And had fewer letters. Four, to be exact.

The man shook his head and tsked. "Not exactly the friendly skies. Haven't caught the spirit yet this morning?"

"Make one more airline-slogan crack and you'll be walking to Chicago," she said.

He nodded once, then pushed his sunglasses onto the top of his tousled hair. The move revealed blue eyes that matched the sky above. And yeah. They were twinkling. Damn it.

"Understood. Just, uh, promise me you'll say 'Coffee, tea or me' at least once, okay? Please?"

Amanda tried to glare, but that twinkle sucked the annoyance right out of her. She could only draw in a slow breath as he climbed into the plane. As she watched her passenger disappear into the small jet, she had to wonder about the trip she was about to take.

Coffee and tea they had, and he was welcome to them.

But her? Well, she'd never even considered making a move on a customer before. Talk about unprofessional.

And yet…

Something inside her suddenly wanted to take a chance, to be a little outrageous.

How long since she had done indecent things—or decent ones, for that matter—with a sexy man? Not since before they'd thrown all their energies into expanding Clear-Blue Air, at the very least. She hadn't had time for a lunch date, much less the kind of lust-fest she'd enjoyed in her younger years. The kind that lasted for entire weekends and involved not leaving a bed except to grab the kind of sensuous food that could be smeared onto—and eaten off—someone else's hot, naked, sweat-tinged body.

She closed her eyes, her hand clenching tight on the railing. Her heart fluttered in her chest and she tried to make herself move. But she couldn't—not climbing up, but not backing away, either. Not physically, and not in her head.

Was she really considering this? God, she hadn't even looked at the stranger's left hand to make sure he was available. She had no idea if he was actually attracted to her or just an irrepressible flirt. Yet something inside was telling her to take a shot with this man.

It was crazy. Something she'd never considered. Yet right now, at this moment, she was definitely considering it. If he was available…could she do it? Seduce a stranger. Have an anonymous fling, like something out of a blue movie on late-night cable?

She didn't know. All she knew was that the flight to

Chicago was a short one so she had to decide quickly. And as she put her foot on the bottom step and began to climb up, Amanda suddenly had to wonder if she was about to embark on the ride of her life.

HARLEQUIN *Presents*®

Sold, bought, bargained for or bartered

He'll take his...

Bride on Approval

Whether there's a debt to be paid,
a will to be obeyed or a business
to be saved...she has no choice
but to say, "I do"!

PURE PRINCESS,
BARTERED BRIDE
by *Caitlin Crews*
#2894

Available February 2010!

HARLEQUIN® *Blaze*™

It all started with a few naughty books....

As a member of the Red Tote Book Club, Carol Snow has been studying works of classic erotic literature…but Carol doesn't believe in love…or marriage. It's going to take another kind of classic—Charles Dickens's *A Christmas Carol*—and a little otherworldly persuasion to convince her to go after her own sexily ever after.

Cuddle up with

Her Sexy Valentine

by STEPHANIE BOND

Available February 2010

red-hot reads

HARLEQUIN® Romance®

ESCAPE AROUND the WORLD

Dream destinations, whirlwind weddings!

The Daredevil Tycoon
by
BARBARA McMAHON

A hot-air balloon race with Amalia Catalon's sexy daredevil boss, Rafael Sandoval, is only the beginning of her exciting Spanish adventure….

*Available in January 2010
wherever books are sold.*

REQUEST YOUR FREE BOOKS!

2 FREE NOVELS PLUS 2 FREE GIFTS!

Silhouette®

n o c t u r n e™

Dramatic and Sensual Tales of Paranormal Romance.

YES! Please send me 2 FREE Silhouette® Nocturne™ novels and my 2 FREE gifts (gifts are worth about $10). After receiving them, if I don't wish to receive any more books, I can return the shipping statement marked "cancel." If I don't cancel, I will receive 4 brand-new novels every other month and be billed just $4.47 per book in the U.S. or $4.99 per book in Canada. That's a saving of about 15% off the cover price! It's quite a bargain! Shipping and handling is just 50¢ per book in the U.S. and 75¢ per book in Canada.* I understand that accepting the 2 free books and gifts places me under no obligation to buy anything. I can always return a shipment and cancel at any time. Even if I never buy another book from Silhouette, the two free books and gifts are mine to keep forever.

238 SDN E37M 338 SDN E37X

Name _____ (PLEASE PRINT) _____

Address _____ Apt. # _____

City _____ State/Prov. _____ Zip/Postal Code _____

Signature (if under 18, a parent or guardian must sign) _____

Mail to the **Silhouette Reader Service:**
IN U.S.A.: P.O. Box 1867, Buffalo, NY 14240-1867
IN CANADA: P.O. Box 609, Fort Erie, Ontario L2A 5X3

Not valid for current subscribers to Silhouette Nocturne books.

Want to try two free books from another line?
Call 1-800-873-8635 or visit www.morefreebooks.com.

* Terms and prices subject to change without notice. Prices do not include applicable taxes. N.Y. residents add applicable sales tax. Canadian residents will be charged applicable provincial taxes and GST. Offer not valid in Quebec. This offer is limited to one order per household. All orders subject to approval. Credit or debit balances in a customer's account(s) may be offset by any other outstanding balance owed by or to the customer. Please allow 4 to 6 weeks for delivery. Offer available while quantities last.

Your Privacy: Silhouette is committed to protecting your privacy. Our Privacy Policy is available online at www.eHarlequin.com or upon request from the Reader Service. From time to time we make our lists of customers available to reputable third parties who may have a product or service of interest to you. If you would prefer we not share your name and address, please check here. ☐

Help us get it right—We strive for accurate, respectful and relevant communications. To clarify or modify your communication preferences, visit us at www.ReaderService.com/consumerschoice.

SN10

HARLEQUIN
Ambassadors

Want to share your passion for reading Harlequin® Books?

Become a Harlequin Ambassador!

Harlequin Ambassadors are a group of passionate and well-connected readers who are willing to share their joy of reading Harlequin® books with family and friends.

You'll be sent all the tools you need to spark great conversation, including free books!

All we ask is that you share the romance with your friends and family!

You'll also be invited to have a say in new book ideas and exchange opinions with women just like you!

To see if you qualify* to be a Harlequin Ambassador, please visit www.HarlequinAmbassadors.com.

*Please note that not everyone who applies to be a Harlequin Ambassador will qualify. For more information please visit www.HarlequinAmbassadors.com.

Thank you for your participation.